TWISTED
INNOCENCE

BOOKS BY TERRI BLACKSTOCK

THE MOONLIGHTERS SERIES

1 *Truth Stained Lies*
2 *Distortion*

THE RESTORATION SERIES

1 *Last Light*
2 *Night Light*
3 *True Light*
4 *Dawn's Light*

THE INTERVENTION SERIES

1 *Intervention*
2 *Vicious Cycle*
3 *Downfall*

THE CAPE REFUGE SERIES

1 *Cape Refuge*
2 *Southern Storm*
3 *River's Edge*
4 *Breaker's Reef*

NEWPOINTE 911

1 *Private Justice*
2 *Shadow of Doubt*
3 *Word of Honor*
4 *Trial by Fire*
5 *Line of Duty*

THE SUN COAST CHRONICLES

1 *Evidence of Mercy*
2 *Justifiable Means*
3 *Ulterior Motives*
4 *Presumption of Guilt*

SECOND CHANCES

1 *Never Again Good-bye*
2 *When Dreams Cross*
3 *Blind Trust*
4 *Broken Wings*

WITH BEVERLY LAHAYE

1 *Seasons Under Heaven*
2 *Showers in Season*
3 *Times and Seasons*
4 *Season of Blessing*

NOVELLA

Seaside

OTHER BOOKS

Shadow in Serenity
Predator
Double Minds
Soul Restoration
Emerald Windows
Miracles (The Listener/The Gifted)
The Heart Reader of Franklin High
The Gifted Sophomores
Covenant Child
Sweet Delights

TWISTED
INNOCENCE

☾ MOONLIGHTERS SERIES, BOOK THREE

New York Times Bestselling Author
TERRI BLACKSTOCK

ZONDERVAN

Twisted Innocence
Copyright © 2015 by Terri Blackstock

This title is also available as a Zondervan e-book. Visit www.zondervan.com.

Requests for information should be addressed to:
Zondervan, *Grand Rapids, Michigan 49546*

Library of Congress Cataloging-in-Publication Data

Blackstock, Terri, 1957-
  Twisted innocence / Terri Blackstock.
     pages. cm. -- (Moonlighters ; book 3)
     ISBN 978-0-310-33236-7 (pbk.)
1. Domestic fiction. I. Title.
PS3552.L34285T95 2015
813'.54--dc23
                                  2014032922

Scripture quotations are taken from The Holy Bible, *New International Version®, NIV®.* Copyright © 1973, 1978, 1984, 2011 by Biblica, Inc.™ Used by permission. All rights reserved worldwide. www.zondervan.com

The New American Standard Bible®, Copyright © 1960, 1962, 1963, 1968, 1971, 1972, 1973, 1975, 1977, 1995 by The Lockman Foundation. Used by permission. (www.Lockman.org).

ISBN: 978-0-310-33237-4 (LE)

Printed in the United States of America

HB 07.25.2018

This book is lovingly dedicated to the Nazarene.

CHAPTER 1

Holly Cramer pulled to the curb of the condemned apartment building, her yellow taxi grinding gears and threatening to die. Though the sun hung bright overhead, the street was colorless, oppressive, with moldy, rotting houses and garbage festering in yards. Men loitered on the road up ahead in front of another boarded house. She shouldn't have accepted this fare, but the customer had called her cell phone personally instead of going through the agency. She must be a repeat customer.

Holly tapped her horn and looked out her passenger window. The house showed no sign of life, but it wasn't the wrong place. The girl had clearly said it was the green house on the corner of Burke and Darby. Holly checked her phone for the caller's number and called her back.

It went straight to voice mail.

Holly sighed. Maybe this was a prank, some kid trying

to yank her chain just to see if she'd come. She had done that enough herself as a kid. Back when she was still Panama City's party girl, she'd done things under the influence that had been even more childish, like calling a guy fourteen times when she knew he was with his girlfriend, just to create trouble in paradise. She and her friends would giggle hysterically at the fight they imagined ensued, but the next day, as she nursed the punishment of a hangover, she would hate herself for it.

Not ready to give up on this fare just yet, Holly honked the horn again. The men up the street turned to look at her. Getting nervous, she reached into the pocket of her door, but of course her pistol wasn't there. It was against the law for a cabbie to carry a firearm inside the car while they were on duty. It was locked safely in her trunk.

She thought of bucking the law and getting it out, but that would call more attention to her. This was stupid. She was a mother now, and the last place she should have been was in the slums, waiting for someone to blow her head off just for target practice.

But what if the woman who'd called wasn't a kid at all, but someone stranded here who desperately needed a ride?

"Two minutes, then I'm leaving," Holly whispered.

The loiterers up ahead were showing too much interest in her, and two swaggered toward her. *That's it. I'm outa here.* She shifted into drive.

"Wait!"

Holly pressed a foot on the brake and looked back, saw a man and woman coming out from behind the abandoned house. They were both skin and bones, and as they hurried closer, she noted their rotting teeth and the sores on their faces. Meth addicts, no doubt. She hoped they had cash.

"I almost left you," she said as the wispy girl slid into the back.

"We came when we heard you." The girl had an irritating smoke-scarred voice.

The guy opened the front door and thunked into her passenger seat. "I'd rather you sat in back," Holly said, moving her money bag and purse to the center console.

"I like it up here," the man said.

"Stevie has a phobia," the girl added, as though that explained it. Holly decided it wasn't worth fighting.

Body odor filled the cab, along with the acrid smell of their habits. Breathing through her mouth, Holly set her meter. "Where to?"

"How much to take us downtown?" Stevie asked as Holly pulled away from the curb, past the dealers.

"Where downtown?"

"Just anywhere."

Holly sighed. She hated nonspecific destinations. "Probably about ten bucks, give or take. Depends on traffic and whether I have to take detours, and where I drop you off."

"Okay, whatever. Just get us out of here."

That didn't sound promising. The man jittered as she turned off the street. "Have I driven you before?" she asked, glancing at the girl in her rearview mirror. "You didn't call through the agency."

"Yeah, you drove me once. Few months ago, you picked me up when my boyfriend ditched me. I still had your card in my purse. Not too many chicks driving cabs."

Yes, she recognized the girl who had run out in front of her cab when Holly was following a subject. She'd had no choice but to give her a ride. The girl had deteriorated since then. Her habit was slowly eating away at her.

Holly didn't try to figure out why they'd wanted a woman driver. Tweekers were always paranoid, so maybe they considered a woman to be safer. Relieved to be out of that neighborhood, she breathed easier and pulled onto a road where businesses had long ago closed. She would be glad when she got back onto more populated streets.

Just as Holly's sense of security returned, Stevie slid up his dirty T-shirt and took hold of something in his waistband. She gasped as he pulled out a .38 revolver, cocked it, and pointed it at her.

"Are you kidding me?" She swerved and almost ran off the road. "What are you doing?"

"Keep both hands on the steering wheel and pull over!" He jabbed at her temple. "Do it!"

That would make as much sense as driving off a bridge. Pulling over would ensure that they stole her car and killed her, leaving Lily to grow up without her mother. Holly slowed and pretended to pull over, then stomped the accelerator, swerving hard to make the man lose his balance as she tried to knock the gun from his hand. Shrieking, the girl leaned forward and threw a belt over Holly's throat, threatening to choke her. "He said pull over!"

Holly groped at the belt but kept her foot on the accelerator. "Are you brain dead?" she choked out. "I'm driving!" The car picked up speed . . . sixty . . . seventy . . . "You kill me and you're both dead too!"

The girl loosened the belt, leaving it around Holly's neck, and the man steadied his aim. Holly deliberately ran off the road, then swerved sharply back onto the asphalt. This time she knocked the gun from his hand. He groped for it on the floorboard, found it, then swung it up into her face, its metal splitting her lip.

Tasting blood, Holly swerved again and stabbed her fingers into the soft tissue of Stevie's eyes. He cried out in pain, and she knocked the gun free again.

The girl jerked the belt, forcing Holly's head back against the headrest. Holly clawed at it and slammed on the brakes, throwing her passengers forward. The girl lost her leverage, and Holly got her fingers between the belt and her throat and ripped it away, then slammed the accelerator again.

The crazed man grabbed the wheel and pulled, forcing her to turn into a parking lot. She stomped to a screeching halt just before ramming into a building.

Holly dove for the gun on the floorboard, but the guy kneed her in the face, then thrust a knuckle punch to her eye. Recoiling, she tried to grab the gun, but he came up with his finger on the trigger. "Give me your cash! All of it!" he shouted.

"I don't have any," she lied.

The girl bent over the seat, snatched the money bag and Holly's purse, and bolted out the back door. Holly watched, astonished, as the girl left Stevie behind and ran behind the building.

Cursing, he flung the door open, lunged out, and ran after the woman. Holly stumbled out, wiping the blood from the bloody gash over her eye. She opened her trunk, grabbed her gun, and aimed at him over the hood. "Stop or I'll shoot!" He disappeared around the building.

"I have to pay my mortgage!" she cried, knowing it was useless.

She couldn't run after them. She'd only given birth four weeks ago. She dropped back into the car and pulled around the building, looking for them. The girl had scaled a fence and dropped to the other side. Now she was running into the woods. The man was almost over the fence.

Holly slammed her fist against the steering wheel and tried to calculate how much money they'd gotten. She would have to start all over . . . be away from Lily twice as long.

She pulled her phone out of her jeans pocket and called the police, then looked at herself in the rearview mirror. Her lip was already swelling and blood was smeared across her cheek. The gash over her eye dripped blood and her lid was puffing shut.

She looked like someone who belonged here. Someone like them.

CHAPTER 2

Holly stopped at a convenience store on the way home and washed her face in the dirty bathroom, splashing away her tears. She looked like she'd been in a drunken fight with a no-good boyfriend. Her sister Juliet would come unglued.

In fact, Holly didn't want to let anyone see her, but the police had encouraged her to go by the bank to cancel her credit cards. She hoped it didn't take long—she needed to see her baby. Maybe then she'd stop shaking. Breathing in strength and trying to look strong, she took care of business, then headed home.

Juliet sat on the floor in Holly's small living room, holding Lily against one shoulder as little Robbie slept in her lap. Only Juliet could pull that off.

"Hey." Holly dropped her keys on the counter, keeping her face down and hidden.

"Just in time. I think Lily's going to want to be fed soon."

"Yeah, sorry I'm late." Holly couldn't keep her face away from Juliet forever. She needed to hold her child. She crossed the room and took Lily from Juliet.

Juliet gasped. "Holly! What happened?"

Lily nuzzled against Holly's neck, and Holly held her for a moment, breathing in the calming scent of her.

"Are you all right?" Juliet said. "Do I need to take you to the hospital?"

"No, I'll be okay. I got mugged."

Juliet came to her feet and laid Robbie on the couch. "Mugged? Holly!"

Holly burst into tears again. "They cleaned me out. Two dopeheads that I should have realized were bad news when I picked them up."

"Oh, honey." Juliet rushed into the kitchen and searched through the cabinets. "We have to clean that. Come here. Did you call the police?"

"Yeah, I called them. They came, but it was too late. The dopeheads had gotten away. I had to go by the bank to cancel my debit card. Real classy, going in with a bloody lip and eye."

Juliet found hydrogen peroxide and poured some over a paper towel. Wadding it, she dabbed at Holly's lip and eyebrow.

"I feel so stupid."

"Holly, I've worried about this very thing happening."

"Well, it finally did. Are you happy? You can say I told you so. But I have to make a living, Juliet." The baby started to cry, and Holly pulled away from Juliet and went to the couch to feed her.

"How many were there? Can you identify them?"

"I'll recognize them if I ever see them again, but the chances of us finding them are pretty slim. They were meth heads. Skinny as toothpicks and pocked with sores. One of them was named Steve or Stevie, but who knows if that was his real name. I doubt the other one would have called him by his real name, knowing they were going to rob me. The money's gone. I'll just have to earn it back."

"Thank God you're okay. That's the important thing. Oh, Holly. I wish I could help you."

Juliet had financial problems of her own. Holly's oldest sibling had once been rich, the wife of an orthopedic surgeon. Now she was a widow with three children and had to live on a budget. She couldn't bail Holly out of her messes anymore.

But that didn't mean she wouldn't try. "Maybe it's time for you to work full-time for Michael. Business is getting to be more than we can handle working part-time."

"You'd think the fact that he's in prison would've put a damper on business, wouldn't you?"

"For any normal guy. But Michael's not a normal guy."

Holly smiled. Everyone in the area knew Michael's whole felony conviction was a farce.

"Anyway, what if you gave up driving the cab and just did that?"

Holly couldn't believe Juliet would suggest such a thing after loaning her the cash to buy the cab. It had been a way for Holly to hold down a job she couldn't be fired from—unlike all the other jobs she'd had. Juliet had a friend from church who owned a taxi service, and they'd agreed to add Holly's cab to their fleet in exchange for a commission when she was on the clock. By the time she paid them, bought gas, maintained her vehicle, paid taxes, and made her loan payment to Juliet, she could barely pay her personal bills.

Welcome to the adult world—a world she had studiously avoided until her pregnancy.

"How would I pay you back?"

"You could sell the cab to the agency and buy a normal car."

Holly sighed. "I can't live on ten bucks an hour."

"Maybe we can raise your pay." Juliet poured more hydrogen peroxide on the paper towel and dabbed at Holly's eyebrow again. "Are you sure you don't need stitches?"

"I don't know. Maybe I'll go to the doctor after I feed Lily. I just don't know how I'll pay for it. I have a huge deductible." How was she going to pay her mortgage, utilities, diapers, babysitters . . . ?

While Holly nursed, Juliet sat on the coffee table across from her. "Holly, what if I can get Michael to raise your pay to fifteen dollars an hour? Could you give up cab driving then?"

"What am I going to do with Lily if we're both working the same hours?"

"We can go in together and get a babysitter. Somebody who can keep Robbie and Lily at one of our houses. And sometimes we can have the babies there at work with us. Robbie has a little separation anxiety, so maybe at first the babysitter can just hang out with us at the office, until the babies are used to her."

"I don't know. That place is moldy."

"It's not moldy. I already had it checked. It's just old."

Holly looked down at the peaceful face of her nursing child. She wanted to cry again, but it would just upset Juliet more. If only she could stay home with her baby and focus on her all the time. But when you had a baby without involving the father . . . well, staying at home was a luxury you couldn't afford.

At least it would be years before Lily knew that her mother was an idiot who always did things in the wrong order.

"It'll be hard for me too, Holly," Juliet said, leaning toward her. "I stayed home with Zach and Abe. It feels all wrong to leave Robbie, but most mothers have to work, and the kids turn out fine."

Holly shot a look at her. "Please don't give me that quality over quantity stuff. I don't want to hear it."

"We can interview babysitters together. Bottom line, I don't want you driving a taxi anymore."

Holly thought about the investment she'd made in the car. She would be way happier working as a PI full-time than as a cabbie, but she had responsibilities, and it didn't really matter what would make her happier. She had to support Lily. "Like it or not," she said, "I make more driving a cab. If Michael will raise my hourly pay, I'll drive less and work for him more, but I can't afford to give up the cab driving altogether."

Juliet clearly didn't like it. She touched Holly's pink-tipped hair. "I guess you're making a mature decision, even though I hate it. You're growing up."

"Twenty-eight years old, it's about time, right?"

Lily looked up at her, her round eyes unfazed by the bruising, bloody wounds. Holly would never get used to that unconditional adoration. That gaze had the feel of God in it, and it calmed her spirit more than anything ever had.

Whatever motherhood cost her, it was worth it.

CHAPTER 3

The doctor, another of Juliet's friends from church, saw Holly right away. He gave her six stitches over her eye, but her lip would have to heal on its own.

Back home, after Juliet and Robbie left, Holly sat in the rocking chair her sister Cathy had bought her. Lily was awake and alert as they rocked, her big eyes focused on Holly as she sang. Holly wasn't a good singer. She'd often taken a turn in karaoke bars when she was loose enough to have flattened inhibitions, but once a friend had videotaped her. She'd watched it later, horrified that she sounded like a bad audition on *American Idol*—one that left crass judges in stitches and was played in mockery on all the morning shows. Still, Lily seemed soothed by her voice.

Holding her daughter was the biggest endorphin rush Holly had ever known.

She dreaded leaving her with a babysitter. None of Holly's

friends was reliable enough to watch her. She knew. She had been just like them.

The doorbell rang, and Holly felt a flash of panic. Her house . . . it was a mess. Who would show up without calling? She stood and glanced in the mirror next to her front door. She looked like she'd just been in a drunken brawl. In the adjoining kitchen, dirty dishes sat piled in the sink. Why hadn't she washed them when she finished eating this morning? The place had a faint odor of dirty diapers. She should have changed the diaper pail.

The bell rang again, followed by an aggressive knock. Whoever it was, they weren't going away.

Reconciling herself to embarrassment and humiliation, Holly raised Lily to her shoulder and headed for the door. She peered out the peephole as more knocking shook the door. Two police officers stood there, looking intimidatingly official.

Worried, she opened the door. "Hi."

"Are you Holly Cramer?"

"Yes. Have you found the muggers already?"

The men looked puzzled. "Muggers? What are you referring to?"

She shrugged. "The robbery today. That's not what you're here about?"

"No, but we'd like to talk to you. Could we come in for a minute?"

Her heart sank. What had she done now? Since she'd found out she was going to be a mother, she'd tried to live a good life, no longer on the razor edge of right and wrong. Had some old choice come back to haunt her?

The taller cop, who identified himself as Sergeant Petri, was dark and somber-looking, a little like Hotch on *Criminal*

Minds. The other one—named Tynes—looked younger but still authoritative. "Can I see your identification?" she asked.

They showed her their badges.

"Southport Police Department? I don't even think I've been to Southport lately. What is it? What do you want to talk to me about?"

"Creed Kershaw," Petri said. "He's not the one who roughed you up, is he?"

She sucked in a breath and pulled Lily tighter. "Creed? No, I haven't seen him in months. I hardly know him."

"If we could come inside, you could sit down."

She glanced back at her living room/kitchen combo. She doubted she could convince the cops to just go away. "All right," she sighed. "It's just . . . it's a mess. With a new baby, only four weeks old . . . and it's been a bad day."

"We won't take long," Petri said.

Sighing, she stepped back and let them in. "I know what you're thinking. How does a person live in this mess? It's just that I'm not getting much sleep, so the dishes aren't really a priority, and the laundry's piling up . . ."

Tynes spoke in a softer voice, surprising her. "I have a three-month-old baby, so I get it. We just want to ask you a few questions about Kershaw."

His smile helped her relax. If they had come to accuse her of some long-forgotten infraction, they would look a little more guarded, wouldn't they?

She moved the blanket draped over the back of the couch, the diaper bag she had thrown there, the vinyl changing pad . . . Cradling Lily in one arm, she moved the vibrating seat on the floor blocking their path. "Here," she said. "You can sit on the couch."

They sat, and she took the rocker again.

Tynes spoke first. "We understand that Kershaw is the father of your baby."

Holly's mouth fell open and she stopped rocking. She hadn't told anyone. Not her sisters, not her best friends . . . nobody. "How is it that you understand that? I haven't identified the father. He's not on the birth certificate. I haven't told anyone who her father is."

"Let me start at the beginning," Petri said. "We're investigating a murder that happened over the weekend in Southport. Creed Kershaw is a person of interest in the case, but he's disappeared. Do you have any knowledge of his whereabouts?"

She let that plunk into her psyche, the ripples moving through her brain. "'A person of interest'? So you think he's the killer? Great. I've always had amazing taste in men."

She saw a glint of amusement in Petri's eyes. "So you did have a relationship with him?"

"No," she said. "I haven't seen him in almost a year."

"Ten months, to be exact?" Tynes asked.

How did they know all this? "What would make you come looking for him here?"

"When we learned he had just become a father, we thought he might be here with you. Are you sure he isn't the one who hurt you?"

"Positive. Do you honestly think I'd defend the person who did this to me?"

She got to her feet, found Lily's pacifier in her swing, offered it to her daughter. Lily took it, her little shoulders hunched.

Tears misted in Holly's eyes as she strapped Lily in her swing, but she wasn't sure if the tears were from anger or fear. "You're barking up the wrong tree. He doesn't know about her. I never told him. I didn't remember his last name until you said it just now. I don't even have a phone number for him. Does he live in Southport?"

"Yes." Their narrow stares indicated they didn't believe her. Petri's gaze broke, and he scanned her living room, registering her pictures, clearly looking for a shot with Creed in it. There weren't any.

She flicked the music button on the swing. "You Are My Sunshine" started playing. Lily seemed content. Holly stood straighter and faced the two men. "Look, I hate this . . . I met him in a stupid bar when I'd been drinking too much, and I made mistakes. But this guy . . . I don't know him. I don't know anything about him. I've never seen him since. He has absolutely no idea."

"Well, that's where you're wrong," Petri said. "We learned of you through a message on his voice mail, left several days ago. It was from a man named Rio, telling Kershaw that you'd given birth, and that he had a daughter."

She felt the blood draining from her face. "You've got to be kidding."

"Do you know Rio Diaz?"

"Yes. He *used* to be a friend. He introduced me to Creed that night in the bar." She had run into Rio once when she was pregnant, and he'd asked when she was due. She shouldn't have told him. Had he counted up the weeks since her night with Creed?

Holly lowered to the edge of her rocker. "Look, I'm trying to change. When I realized I was having a baby, I tried to do better, you know? I didn't want him to know because he seemed like bad news, like all the other guys I'm usually attracted to. The bad dudes I could never bring home to meet my sisters and brother. I figured he'd never know." There was no sign of sympathy in their eyes. How could they understand? "If he knows about her, I doubt he'd even care. Wouldn't he have called or something if he did? And if he's hiding, he sure wouldn't come to me."

"If you see him, if he shows up here, we need for you to call us right away."

She took the card Petri offered across the coffee table. "Is he dangerous?"

"We believe he could be. By now, he knows we're looking for him. He's probably armed."

They got to their feet, and Holly checked on Lily, who had drifted off to sleep. She walked them to the door. "So . . . you'll keep this quiet, right? About Lily? If he hasn't told his family, I'd rather they didn't know."

Tynes looked back at her. "I can't guarantee his family didn't hear the voice mail. They've been looking for him."

Her heart plunged. "Great."

"They're just focused on finding their son right now."

She nodded, hating herself. *Great job, Holly. You found the only murderer in the room, got drunk with him, and conceived a child. How does it get better than that?*

She let them out and stood on the front stoop as they strode to their squad car. When they drove away, she went back in and studied herself in the mirror.

"Good job!" she bit out, angry tears rimming her eyes. "Look at you now." She hated herself, from the tattoos on her biceps to the pink tips on her blonde hair. She wished she could shed her skin like a snake and become someone else, but she would still be a mess.

Lily's pacifier fell, and the baby started to cry. Wiping her own tears, Holly shook herself out of her self-loathing and took care of her child.

CHAPTER 4

It took a couple of hours for Holly to find Rio Diaz's phone number. She had to call friends of her friends until she found one who knew how to reach him. He didn't answer when she called, so she left a message, trying to keep it upbeat so he wouldn't duck her call. "Hey, Rio, how's it going? It's Holly Cramer. Listen, would you give me a call? I need to ask you something. Thanks!"

When he didn't call back right away, she texted him. "Hey, Rio! This is Holly Cramer. Give me a call, will you? It's important."

While she waited for his return call, she walked Lily around the house, bouncing her gently. What should she do now? She had no intention of sharing this news with her siblings. Juliet would just remind her that her bad decisions had lousy consequences.

Holly knew about consequences. Hadn't she had enough of them?

It was hard to convince people you were trying to change when you kept repeating the same mistakes. Pregnancy was like a neon sign saying, "You were right! There are consequences!"

But pregnancy had been the first thing that had ever made Holly want to change.

She didn't want to drag it all up again with her sisters or her brother. Wasn't it bad enough that one drunken, careless night had resulted in a life change? They already thought that picking up guys in bars for one-night stands was common practice for her. Truth be known, it wasn't. She didn't normally take strangers home. Even now, she didn't know what had gotten into her that night.

And then . . . she'd tried to put it out of her mind until nausea began to greet her each morning. The reality of her pregnancy had hit her hard. She had fully intended to abort . . . but she couldn't go through with it. The knowledge that there was a baby in her belly—a baby with fingers and toes and nerve endings and a developing brain, and even a personality and potential—had overwhelmed and defeated her plan to end this quietly.

Her siblings had been great about it. What could they do when a little life was involved? But she knew that they had pretty much thrown up their hands at her latest crisis. They'd teamed up to help clean up another of Holly's messes. At this very moment, they were probably begging God not to let her fail at motherhood.

They all assumed she was so promiscuous that she didn't know the name of the father. She had never told them that, but she let them believe it.

The phone suddenly rang, startling her, but her twitch didn't wake the baby. She grabbed the phone. Rio!

She swiped to answer and put it to her ear. "Hey, Rio. Long time no hear from."

She heard the hesitation in his voice. "Hey, Holly. How are you?"

She thought of skipping over the giving-birth part, but that would be suspect, since he clearly already knew. "Oh, I'm okay. Had a baby four weeks ago. Little girl. Getting used to motherhood and all that."

He hesitated again, then said, "Really? I knew you were pregnant, but didn't know you'd had it already."

That made her angry, ripping her thin membrane of pleasantries. "Okay, cut the ruse, Rio."

"What?"

"You know good and well I've had the baby, because you called Creed Kershaw. Where do you get off making the assumption that he's the father and running to tell him?"

He sighed. "Have you heard from him, then?"

"No, I haven't heard from him. He's apparently missing and wanted for murder. Thanks for introducing us, by the way."

"Holly, I didn't know he was into anything illegal—and maybe he's not. He's just a person of interest, right? And besides, I wasn't fixing you up with him. I just introduced you."

"What made you think he had anything to do with my pregnancy?"

"The timing," he said. "When I saw you pregnant and you told me the due date, I sorta counted back, and it seemed like it was around that time."

"So?"

"So, I know you. You're not the type to just . . . Even that night I was surprised. When I heard you'd had the baby, I decided to tell him. I figured if he was the dad, he needed to know."

The thought made her sick. "What did he say?"

"Nothing. I left a message, but he never called back. If he's hiding out and evading a murder charge, the baby might be the last thing on his mind."

Her head was beginning to throb. "How did you even know I had her?"

"I heard it from Mattie at the Dock."

The Dock had been one of her favorite bars, back when she was the party queen. "Yeah, she came to see me in the hospital."

"She showed me a picture. Cute baby. Looks just like you, except for the pink hair."

Holly couldn't help the pride welling up in her heart.

"So the cops talked to you?" Rio asked.

"Yeah, they did, because of you. When's the last time you talked to Creed?"

"It's been a few months."

"Did you tell anyone else about this?"

"No, nobody. I swear, Holly. I wasn't even sure, so I only told him."

"This isn't just gossip, Rio. It's my baby's life. She deserves better, and I don't want some stranger suing me for visitation rights."

She knew how ridiculous this sounded. If he were such a stranger, why had she gotten so intimate? The irony didn't escape her.

"I meant well, Holly. He was a good guy when I knew him in high school. I don't know what happened."

"Next time mind your own stinking business." Her words got caught in her throat. "Whatever. Thanks for the info."

She hung up and drew in a deep, ragged breath and dabbed

at her eyes. Now what? She rejected her first instinct to call one of her sisters or her brother.

She went to the window, peered out. Her street looked quiet. It had started to rain, so the road was empty of playing children and neighbors walking their dogs. She checked her locks, then armed her security system, the one that Juliet had insisted she have installed. Even if Creed didn't come, she could always count on the meth heads showing up for an encore.

She got her gun out of her purse and made sure it was loaded.

Maybe the murder investigation had distracted Creed completely. Maybe a new daughter was the furthest thing from Creed Kershaw's mind, wherever he was. But she couldn't depend on that. And the dopers . . . they'd probably thrown away anything that couldn't help them buy drugs right away. Still, her address had been in her purse. She prayed they wouldn't use it.

Anger spiraled through her chest. She couldn't just sit here waiting. She had to *do* something. She didn't know where to find her muggers, but she might be able to help track Creed down.

She'd gotten pretty good at finding missing persons and tracking those who hid from creditors and ex-wives. Creed's knowledge of Lily was a frightening thing, something she'd never expected. Making sure he was arrested for whatever he'd done was one way to ensure that he put no claims on her daughter's life.

Then again, hunting him could be dangerous.

The police would find him eventually. But if she left it up to them, she might be looking over her shoulder for days, even weeks. No, she had to be proactive. Somehow she had to move this along and make sure Creed didn't pop up when she least expected it.

CHAPTER 5

Michael Hogan grabbed a wad of trash and stuffed it into his flimsy garbage bag. It was raining, but the work wasn't finished, so there was no way Lieutenant Rafferty would take the work crew back to the jail. Michael worked faster, hoping to get the job done. But some of the others continued to work slowly, as if they'd rather get soaked than go back to that place.

Being a trustee allowed to go out on the work crew was a privilege, earned only through months of good behavior. It broke up the hours of monotony, sitting in the cell with the same faces day after day, the same fights, the same insanity among the mentally ill, the same rage of hungry addicts, and the bitter, angry offenders who found themselves locked up.

Someone honked a horn, and Michael looked up. A car full of teenaged girls drove by, laughing and waving, mocking them. He looked down at his green-and-white-striped

Dr. Seuss pants, society's assurance that none of the inmates would ever be mistaken for the general public.

When he got out of jail, he would never wear stripes again.

He was here for breaking the law, illegally using a firearm when he was a convicted felon. Though he'd been helping break up the biggest drug ring ever to work this area, and defending his friend and her kidnapped children, he couldn't deny that he'd violated probation. There was a penalty for that, and he had to accept it. Juliet and her kids were safe, which made a year behind bars worth it.

He'd filled his bag, so he tied it up and left it where the garbage men could pick it up, then went back to the truck to get another one. The drivers waiting for the light to change kept their eyes focused ahead of them, as if afraid to glance in the prisoners' direction. He heard a click—someone locking his doors.

Michael pulled a garbage bag off its roll, shook it out. "Hogan, cross the street and start over there," Rafferty shouted.

Michael nodded. Rafferty wouldn't let cars get between himself and most of the other inmates, but he trusted Michael. He'd known him back when Michael was a detective on the Panama City police force. He'd been one of Michael's sympathizers when he was convicted, and he'd vouched for him and gotten him on the work crew at the earliest opportunity.

Michael went to the crosswalk and waited for the light to change again. It turned yellow, and cars turning left passed in front of him.

When the crossing light turned green, he stepped out into the street. But the approaching SUV didn't slow, and Michael jumped back just as it rounded the corner. His gaze connected with the driver.

No way. It couldn't be him!

Michael stared at the driver as the SUV passed. His hair was blond and longer than it had been before . . . He took a few steps in the direction of the SUV, memorizing the tag. LTH 425.

LTH 425 . . . LTH 425 . . . LTH 425. If only he had a pen.

He'd have to remember it. Heart racing, he crossed the street and worked on the road cleanup, repeating the number in his mind over and over as he finished his work, constantly glancing up to watch the passing cars. LTH 425. Black Lincoln Navigator, 2012 or 2013.

Leonard Miller. Did he have the gall to come back into town when he knew so many were looking for him? Was he so pompous that he thought he was invincible?

If that *was* him, Michael would find him. Miller wouldn't get away again. Even from the inside, there were things Michael could do. He wouldn't rest until his brother's killer faced the justice he deserved.

CHAPTER 6

Cathy Cramer had never felt so determined. Ever since Michael, her fiancé, had been sentenced to prison, she'd spent every waking moment thinking about how to save him.

It had been her sister Holly's idea to start a letter-writing campaign, and even though it was a long shot, she had to believe that a pardon was possible if the governor was barraged with mountains of letters on Michael's behalf.

Her blog, *Cat's Curious*, was her best means to that end.

Dear Friends,

Many thanks to those of you who've already contacted the governor of Florida to request a pardon for Michael Hogan. To the rest of you, I'm begging you to write a simple letter on paper—not just e-mail—and send it to the governor's office. At the very least, it will get his attention and make him consider Michael's case.

The man is a hero. He has spent his life fighting crime and locking up bad guys, and now he lives among those he helped put away. Everyone who watched Leonard Miller's trial two and a half years ago knows that Michael didn't deliberately lie during his testimony. He didn't suppress evidence. He forgot the affidavit a woman with dementia had signed, describing someone other than Leonard Miller as the one who'd shot Joe. Michael realized that she wasn't reliable; every other witness identified Miller without hesitation.

Forgive me for rehashing this, but my newer *Cat's Curious* readers may not know the details of the case. When the defense attorney called the mistaken woman's daughter to the stand, Michael didn't even remember meeting her. She testified that Michael hadn't followed through on her mother's affidavit, thereby effectively refuting Michael's claim under oath that he'd never in his life suppressed evidence.

Because of the woman's testimony and the defense attorney's focus on this, the jury had reasonable doubt about the police department's integrity and found Leonard Miller not guilty. After the trial, Michael was convicted of lying under oath. He lost his job at the police department since, as a convicted felon, he could no longer carry a weapon.

Needless to say, Miller went on to kill and kidnap others as he climbed the ladder of his deadly drug-trafficking ring. When Michael Hogan later took up arms to save my sister Juliet and her children from Miller's murderous cruelty, he violated probation. Michael pled guilty and took the sentence without hesitation or regret, even though I begged him to fight it. His marriage proposal to me came as they hauled him off to jail.

Again, a cold-blooded, brutal bottom dweller escaped

justice, while a hero is in jail. And they wonder why I lost faith in the justice system and quit practicing law.

If there was ever a man who was wrongfully incarcerated, it's Michael Hogan. If there's ever been a man who deserves not just freedom, but a complete pardon, it's Michael.

Please take fifteen minutes to draft a letter to the governor, begging him to offer that pardon. You don't have to be from Florida to do it. Just add your voice to all the other voices, and let's get Michael free.

Curious Cat

She sat back in her chair and closed her eyes. Would this even work? She had accumulated over two million readers since she'd devoted herself to investigative blogging, enough that big advertisers sought her out to buy ad space on her site. If only a fraction of those readers responded and wrote a letter, surely it would get the governor's attention.

But Governor Larimore was known to eschew his pardoning powers. During his campaign, he complained often about the number of pardons the previous governor had granted—some to convicted murderers and rapists. Larimore's vow to not grant a single pardon was one of the reasons he'd won the governor's seat.

Was getting him to make an exception even possible?

Anxiety ebbed in her again, and she looked down at the photo album the florist had given her. She was supposed to be picking out the colors she wanted, the kind of flowers, the shape of the bouquet, but she couldn't think about any of that when Michael was in jail. His release nine months from now seemed so far away.

Her computer pinged as readers commented on the blog

she'd just posted—pledges from readers to write that letter. She hoped she could fill up the governor's mail room.

She checked her watch. Almost time to visit Michael. She wouldn't be able to use her attorney privileges to get into the same room with him today, so she'd have to visit like any other loved one. She couldn't hug him or kiss him or touch the stubble on his face or smell his unique scent.

She shut down her computer, letting the readers take it from there, and headed to the jail.

CHAPTER 7

Cathy drank in the sight of Michael like a parched desert traveler. He sat behind the dirty glass, phone to his ear, his gaze locked to hers. "Are you sure it was Miller?" she asked into the phone.

"No, not completely."

"It's just that . . . you want to find him so badly, maybe you just *think* it looked like him."

"He almost ran over me. I was only three feet from him. I saw his face."

"Still . . . you said his hair was a lighter color. It could have been someone else. I just . . . I don't think he'd come back. It's too dangerous. He's wanted for drug trafficking, distribution, conspiracy, kidnapping, and murder . . . and that's not all. His face has been all over the news. He barely escaped last time. He'd be insane to come back now."

"But he *is* insane, and there are millions of dollars more to be made if he stays in the game. Think about it. A guy like

30

Miller, who was basically just a street dealer, who then rises to the level of distributor in an international drug ring? And then he gets chased out of town. He wouldn't just disappear, knowing there was more to be had."

"But he got *away* with so much. Enough to live on comfortably for the rest of his life."

"He doesn't think like we do. He gets a rush out of living dangerously."

Cathy felt that knot forming in her throat, and she swallowed hard. The pain of losing her former fiancé—Michael's brother—had grown duller over the last two and a half years, but remembering how his killer walked free still refilled that grief well.

And that had only been the beginning.

She looked down at the paper she'd printed out. "So the SUV is a 2013 Lincoln Navigator registered to Sidney Hutchinson, forty-five. He lives at 1366 Pendleton Street. Only there isn't a 1366 Pendleton Street. There was, but it was recently demolished. They're building a CVS Pharmacy there."

Michael leaned forward, clutching the phone to his ear. "See? If this wasn't Miller, the tag would check out."

"I agree. So we're looking for him, and so is Max, but I don't want you to get your hopes up." Her eyes glistened with tears, and she touched the glass.

He met her fingertips on the other side and smiled, always the comforter. Even in prison clothes, he looked strong and healthy, as though he could protect her from inside. There seemed to be no hint of weakness from the gunshot wound to his chest. He'd been getting some sun, and his face was tan, his cheekbones slightly burned.

She wished they would let him have sunscreen.

"So . . . tell me about the wedding plans," he said.

That was just like him, to change the subject when he saw the tears coming on. It worked. She dropped her hand and grinned. He had asked her to marry him at his sentencing, and they'd scheduled the wedding for the month after he was to be released. "Well, I heard back from the venue. Looks like the Sterling Reef is available that day. It's nice and it's on the beach. I want something with a beautiful ocean view from inside, so we can get the outdoor feel but still have air conditioning."

"I'm all for AC. Did you put down a deposit?"

She twisted her mouth. "No. I'm still thinking about it."

"Why?"

"Money, for one."

She wished she hadn't brought it up. It only made him feel inadequate. "But business is good," she went on. "Your clients are still calling, and Juliet, Holly, and I are keeping things going. Business is almost too good. We're having trouble keeping up with all of it."

"Don't forget to bill them."

"Yeah, Juliet is taking care of that. She's the most organized."

"She also has three kids now."

"She's managing. We're all managing."

"So . . . we should have enough for the wedding, right?"

"Yes, but do we want to spend it on that? We'll be just as married if we do it more simply. We could walk across the street from my house and do it on our beach."

"But we couldn't invite all our friends. We couldn't even manage much family without needing some kind of permit. And once you're into all that, you might as well have a nice venue."

"Yeah," she said. "I'll think about it some more."

"We could still get married in my church," he said.

Cathy met his eyes, aware that he wanted it to be *her* church too, but she hadn't made it her own yet. "Yeah, that's a possibility. Or Juliet's. She'd love it. She'd surely fill the place up with her friends."

"I want people to celebrate with us," he said into the phone.

"Maybe."

He moved closer to the dirty glass, tapped on it. She met his eyes. "You sure you're okay with this?" he said. "Getting married, I mean?"

"Of course I am." Her smile caught in her eyes, and those tears shimmered back. "It's just . . . kind of nostalgic, you know? I've planned a wedding before. Instead of happy, all these decisions just make me . . . kind of sad. And when you're not able to plan with me . . ."

"I know."

"I made all these decisions once. All the things I'd dreamed of, but I can't do those same things now because . . . well, it just seems weird."

"Yeah."

"So I'm trying to make different decisions. Only I still like the same things."

His gaze held her for a long moment. "Joe wouldn't mind if you planned the same kind of wedding."

"I know. I just don't want to be thinking of him that day. I don't want to be sad on our wedding day. And I don't want you to be."

"Maybe that's the wrong approach. Maybe we do need to think of him. Maybe we need to make him part of it somehow."

She didn't know what that would look like, but as she left the jail, she tried to shake herself out of her melancholy. Part of it, of course, was that she hadn't been able to hug Michael more than a few times since he was incarcerated, and then only because she was his attorney and was able to get into the same room with him now and then. The rest of the time, she had to sit with virus-crusted glass between them and talk to him on the phone.

She opened her purse and pulled out her latest letter to the governor that she had typed and sealed. She said a silent prayer over it, then drove to the nearest postal box and dropped it in. *Please, God . . . I'm begging you . . .*

Michael's fate was in God's hands. She would have to trust him, but meanwhile, she would follow up on every avenue he put into her mind.

CHAPTER 8

Holly stood in front of the bathroom mirror, the box of hair dye in her hands. The bleach should erase the pink tips. She had been dyeing the bottom half of her hair pink since before her pregnancy, giving her an edgy, two-tone look that set her apart. Maybe it had something to do with being a preacher's kid. Her father's betrayal of the family had created a rebellious streak in her. Pink hair and tattoos had been a way of thumbing her nose at those who judged her, but now she was sick of them. Her old life was wilted around the edges, like decaying flowers.

Hurrying to finish before Lily woke up, she opened the box and pulled out the bottles of peroxide and bleach. If she was going to locate Creed Kershaw, she needed to blend in. The tattoos were easy enough to cover with sleeves, but the pink hair was too memorable.

She read over the instructions then poured the bleach over

her hair and worked it through, making sure it covered all the pink. As she waited for the developer to work, she got on the computer and searched for anything she could find about Creed Kershaw. Though she had access to a lot of Michael's databases from home, she would probably have to go into the office to gain entry to sites only accessible from his computer.

When she found Creed, she would call Petri and Tynes and tell them where he was. Then she'd know for sure that he wasn't about to intrude on Lily's life. If he truly was guilty of murder, a prison sentence would solve the problem for her.

Holly suspected that if her sisters knew about Creed, they'd tell her that failing to tell her baby's father about Lily was deceptive. He had a right to know, they would say. But they didn't get it. The idea of having some stranger in her life sharing custody with her was unbearable.

When the time was up for the color to develop, she rinsed out her hair and checked to see if the pink was gone. Good—it was now a soft champagne color.

She dried it quickly, wincing at the look of normalcy. It wasn't bad. It might even be pretty . . . but pretty had never been what Holly valued most.

Lily woke and began crying before Holly's hair was completely dry, so she abandoned the dryer and went to get her daughter. As she comforted Lily, she sat near the window, looking out through the curtains, making sure that no murderers or muggers or estranged fathers lurked nearby, watching.

It had been a long time since she'd kept her sisters and brother in the dark about her deepest emotions. The isolation was heavy. She had never felt more lonely.

CHAPTER 9

Holly went to Michael's office after she fed Lily. She parked out by the defunct gas pumps under the sign that said "Hogan Investigative Services." The building, which had once been a convenience store and gas station, had seen better days. The grass had grown taller in the cracked and weed-riddled pavement. They needed to have an outside workday to care for the property, but the work inside took priority. Clients still came asking for their help to locate biological parents, to check out backgrounds on employees, to investigate workers' comp fraud cases, and a million other little things that kept them in business. Their PR about disrupting Miller's drug ring a few months ago had increased business almost a hundred percent, at the worst possible time.

She clicked Lily's car seat out of the cab and took her inside. Juliet sat at Michael's desk, papers covering it. "Thank goodness you're here," she said without looking up. "Got in three new clients this afternoon. Easy stuff, I think. We can pull them off in a couple hours each. I'm trying to bill for the stuff we did last week, and I don't feel like I'm ever gonna catch up."

When Holly didn't answer, Juliet looked up at her.

"Wait. Your hair! That's not your wig, is it?"

"No, it's me." Holly struck a pose. "What do you think?"

"Pretty! I like it a lot, but your face looks awful."

Holly had almost forgotten the cuts and bruises. "Yeah, well. What else is new?"

"Have the police found the people who mugged you?"

"Haven't heard from them about it, but I doubt it."

"Why did you do it? The hair thing?"

Holly shrugged. "Tired of it. And the wigs get hot when I'm doing surveillance."

Juliet just grinned—she had always hated the pink tips—but she had the grace not to say anything else.

Holly went to the computer in the other room, sat down, and typed in "Creed Kershaw Southport Florida." A few things came up, and she studied them. He had a possession of marijuana charge three years ago but had gotten a deferment in favor of drug treatment. He didn't have any charges for drug dealing. She did a newspaper search on Southport murders, found one article: "Police Search for Clues into Southport Murder." She read over it. At the writing of the article, the reporter hadn't known much about the case other than the fact that a man named Emilio Juarez had been found dead in an abandoned parking lot, shot through the back of his head. Police speculated that it had to do with a drug deal. There were no suspects listed.

She searched the newspaper again, looking for any other murders, but none had occurred in the last month. This had to be the one. She wrote down the name of the dead person and did a quick search on him. Juarez did have a rap sheet. He'd spent a year in prison for drug distribution and had been arrested twice more. Someone had hired him a high-powered attorney—Jack Humphrey, who was renowned for representing sleazeballs—and he'd gotten off both times.

She jumped when Juliet came into the room. "What're you doing?"

Holly shook her head. "Nothing. Just trying to get a few things done."

"That one of our jobs?" Juliet asked, looking at the screen.

Holly closed out the window she was looking at. "Yeah, the Simon case."

"Oh. Nothing resolved yet?"

"No," Holly said. "Still working on it."

Juliet put three files down on a folding table that functioned as a desk. "Can you take these? They're pretty easy background searches for employment. You can probably knock them out pretty fast."

"Sure," Holly said.

Juliet disappeared back into Michael's office. "I have to go soon," she said. "I have to pick the kids up. I've got a neighbor looking after Robbie, but I promised her I'd only be gone a couple of hours." She came back out with her purse under her arm. "So when do you want to do our interviews?"

Holly glanced back at her. "Interviews for what?"

"Our nanny."

Holly sighed and looked down at Lily, still content in her infant seat. "I don't know. I'm not really ready yet. She's so little."

"But we talked about this. We both need sitters. Let's choose someone together. Someone we trust and like. Even if you don't go full-time here, you'll need somebody when you drive."

"You go ahead and interview them," Holly said. "When you narrow it down, I'll meet them."

When Juliet left, Holly went into Michael's office and sat at the desk. She used his computer to go through his deeper databases looking for information on Creed Kershaw and Emilio Juarez.

When the front door creaked open, she jumped, then peered through Michael's office doorway. His brother Max, a detective in the major crimes unit at the Panama City Police Department, stood just inside the front door. "Max, I didn't see you drive up."

"Didn't mean to scare you," he said. "You looked deep in thought." He stared at her for a moment. "Hey, what happened to you?"

"Mugged this morning in my cab. I filed a report. Two meth heads. They got three hundred bucks."

Max lowered himself into a chair. "Did you know them?"

"No. I've driven the girl before, but I don't remember her name. She called the guy Stevie." She looked up at him. "What are you doing here?"

"I had some time off and I thought maybe I could come and give you guys a hand. I think it's pretty cool that you're trying to keep Michael's business going. He said business is actually good and that you're a little overwhelmed."

"True story," she said. "It doesn't help that I just had a baby and Juliet's dealing with a new one of her own."

"Yeah, I heard about her adoption. That's really something. Takes a special kind of person to adopt the baby her husband had with his mistress."

"That's what she is," Holly said. "A special kind of person. But these babies kind of tug at your heartstrings, you know?"

When she looked down at her own sleeping child, Max moved out of his chair and squatted down next to Lily. She was asleep, but he gently touched her hair. "She looks like you, Holly," he said. "At least like the left side of your face."

She grinned. "Poor kid."

Max grinned back. "I like your hair, by the way. Kind of takes the focus off your black eye and busted lip."

"Really? So you were a hater of the pink tips too?"

"Didn't hate them," he said. "I just didn't quite understand what you were going for."

She shrugged. "Seemed like a good idea at the time."

"So what made you get rid of the pink?"

She sat back, stared at Max, wondering if she should tell him what was going on. He was a detective, after all, and he had access to more information than she could get here. Maybe he could tell her something about Creed Kershaw's case, find out if she had anything to fear. "I've really been thinking about dyeing my hair for a while now," she said. "Pink hair gives people the wrong idea about me. I'd rather be taken seriously."

"I understand."

She set her chin on her palm. "Listen, I'm glad you're here. Something happened today."

"Besides the mugging?"

"Yeah, something else." She leaned forward on the desk. "If I tell you this, would you promise not to tell anybody else?"

Max frowned. "I don't know if I can promise that, Holly."

"Nothing illegal," she said. "I mean, nothing I've done. I just don't want my sisters or my brother finding out. Not even Michael."

"What does it have to do with?"

She hesitated, glanced at her daughter, then looked back at Max. "Lily's father."

Max sat straighter. "Oh yeah?"

"I don't want anybody to know who he is. I'm ashamed of the whole situation."

Max had nothing to say to that.

"I haven't told my sisters or anybody who he is. I thought I could just forget about him, but today the police came to my house—"

"The police?"

"The Southport police." She told him what they'd said about Creed Kershaw and her phone call with Rio. "It makes me sick," she said. "It scares me to death—first of all that he's a killer. Of course that's the kind of guy I would be attracted to. It's just like me."

Max chuckled. "You're being hard on yourself."

"Somebody's gotta do it," she said. "The other thing is . . . now that he knows about Lily . . . the idea that he might come in and want to get involved in her life scares me to death. I can't stand the thought of him having anything to do with her, especially now that I know he could be a criminal."

"So what do you want me to do?"

"I was just wondering . . . could you look him up and find out about this murder? Find out what they have on him, what the chances are that he's really the one? I just want to know who I'm dealing with."

"If he winds up in prison, you don't have much to worry about."

"Yeah, but even if he's in prison, his family could try to get involved with Lily."

"Doubtful," he said. "I'm no lawyer—Cathy could tell you

for sure—but if his name's not on the birth certificate and he hasn't been part of her life—that family might not have any rights to her."

"Still, it could turn into some big hairy deal if they decided to get a lawyer and paternity tests and all, and I hate the thought of it. Will you help me?"

Max shrugged. "Sure, I'll see what I can find out for you."

"Thank you." She breathed a sigh of relief. "It's kind of urgent."

"I'll work fast," he said. "But in the meantime, do you have any cases I could help resolve with my resources, just to help my brother out a little bit and keep you guys going?"

"That would be great," Holly said. "Juliet and Cathy would really appreciate it. We're all in over our heads right now." She looked closely at Max, watching for a reaction as she said, "I'm glad you and Michael are getting along better now."

He rubbed his mouth. "Let's just say his incarceration has made me reevaluate things. The least I can do is what you guys are doing."

Holly was surprised. She had never been close to Max. He had seemed all business, a little arrogant, and she'd hated the way he and his parents had treated Michael, as if he were responsible for Joe's killer walking free. But Max had made mistakes too. Maybe they'd made him humble.

"So whatcha got?" he said again.

She handed him the three cases that Juliet had just given her. "If you could get these off my desk, I'd appreciate it. Routine employment background searches for our biggest corporate account."

"Seems doable. I can probably knock these out tonight, then you can bill them tomorrow."

"You can talk to Juliet about compensation."

He shook his head. "I don't want any. I've got a job. I just want to help my brother."

Lily started to cry, and Holly jumped up and got her out of the car seat. She needed to nurse, but she wouldn't do it in front of Max.

As if on cue, he got to his feet. "Guess I'll go get started on these at home so you can do your mom thing."

She smiled, felt a blush on her cheeks. "Yeah, thanks."

He stepped to the door, looked out at her taxi. "Still gonna be driving a cab after the mugging?"

"Some," she said, "but I sure would like it if I could transition to full-time with Michael. I like this gig a whole lot better. Especially today."

"If business is as good as he says, that might work." He motioned to her face. "Might want to put some ice on that eye." He opened the door.

"Hey, Max?"

He turned back.

"Thanks for helping me on that Creed Kershaw thing. I really appreciate it. And I appreciate the secrecy."

He nodded. "No problem."

"I just want you to know I'm not really like that."

"Like what?"

"I'm not the kind of girl who just goes home with a random guy. I don't know what got into me that night. Too much alcohol, probably, but it was a rare thing." She looked down at Lily. "I just want you to know that."

"I'm not judging you," he said. "Everybody makes mistakes. You're no different."

He strode out to his car, got in. Holly stood looking through the window. No different? That was the last thing she wanted to hear.

She went to the bathroom mirror, bouncing her baby. Her face looked ridiculous. Her right eye had swollen shut, and the stitches across her eyebrow were Frankensteinish. The purple and black gash on her fat lip was lovely. She studied her hair again, longing for her pink tips. They made her different, didn't they? At the very least, they would distract from her face.

Sighing, she decided to stick with her plan to stay a blonde for now. She could always change her mind later.

CHAPTER 10

Max talked to the cops who'd taken Holly's complaint and learned they had no leads on the two who'd mugged her. Holly's abusers had gotten away with it.

He knocked out the cases that Holly had given him in less than an hour, e-mailed her the results, then got to work on Creed Kershaw. The first thing he found was Kershaw's picture on his driver's license. He studied it for a moment, trying to think like Holly. What had she seen in this guy the night she met him that made her go home with him? She probably saw him as good looking. He was six feet tall, had dark brown hair and blue eyes that girls probably found dreamy, and he teetered on the edge between clean-cut and thug. One part jock with one part bad boy. Enough for Holly to be snowed.

Max pulled up Kershaw's rap sheet and looked it over. A possession charge and a probation violation.

The charges were from three years ago. Kershaw had been fairly clean since, except for a few driving violations.

There hadn't been a warrant issued for his arrest for this recent murder. They must just want to question him. The dead guy—Emilio Juarez—was a drug dealer who had lived in Southport but was known on the streets of Panama City too. He'd been known in the drug community as Loco, an interesting distinction, considering so many in the drug culture were crazy.

Max did a quick search on Loco and found the report the first responders had filed after discovering his body. He'd been murdered execution style—shot in the back of the head—and his body had been left in a parking lot behind a shopping center.

Max picked up the phone and called Holly.

"You got something already?" she asked him.

"Yeah, listen to this." He told her what he'd found. "There's no warrant for his arrest yet. He's just a person of interest, but his DNA was all over the crime scene."

"So do you think he killed him?"

"Don't know, but his sudden disappearance after the murder raised suspicion."

"How do they know he isn't dead too?"

"It says he called his family once after the murder, babbling something about how he was sorry he'd disappointed them. They were afraid of suicide, so they reported it to the police, but he's used his credit card around town and made phone calls, so they believe he's still alive and in the area. Looks like he's in hiding."

"So they think this was a drug deal gone bad?" Holly asked.

"Looks like it. Loco was well-known around here. Sold a lot of dope. If Kershaw wound up doing an execution, that would mean he works for someone higher up, the one who ordered the hit. You know how these things work."

Holly's silence told him she did. She'd done enough work on Miller's drug ring that he didn't have to explain things to her.

"Do I have good taste in men or what?"

He chuckled. "Hey, it's not like the guy *looks* like a killer." He pulled up Kershaw's mug shot from his arrest. "He doesn't look so bad. I can see how you'd be fooled. He came from a middle-class family in Southport. Has a high school diploma, couple years of college. He probably seemed like a decent guy."

"That doesn't help a lot, but thanks for trying. How stupid is it that women go home with strangers they've never even held hands with? It doesn't make any logical sense if you think about it when you're sober. As Juliet always says, everything has a consequence. I just wish this didn't have to be Lily's consequence too."

"Frankly, I think he's probably got too much on his mind to even be thinking about you."

"But I can't be sure, can I?"

"No, I guess not."

"Guess I'll have to find him and make sure."

Max sat straighter. "Holly, that's not a good idea. Don't go looking for trouble."

"If he's worried about his own life or going to prison for the rest of it, how do I know he won't try to see his child before he gets caught? I know the power these little lives have over parents. If he has any normal instincts, that feeling could be pretty intense. He could have been watching us already. I just want to stop worrying about it and make sure he doesn't show up. Do you have a last-known address for him?"

Max frowned. "Yeah, but I don't think I should give it to you. I don't want you showing up at his house."

"I have one already, Max. I just want to confirm it. Is it 366 Bay Drive?"

He sighed. "Yep, that's what I have. Holly, I'm sure they'll locate him soon and take him in. You don't have to worry."

"I wish I could be sure of that. But thanks for your help. I appreciate your looking him up."

"You sure you don't want to tell your sisters? I mean, they would have your back."

"No. I know it wouldn't surprise them—none of it. But I've been doing better for the last few months. That's what I want them to think of when they think of me—the good things, and my being a good mom, instead of dredging up memories of all my old choices."

Max smiled. "I get it. I won't say anything."

"Thank you, Max."

"Well, I'll see what else I can find out and let you know. Take care, okay? Don't do anything stupid."

When she hung up, he held the phone under his chin, thinking about this girl who had put herself in harm's way for her family on several occasions in the last year. Yet she had so much fear over her family finding out the details of her past.

He typed a few things into his computer, pulled up more about Creed Kershaw. He would find out everything he could to help Holly so she wouldn't feel the need to go after him herself.

CHAPTER 11

The idea that Leonard Miller was back in town kept Michael from sleeping. He sat up on his bottom bunk late into the night, studying the notes he kept under his mattress about the man who'd killed his brother and terrorized Cathy's family.

His chest hurt, and he rubbed the surgical scar from a few months ago—the consequence of a gunshot wound.

His new cell mate hung his feet over the top bunk.

Michael looked up. "Sorry, man. Did the light wake you?"

"Naw, I just can't sleep. Sick to my stomach, shaking like a leaf . . ."

"Would you rather have the bottom bunk so you can get to the bathroom faster?"

The man slid down to the floor, then considered that. "Yeah, maybe."

Michael had waited until his last cell mate was released to claim the bottom bunk, but he figured it hardly mattered now.

Craven was covered with sweat. As he stumbled to the toilet again, Michael got up and moved the papers he'd been reading. "Here, take it," he said when Craven was upright again.

"Thanks, man."

"So what are you withdrawing from?"

Craven moved the few supplies they'd given him from the upper bunk. "Heroin, Xanax, alcohol."

Cold turkey from any one of those could make him sick, but all three could make a person wish he was dead. "Did you see the nurse when they brought you in?"

"No. I see him tomorrow. Will he give me something that helps?"

"Maybe."

Craven scratched his arms. "You go through this when you came in, dude?"

"No, I don't use."

That seemed to shut the conversation down. Michael dreaded Craven learning he had been a cop. The moment his last cell mate found that out, he'd accused Michael of being a plant by the DA to snitch on him. That bit of gossip had spread through Michael's pod like fire, marking a target on his back.

Michael sat down at the metal desk built into the wall and studied his notebook. Craven looked over his shoulder. "Why are you writing about Lenny Miller?"

Michael looked back at him. "You know him?"

"I know *of* him." Craven wiped the sweat off his forehead with a towel. "Saw him the other day."

"You did? Here in town?"

"Yeah." Craven went to the toilet and heaved.

Michael waited, telling himself not to show cop-like interest, pausing while Craven slumped onto the bottom bunk and curled up in a fetal position. He could hear the man's teeth chattering.

Michael washed out a small Styrofoam coffee cup and filled it with water. "Here, drink something."

Craven sat up and took the cup, sloshing the water out. He was trembling too badly to hold it, so Michael helped him.

Craven wiped his mouth. "Thanks, man."

"Sure. Detoxing in jail is no picnic." After a moment, Michael said, "I thought I saw Miller the other day when I was out with the crew. His hair was lighter."

"Yeah, blond."

"Is he still distributing, or is he a broker now?"

"Got me. All's I know is you don't mess with the dude."

"So where did you see him?"

"In Bayou Park. I was sleeping there. They were . . . exterminating my place."

So Craven was homeless. "Yeah? And you saw him there?"

"Yeah, talking to some scary dudes. I stayed back. Didn't want to be noticed."

"How did you know it was him?"

"Recognized him from all that time he was on TV during the trial. At first I was like, who is that guy? I know I seen him before. I thought maybe he was an actor or some athlete or somethin', but then it hits me. That's that Miller dude from that trial." Suddenly Craven turned over and squinted at Michael. "Hey, that's where I seen you too. That's who *you* are!"

Michael turned back to his notebook.

"During that trial, coupla years ago. You was that cop."

Michael didn't look up. "That trial is what got me here."

"Oh yeah, I remember. Perjury, right?"

Michael didn't answer. A few minutes later, Craven heaved

in the toilet again, and when he was back on the bed, he seemed to have forgotten what they'd been talking about. He wrapped up in his thin blanket and turned to the wall.

Eventually Michael climbed onto the upper bunk and lay on his back, staring at the ceiling. If he were out of here, he would find Miller. He'd make sure he got justice. There were several warrants out on the man, and if they ever found and convicted him, he'd go to prison for life.

But Miller wasn't stupid. Even staying here in town, he would manage to elude the authorities.

Michael tried to quell the sense of absurdity that he was locked up instead of the man who had murdered, kidnapped, trafficked cocaine, and evaded the law so many times. But that was the way things worked.

He would see if he could get more information about Miller out of anyone else in the jail population, then let Cathy know tomorrow about Craven's confirmation that Miller was back. Max might also be able to find Miller in his official capacity with the Panama City PD, now that they knew he really was in town. If Max knew, he'd be all over it. Next to Cathy and himself, Max wanted to find his brother's killer most of all, and they all wanted the arrest to be incontestable. They wouldn't let him get off on a technicality again.

CHAPTER 12

Holly hated lying to Juliet, but it wasn't the first time. Her lying muscles had grown weak over the last few months, but it was like getting back on a bicycle.

"You want to drive at night after you got mugged?" Juliet asked her. "I thought we talked about this. You were going to transition to full-time at the office and quit driving the cab."

"That's not what I said, Juliet. I said I'd work more for Michael, but that I'd still have to drive. I worked all day at the office, but I need cash now. I lost a lot in the robbery, and I need to make it up."

"But aren't you scared?" Juliet asked as she took Lily.

"I have to get back in the saddle. I'll be careful who I pick up. No more dodgy neighborhoods. I'll stick to the airport tonight."

Holly headed to Southport, her notes open on her seat. She'd found Creed's last-known employment, a restaurant where he'd worked as a server. She would go there first and see what she could find out. Then she'd go by his parents' house—the address he'd used last—and see if she could catch a glimpse of him coming or going. Yes, the police were probably watching him too, but they were a small-town force. They might not have the manpower for twenty-four-hour surveillance.

The taxi could stand out like a sore thumb in certain areas, but there were times when it became invisible, like at hotels or the airport, and sometimes people overlooked it in neighborhoods too. She hoped that would be the case tonight.

Holly easily found the Gourmet Crab Bar and Grill in Southport. There weren't that many patrons taking up spaces. She went inside, looked around. The place was nice, with a good atmosphere, and classic rock music played throughout. A couple of groups sat at tables, three or four around the bar.

Holly slipped onto a stool and waited for the bartender to notice her. Finally, the girl—who sported a name tag that said Brittany—came to her. "What can I get you?"

"Coke," Holly said.

Brittany crossed her pit and filled up a glass. When she came back, Holly tossed out the question. "Hey, is Creed working today?"

The girl paused and gave Holly a narrow gaze. "No."

Holly sipped her drink. "He works here, right? I was just gonna say hi. When will he be back in?"

"Are you a cop?"

Holly almost spat out her drink. "A cop? No, do I look like one? Why? Are they looking for him?"

Brittany got a dishrag and wiped off the counter. "I don't know where he is, all right? I haven't seen him in days. I've already been questioned, and I told them everything I know."

Holly took that in. Brittany'd been questioned . . . but why? Had they questioned all his coworkers?

Something about the uncomfortable look on Brittany's face told Holly there was more. "So what's going on? Is he in some kind of trouble?"

"He didn't do what they're saying."

Holly tried to look irritated. "And that would be . . ."

The girl wasn't buying it. She looked over her shoulder, as if looking for her boss. Then she turned back to Holly and leaned on the counter. "Who are you?"

Holly thought of lying, but she wanted to see if her name got a reaction. "I'm Holly Cramer."

Brittany stopped wiping and stared at her. "You had the baby."

Holly felt the blood draining from her face. So he had told others. A guy who didn't care, who wasn't going to intrude on her life, would have kept it to himself, maybe even denied that he could be the father. But someone who shared it with a confidante . . .

"He told you that?"

"Yes, last week. He said it was a girl. What do you want? Child support, when you didn't even bother to tell him he was a father?"

"No, that's not why I'm here." Holly's lips tightened, and she reached into her purse for her cash. She slid the cost of the drink across the table. "I just want to know what his intentions are."

"Who knows? They're trying to nail him with a murder rap."

"Murder?" Holly asked, trying to look surprised.

"He hasn't been charged with anything. Not yet."

Holly slid off her stool. "Do you know how I can reach him?"

"Of course not." That was all. The speed with which she

answered made Holly think she was lying. This girl knew where he was. Maybe she would lead her to him.

Holly went back out and sat in her car. Brittany probably worked the dinner shift. Maybe Holly could come back later and see where she went after work.

While she waited, Holly drove to Creed's parents' address. Surprisingly, it was in a nice middle-class neighborhood, where people took pride in their lawns and homes. She found the address and slowed as she drove past. There was one car in the open garage, another in the driveway. She wrote down their tag numbers, then drove around the block.

As she approached the house on her second drive-by, she saw that someone was walking to the car in the driveway. Dark hair, same height as Creed, but twenty-five years older. Creed's dad? The man was clean-cut, dressed in a T-shirt and khaki shorts. As she drew closer, a blonde middle-aged woman came out of the house and got into the passenger seat.

Holly pulled into a driveway a few houses up from them, idled there a moment. When the Kershaws had pulled out of their driveway, she followed them. Hopefully they would think she had picked up a neighbor, if they noticed her at all.

Would his parents know where he was staying? Would Creed have dared to tell them? Maybe they were paying for a hotel or something. Surely they were worried about their son's situation.

But no—hadn't the two Southport cops told her that his parents had called them, worried about suicide? Maybe they were in the dark about where he was.

When Creed's parents reached an athletic park with several baseball fields, she followed them in and parked at a diamond adjacent to the one they went to. She watched as they went to the bleachers of a smaller field, where little kids gathered with their parents for a T-ball game.

She got out and crossed the field to the game. Creed's parents stood apart from the stands, their expressions grim. They both looked tired, as if they hadn't been sleeping, but when a little boy called out, "Grandma! Grandpa!" their expressions changed. They smiled as he ran to them for hugs.

As the boy went to join his team, a younger man and woman—the boy's parents, probably—talked quietly with the Kershaws. Holly took a seat on the bleachers as they set up lawn chairs away from the others. She couldn't hear them talking, but Mrs. Kershaw wiped tears, then hugged the young woman. Creed's sister?

She sat for a while, half-following the hilarity of the game—kids chasing butterflies in the outfield, hitting the ball and running to third base instead of first, parents cheering madly even when their kids didn't hit the ball. She couldn't wait until Lily could play. She watched from behind her sunglasses as the Kershaws cheered for their grandchild, even though she knew their hearts were breaking over their son's plight. Did they fear he was dead? Did they assume he was hiding? Was this just one more thing in a long history of catastrophes he'd brought on their family?

She could see how focused they were on their grandchild. And they were Lily's grandparents too. Watching them made her more determined than ever to keep them from claiming Lily. This couple would never simply walk away from a grandchild.

When the game was over, she drove back to the restaurant. From the cab in the parking lot, she used their Wi-Fi signal to find out what she could about Creed's parents and sister. Frank

Kershaw was a building contractor, and Sandra, his mother, was a third-grade teacher. They had no arrests—not even any traffic violations. Neither did his sister, Kelsey.

Creed must be a huge disappointment to them.

As darkness fell, she watched the door for the employees to leave. At nine o'clock, Brittany came out, got into her car, and sat there a moment. Holly wrote down her tag number to look up later. When Brittany pulled away, Holly followed.

"Take me to Creed, girl," Holly muttered as she drove.

But Brittany didn't take her to Creed. She only went to another bar. Holly went in a few minutes behind her and stopped in the front area behind a plant, looking around the dark room.

There she was, joining a table of women, each of whom hugged her when she arrived, as if consoling her for some loss. They were there to commiserate with her. It was unlikely Creed would be here.

Disappointed, Holly headed back home. Tonight was a dead end, but she wouldn't give up. She would try again tomorrow.

CHAPTER 13

The last thing Cathy wanted tonight was to dress up in formal wear and schmooze at the governor's dinner, but it had to be done. She looked in her rearview mirror at the earrings she wore, hanging to her jawline and catching the light. She wore a necklace that looked expensive, although she'd bought it secondhand in a thrift shop. She drove through the gates of the mansion and up the circular drive. When she stopped, a valet came to her door. She grabbed her clutch bag and slipped out, trying not to wobble on her heels. Why had she worn these anyway? They were too high and she hadn't worn them in months, but she stretched herself to her full height and tried to walk like a runway model up the steps and into the white mansion. Men in tuxedos stood at the door, checking invitations. She pulled her press pass out of her bag and showed it to one of them.

"Yes, Ms. Cramer. Take the doors to the right and you'll see your table."

"Thank you." She walked into the foyer crowded with people waiting to enter the ballroom. Most of the guests looked as though they'd had red-carpet consultants. Cathy had worn her go-to black formal and hoped she looked as though she'd tried.

The mansion was warm. She would have thought they would adjust the thermostat with so many people crowded in, but Florida heat was difficult to battle. She fanned herself with her credentials as she waited to make her way to the door. As she did, she scanned faces. If she could just get an introduction to the governor . . . if she could just speak to him for two minutes . . . Then she could leave and she wouldn't have to suffer through the whole program.

Once past the bottleneck at the door, she scouted out her table and found her name card. She'd been seated between two other press members—one of the anchors from the local NBC affiliate, and a newspaper editor. Disappointed, she checked the name cards around the rest of the table. The one directly across from her was the governor's press secretary, Jeremy Brix. Quickly, she swapped his card with the one next to her, ensuring that she was seated next to him.

If no one moved his card back to where it had been, she would at least have the chance to pitch Michael's story to him. It was one more avenue to get to the governor, to put a bug in his ear. She scanned the crowd. It didn't appear that the governor had shown up yet. He would probably make his entrance at the last moment.

She recognized some of the astronauts who were the evening's guests of honor—they all wore special name tags. She had no professional interest in what they would say tonight, even though, under different circumstances, she was sure she would have hung on every word.

"So I see you made it."

She turned to see Ned Garrison, the governor's administrative assistant. "Hi, Ned," she said, applying her most charming smile. "Thanks so much for getting me a pass. I really appreciate it."

"Well, don't abuse it, okay? The governor is focused on the space program tonight."

"I know, but if I could just speak to him for two minutes."

"Good luck with that. Everybody here wants to see him for two minutes. And by the way, your fans have broadsided us with mail. It's getting a little annoying."

"Great," Cathy said. "At least it's gotten your attention. And they're my *readers*, not fans. They just agree with me that Michael shouldn't be in jail."

"Everybody in jail feels they shouldn't be there. The bottom line is that he broke the law, and that's all that matters."

"It is *not* all that matters!" Cathy said too loudly. "He shouldn't have had a felony conviction in the first place. He didn't do anything wrong—*everybody* knows that. The woman had dementia—"

He raised his hand, cutting her off. "Cathy, I don't have time for this. Enjoy yourself, but please, don't make me sorry I got you the pass."

Cathy shrank back, scowling at him as he walked away. She had gone to college with Ned—the only reason he was doing her a favor now. He had majored in political science, then gone to work for the governor's office a few years ago in a lower-level position. He'd managed to climb his way up, and she didn't blame him for not wanting to mess that up. But how could pardoning a wrongly convicted man mess things up?

While she waited for the program to start, she made her

way to everyone she could identify in the room who might have some clout with the governor. She talked to both of her senators, two congressmen, the Panama City mayor, and every staff member she could identify. They all expressed sympathy and compassion for Michael. They had all heard of his case. They all said they would put in a word with the governor, but she doubted any of them would remember. What was he to them? Just another man behind bars. But he wasn't just another man. He was a hero, a man who had saved so many lives, who had temporarily disrupted the drug flow into the entire panhandle.

A man who was the love of her life.

Before the governor finally made his entrance, everyone was asked to take their seats. Cathy gravitated back to her table, where some of her press colleagues were already in their places. Thankfully, the cards hadn't been moved—the press secretary came a few minutes after the waitstaff began serving dinner and took his place beside her. He introduced himself to everyone around the table as if they didn't already know him.

Cathy waited until they were halfway through the dinner, chatting about the space program and all that it meant to the US, before she brought up Michael. "Listen, Jeremy," she said, leaning toward him and lowering her voice, "I have an idea for a great PR story for the governor. A good news opportunity that would really make him look like a prince in the next election."

Jeremy gave her a sideways look. "Really? Let's hear it."

"Do you remember Michael Hogan?"

"The cop?" Jeremy asked.

She nodded. "Michael is serving time in prison right now." She quickly updated him on the felony conviction that should never have been, and the case a few months ago when he had violated probation by using a weapon to rescue her sister. "He even got shot himself. It was a matter of life and death. He shouldn't be in prison because of it."

"I remember all that. No question, the guy's a real hero," Jeremy said. "But what do you want the governor to do? He doesn't give pardons. That was one of his campaign promises. He's not going to go back on that."

"But if he made this one exception, I think it would spread goodwill. There are a lot of people who know that Michael shouldn't be behind bars. He's already served two months. That's more than enough. We need people like him out there fighting crime in our community, not being lumped in with the bad guys himself. If Michael got a pardon, his felony record would be wiped clean, and he could go back to carrying a weapon and being a cop. He could get back to hunting down bad guys, rather than being considered one of them."

Jeremy considered that as he cut into his chicken. "I can't argue with that, but the governor is a stickler about keeping campaign promises. His opponents would jump on it if he went back on his word."

"So you believe the governor cares more about political expediency than about doing the right thing?" When Jeremy rolled his eyes, Cathy wondered if she'd gone too far. "Can't he just explain that he got a dose of common sense and decided that this wrong needs to be righted?"

"Then he'd be barraged with pardon requests."

"Isn't he already? And anyway, what difference does that make? He doesn't have to process those himself. This is one case where he could break that pledge and people would applaud him. A good man's life is at stake."

Jeremy shook his head. "No, it's not. He got a year. He'll serve six months."

"But he'll be a felon for the rest of his life! He lost his police career over this, and he was good at what he did. Even after leaving the police force—even without a weapon—he got scumbags off the street."

Jeremy took a bite of his dessert, chewed for a moment. Was he considering her request or had she lost him already? Tears rimmed her eyes. "Jeremy, he's a good man. He needs consideration. And if he got pardoned, I would make you and the governor absolute heroes. I would talk it up on my blog, and people would be touting the governor as compassionate and clear minded."

Jeremy took another bite, chewed for a long moment. "Let me think about it," he said. Then he turned and started a conversation with the person on the other side of him.

Cathy let out a hard sigh. That had gone nowhere. As those around her chatted and worked on their cheesecake, she noticed that several people had crossed the room for photo ops with the governor.

Sliding her chair back, she excused herself and went out as if going to the restroom, then went back in through the door closer to where the governor stood. She made her way along the wall, up toward the group around him.

She waited as two or three more people had pictures taken with him, praying that he wouldn't be called to the next activity before her turn. Finally, she made her way to his side.

"Governor Larimore, hi," she said in her most charming voice. "Cathy Cramer."

He smiled and lifted his chin. "Of the blog, *Cat's Curious?*"

She smiled. "Yes, you read my blog?"

"I don't have the time I once did, but I used to. I like your work."

"I'm honored," she said.

"Did you want a picture?" one of his aides asked her.

"Sure." She smiled and leaned in as the photographer came closer. "Governor," she said quickly before someone else could intrude, "I just wanted to call your attention to a letter-writing campaign going on right now. A lot of people are trying to get Michael Hogan under consideration as someone you should pardon."

The governor shook his head. "Cathy, you know I made a promise."

"I know," she cut in, launching into her sales pitch. "It was all a terrible mistake, as everybody who followed that trial was aware. Wouldn't it be a great PR move for you if you agreed to make an exception for a local hero?"

The governor narrowed his eyes. "Aren't you engaged to him? Didn't I read that somewhere?"

She hoped that wouldn't make a difference. "Yes, as a matter of fact. But I would do this for him even if we weren't getting married. My first fiancé was Michael's brother, and he was murdered. Michael lost his career because of that case, and the killer is still on the street, literally getting away with murder, not to mention several other crimes. It's just so wrong that Michael is serving time—"

"Excuse me," an aide said, cutting in to her speech. "Governor, it's time for you to speak."

Governor Larimore touched Cathy's elbow. "It's nice to meet you, Cathy."

She couldn't let him go. "Governor, please consider it. Just read the letters and the package that I sent you."

"Thank you, Cathy," he said. "No promises." He walked away.

Cathy stood clutching her purse and trying not to cry. She

lifted her chin and looked around. Was there anyone else in the room she should talk to?

The lights began to lower and the spotlight at the podium came on. The program was about to begin.

Quickly, she headed out of the room and down the steps of the mansion. The valet brought her car. She didn't let herself cry until she got behind the wheel.

CHAPTER 14

"What am I supposed to do with these?" Cathy stood the next morning at Juliet's kitchen table, puzzling over the rolled-up diapers, the tutu, and the pink headbands and bows.

Juliet was holding Robbie on her hip while decorating her end table. "You make it into a centerpiece. Stand the diaper rolls on end and put the tutu around them. The headbands go around the top." She thrust a green stuffed bear at her. "Stick this in the top. You can figure it out."

Cathy tried to follow the instructions. "How come I didn't get the decorating gene?"

"It's not genetic. It's Pinterest." Juliet went to the kitchen counter, where the ingredients for the punch were laid out. "Just before they get here, I'll put the ice cream and rubber duckies in, and they'll look like they're floating in suds."

"Really? Are you sure?"

"Yes, I've done it dozens of times."

"Holly's friends might spike it."

Juliet chuckled and pointed at the two-liter bottles on the counter. "We'll also have soda, just in case. Remind me to put out a bucket of ice."

The doorbell rang, and Cathy gasped. "Who's that? It's an hour and a half early."

"Probably the first babysitter I'm interviewing."

"Now?"

"Yes, I had to fit it in. If the oven timer goes off, get the brownies out and put the quiche in for fifteen minutes on three-fifty." As she headed for the front door, she called out, "Zach? Come get your shoes out of here!" The bell rang again.

Cathy worked on the centerpiece, not certain she was doing it right. How did Juliet do all this? She just had a flair for it, and she loved to entertain, though her new house was half the size of her former one and didn't flow as well. Still, Cathy had no doubt that Juliet would pull off Holly's baby shower, and she would do it without giving the slightest hint of the stress she was under with her husband's death, her responsibility for her children's well-being, the adoption of a baby, and the financial problems bearing down on her.

The timer went off, and Cathy abandoned the centerpiece and hurried to the oven. She heard voices . . .

A shrieking, nasal voice almost shook the house. "Oh my soul, look at that adorable little guy!"

Robbie started screaming. Not a good start.

Cathy looked over her shoulder as Juliet led the woman into the living area and offered her a seat. Juliet quickly introduced Cathy, then sat as she tried to comfort Robbie. "So . . . how long have you been working as a nanny?"

"Seven years," the woman nasaled. "Ten kids."

"All in one family?"

"No, separate families. Some didn't work out, so I moved on."

Cathy glanced at Juliet, saw the concern on her face. She checked the oven, trying to eavesdrop over Robbie's crying.

Zach came into the room in his sock feet and slipped on his shoes, then took Robbie from his mother. "Whatsa matter, buddy?" he asked, instantly calming his little brother.

"I smell cigarette smoke," Juliet said. "I told the agency I don't want a smoker."

"I never smoke around my babies, don't worry about that."

"So . . . what do you do when you need to smoke? Do you leave them alone and go outside?"

"Only when they're sleeping, sweetie." The woman looked around and sprang up at the sight of the centerpiece. "Would you look at that? That's just about the cutest thing I've ever seen."

Her voice grated. Cathy could smell her smoke-covered clothes and hair from the kitchen. She clearly wasn't just an occasional smoker. How long would Juliet go on with this?

As if reading Cathy's thoughts, Juliet stood up. "Anita, I so appreciate your coming by, but I don't think you're what we're looking for. The smoking worries me, since there are two babies you'll be caring for. Robbie and my niece, Lily. It'll be rare that they're asleep at the same time—"

Anita waved her off. "Honey, we can work that out."

"No, I don't think we can. Robbie isn't reacting well to you, either."

"Look, I can take care of your kids. The agency wouldn't have sent me if I wasn't qualified."

"I appreciate that," Juliet said. "We have some more people to interview."

Cathy suppressed her grin and put the quiche into the oven.

When Juliet came back from letting Anita out, she opened the back door. "Now the house smells like smoke. I want it to smell like brownies and cake."

"So I take it you're not hiring Anita?"

"Give me a break. Her voice knocked her out of the game when it sent Robbie into hysterics." She went to the hallway. "Abe! Come move your backpack!" She checked the centerpiece. "Anita was right—that's perfect. I think you do have the gene after all."

"Thank you. I had no idea if I was doing it right. I don't want a bunch of church ladies gossiping about my artwork."

"They're not 'church ladies,' they're my friends, and they're not gossips. They really aren't. Cathy, you'll like them. They're good people. They just want to bless Holly."

Cathy hoped Juliet was right and that the mix of Holly's friends with Juliet's wouldn't be disastrous.

CHAPTER 15

Holly was glad she had listened to Juliet and worn the dress she'd picked out. She had been dreading the baby shower that her sisters had insisted on giving her. Even with thick makeup, her black eye was still visible, and her gash was healing with a thick scab. The story of her mugging was true and believable—but Juliet's friends didn't go places where muggings were common. It made Holly feel cheap.

"Every mother needs a baby shower," Juliet had said. "My friends know how to do it better than anybody. They want to do this for you."

"But I don't know them," Holly muttered. "I don't want them judging me. I can just see it now, all the noses turned up as the church divas march in."

Juliet grunted. "Holly, it's not like that. You have the wrong idea. This is not our old church. Besides, it's at my house, and I won't let anybody treat you badly. These are nice people. I only invited people I knew would support you."

"Support me in what? Having a baby out of wedlock? Are they holding their noses? Or am I their next project?"

Juliet set her hand on her hip. "I know you don't realize this, but you're the one judging here. They want to bring you gifts and celebrate Lily's life. You need things. I just wish I had been in a position to give you the shower before she was born, but I wasn't."

Holly mentally kicked herself for giving Juliet a hard time. "I'm sorry. I'm just nervous. Your friends are probably super-Christians, and I'm so . . . *not*."

Juliet leaned on the edge of her counter. "Honey, we didn't all start out at the same place. We had totally different journeys. Stop looking at yourself as inferior. God doesn't do that."

Holly knew Juliet meant well, but it didn't change how she saw herself. "We were raised the same way, in the same family."

"Oh, Holly. No, we weren't." Juliet lifted Holly's chin. "Look at me."

Holly met Juliet's moist eyes. "What?"

"I was raised by two parents who loved the Lord and taught me to. *You* were raised by a single mom after your preacher dad betrayed the family."

"He was your preacher dad too."

"But I was cooked by then, honey. I'd had a stable, solid upbringing. By the time Dad left us, I already knew Jesus and my faith was deep. It was in God more than in Dad. But you were just a little girl. Things were totally different on your journey."

Holly tried to hold back her tears. "So you're completely letting me off the hook for my detours?"

"That's not my job. I'm just saying that God knows where you started and how you got here. He's not disgusted, and neither are my friends. And when they get to know you, they'll delight in you like God does."

The tears came despite Holly's efforts. As she dabbed at them, she turned and saw Cathy listening from a few feet away, a poignant smile on her face.

"I really want this to be fun for you," Juliet added. "And don't tell anybody, but I also want to show Lily off to all our friends. I want them to see how adorable she is."

Now, Holly tried to focus on the assurances Juliet had given her as the guests began to arrive. Would any of her own friends actually make the effort to come? Most of them hated mornings, and they would consider a shower to be on their Top 10 List of Most Awkward Situations.

As Juliet's church friends arrived, that insecurity crept back in. Holly wished she'd worn a sweater to cover the tattoos on her biceps. It surprised her that Juliet hadn't made her do that already. Maybe she'd warned them. *Holly looks like a biker chick, but try to look past that.*

There she went again, judging them for things she expected them to think. Maybe she was wrong. Maybe they were all sweet, like Juliet.

Despite her tension, she found herself relaxing as they gushed over Lily.

"She locks in on you when you talk to her, like she understands every word."

"I can see the resemblance, Holly."

"Right? Look at those eyes. She's gorgeous."

Holly couldn't help smiling. "Yeah, I kind of think she looks like me too. Poor kid."

"Poor kid?" one of the women said. "Are you crazy? Look at you!"

This wasn't so bad, Holly thought as more of the women came in. A few of them asked about her mugging and commented on her bruise and busted lip, but she didn't feel judged. She grew less uncomfortable with the inevitable hugs. She wondered if Juliet had lectured them about how to treat her. *Don't say anything about her having the baby alone, and for heaven's sake don't mention her driving a taxi.*

Juliet wasn't above scheming with her friends to get Holly back to church, but they seemed sincere.

Just as Juliet was asking them all to sit, the doorbell rang again, and three of Holly's friends from the Dock came in. Thrilled to see familiar faces, she ran across the room and hugged each of them. "I didn't for a minute think you'd come!" she whispered. "It's so good to have people I really know here."

Her friend Spree spoke a little too loudly. "Girl, we wouldn't miss it. We had to see you acting all mommy-like. Cracks us up."

Georgia took Holly by the shoulders and studied her face. "What happened to you?"

"Long, sad story," Holly said. "I got mugged."

"I hope you got in a coupla licks," Mattie said.

Holly smiled. "I tried."

"So let's see the little beauty," Spree said.

Holly took them into the living room and showed them her baby. Spree wanted to hold her. Holly didn't like passing Lily around like a vegetable dish, but she allowed it anyway. Spree, who didn't have a good filter for what was appropriate, bounced her so hard and talked so loudly that Lily began to scream. Holly quickly took her back and held her close to comfort her.

When it seemed that everyone had arrived, Juliet seated

them around in chairs in a circle and played a few games that broke the ice and made everyone laugh. Holly noticed her friends whispering in the corner. They'd have a lot to say about this later, she was sure.

When it was time to open gifts, Cathy sat next to her, writing down the names of people to thank. There was a mountain of gifts, things she'd never thought she would get, but they were all things she needed. Lily would have enough onesies to get her through the first year, and there was no shortage of hoodie towels and receiving blankets and diapers.

By the time Holly had opened all her gifts, she was moved to tears at the generosity of these people. If they reflected God's love, maybe Juliet was right. Maybe he wasn't disgusted by her.

As Juliet's friends began to leave, Holly looked for her friends and found them smoking on the patio.

She went out and sat down next to them. "Well, that turned out better than I expected. They all seemed nice."

"If you take all that loot back to the store, you'll wind up with a fortune," Spree said too loudly.

"I like all of it. I'm keeping it."

"She has more clothes now than the Kardashian baby," Mattie said. "She's a one-month-old fashion diva. Want a smoke?"

Holly shook her head. "No, I quit when I was pregnant and haven't started back."

"So did you dye away the pink just for this shower?"

"No, I was just tired of the pink. Guess I outgrew it."

"Don't you start acting all churchy now," Spree said.

Holly breathed a laugh. "I used to think that was a bad thing. But you gotta admit, these people were nice. They weren't like I expected. Who knows? Maybe I could go to church and not feel like an outcast."

"Wanna lay bets that the whole act will disappear as you get to know them?"

Holly sighed. "Don't be such a cynic. Maybe they were authentic."

"Sounds to me like Holly needs a night out to get her head straight," Mattie said. "Let's have a girls' night tonight. It's ladies' night at Club Onyx."

Holly shook her head. "Can't. I have too much going on. I can't party like I used to."

"There she goes," Spree told the other two. "They've turned her."

"I haven't turned," Holly said. "I have two jobs and a baby."

"So come for a little while and turn in early. Surely you have enough babysitters."

Juliet opened the sliding glass door and leaned out, holding Lily, who was crying. "Holly, Lily needs you."

Holly took her baby, quieting her.

"So what do you say?" Georgia asked. "Get big sis to babysit and come out with us tonight?"

Holly shot Juliet an uncomfortable look. "Not tonight, you guys. Maybe later."

Juliet seemed stiffer as she went back in.

Disheartened, Holly walked her friends to the door and let them out, still fending off their protests. Even if she wanted a night of partying—which she didn't—she still had Creed to worry about.

As she went back into the kitchen where the last of Juliet's friends were cleaning up, Holly wondered what they would think if they knew the father of her baby was wanted for murder, and that she feared he would intrude on her life and disrupt everything. Would they treat her as kindly?

Or would they welcome her into their midst, then whisper behind her back?

She didn't know, and she was too tired to puzzle it all out. Instead of forcing herself back in among them, Holly slipped into Juliet's bedroom to nurse her baby.

CHAPTER 16

The conversation Juliet had overheard at the shower didn't help Holly's case when she asked her to babysit that night. "Are you going to the Dock with those girls?" Juliet asked point-blank.

Holly grunted. "No, Juliet. There's a lawyers' convention starting in town, and maybe I can earn back some of the money I lost in the mugging."

Juliet wasn't buying it. "So you promise me you're not going out drinking with your friends?"

Holly raised her right hand. "I promise I'm not going out drinking with my friends."

"Because you're breastfeeding, you know. Plus, I don't mind sitting while you work, but it's another thing if you just want a night out. It's been a long day and I need to focus on my kids tonight."

"Juliet, it's not just a night out, okay? It's important."

Juliet hesitated, then sighed. "All right, but will you be home by eleven? If you can get Lily before I go to bed, it'll help me. We have church in the morning."

"Absolutely."

Juliet took the baby, held her to her shoulder. Lily kept her knees up and rooted toward Juliet's face. Holly almost couldn't bear to let her go.

"So have you had any luck with the police?" Juliet asked.

Holly's heart jolted. "What police?"

"About the mugging. Have they found the couple yet?"

Holly let herself breathe. "I haven't heard from them since the report. People like that, they're probably off the grid."

"You mean homeless?"

"Maybe. And by now they've probably already smoked away every penny of the money I made."

As Holly went back out to her car, she realized she hadn't given the muggers much thought. The threat of Creed Kershaw coming into Lily's life was a much greater threat than someone beating and robbing her mom.

How had her life come to this?

After working the airport for three hours, Holly went back to the restaurant where Creed had worked. She found Brittany's car and parked a few spaces down, waiting for the bartender to come out when she got off work.

As she waited, Holly thought back over today's shower, wondered what her friends were saying about her, and what the church people were saying about her friends. She leaned her head back on the seat and thought about the lifestyle she'd led until Lily's conception. She'd gone from one drinking binge to another, had hangovers every morning. It didn't seem so attractive now.

So why did she long for her friends' companionship? Why did she wish she could go out with them tonight . . . just this once?

Her friends' lives weren't really working either, but they couldn't see it. Chaos was no way to live. Drowning pain, numbing feelings, snorting out regrets, and then creating more regrets . . . it was a cycle that was hard to break. It had taken Lily to make Holly break it, but she knew she could easily be drawn back in.

One invitation at a time, she told herself. *No* would get easier to say.

At nine o'clock, the side employees' door opened and she saw Brittany walking out, her purse tight under her arm as she crossed the dark parking lot to her car. Holly gave her a chance to pull out, then followed.

Come on, girl. Show me where he is this time.

This time Brittany didn't go to the bar to meet her friends. She drove farther out toward the beach, a few miles west on Gulf Coast Highway. Holly had looked up Brittany's address earlier, and she didn't live in this area. Maybe . . . just maybe . . .

Brittany pulled into an RV park where recreational vehicles and motor homes were lined up in spaces with an ocean view. Holly stayed back and cut off her headlights, letting Brittany get a good distance ahead of her. Brittany stopped in front of a motor home.

Holly pulled into a space that allowed a clear view of Brittany's car and idled there as if waiting for a fare. Brittany got out of her car. Under the streetlight that illuminated her space and the motor home, she looked both ways. Her gaze didn't linger in the direction of Holly's cab.

Finally, she went to the door, knocked, and was let in.

Turning off her interior light, Holly got out of the car and got her camera bag and gun out of the trunk, just in case. She got back in and snapped on a telephoto lens. She zoomed, trying to focus on the motor home's license plate or any other identifier.

Holly hadn't seen who had opened the door, so she turned off her ignition and turned her phone to silent. She got out of the car with the camera and walked up to the road past the motor home, then looked back, trying to see through the unadorned windows. In the dim light inside, she saw Brittany talking and gesturing, but couldn't see who she was talking to. Holly stole closer to the camper and got the tag, hoping it showed up in the picture.

There was a park bench nearby, so Holly sat down in the darkness, watching and waiting, her eyes fixed on those windows. If she got even one glimpse of him, she could snap a photo and call the police.

But she never saw him.

After half an hour, Brittany came back out and returned to her car.

Who was inside? Holly couldn't be sure it was Creed. The camper might belong to a relative or friend of Brittany's who'd come to visit, but there was no car here and the lights were dim, and the motor home wasn't hooked up to electricity or water.

As Brittany drove away, Holly looked up and down the lane to make sure no one was out jogging or walking a dog. She walked closer to the motor home, trying to get a different angle inside the window from the street. She still saw no one.

She couldn't get closer without trespassing or breaking a Peeping Tom law, so, frustrated, she headed back toward her car.

She would just sit in her cab and watch the motor home

for the next hour or so, until she had to go get Lily. Then maybe she could drive back over with Lily asleep in the backseat. All she needed was one sighting.

As she opened her cab door, she checked her watch. Nine thirty. She had a good hour before she would have to leave. She slipped into the driver's seat, set the camera down . . .

"Don't move! I've got your gun."

Holly caught her breath and looked in the rearview mirror. Creed Kershaw sat in her backseat, sweat covering his face as he held her Glock .38 just inches from the back of her head.

CHAPTER 17

Robbie didn't like carrots. They were all over his face, down the front of his shirt, and splattered on Juliet's blouse. "Come on, Robbie, open up. Here comes the helicopter." She flew the spoon toward his mouth, but he twisted and turned his face away.

"Mom, why do I have to take algebra?" Zach called from the adjacent den. "When am I ever gonna need this in my life?"

"It's good to exercise your brain. And you'll need it to get into a good college."

Lily started to cry, and Juliet quickly wiped Robbie's face and hands, then lifted Lily out of her swing. "Come on, honey. Mommy will be back soon."

Where was Lily's bottle? Holly had put it in the refrigerator, hadn't she? Juliet looked inside and found the bottle. Now she'd have to warm it.

"But we're not supposed to have homework on weekends."

"You had three days to do it. It's not your teacher's fault you waited until the weekend."

"If I fail, I'm not gonna get into *any* college."

"You're taking algebra, Zach. End of discussion."

"Mom!" Abe called from his room. "Can you come here?"

"No!" she called back.

"Brody pooped on the floor."

"Clean it up and take him out!" she called.

"But I'm busy!"

Juliet wanted to scream. She put the bottle in the bottle warmer. By now, Robbie was crying, squirming to get out of his chair.

"He wants out," Zach said. "Want me to get him?"

"Yes, but be careful. He's covered with carrots."

"I'd rather be covered with smashed carrots than do algebra." Zach got Robbie out, and Juliet jostled Lily, trying to make her stop crying. The bottle warmer beeped.

Abe was in the kitchen now with soiled paper towels. "I hate cleaning up poop. It's on the carpet."

That was one reason Juliet hated carpet, but when she'd sold her house, she hadn't been able to find anything she liked with hardwood or tile floors. "What's wrong with him? Why is he suddenly going in the house?"

Zach shrugged. "Because Abe didn't take him out. What's he supposed to do?"

The Yorkie came into the kitchen and went straight for the splattered carrots on the floor. "Did you feed him, Zach?"

"Yes, which is why he had something to poop."

She tried to give Lily the bottle, but the baby rejected it and cried a higher octave. Juliet swayed from side to side. "Zach, will you go start a bath for Robbie?"

"What about my algebra?"

"It'll only take a minute. Please. Just put him in his walker."

Zach struggled with Robbie, finally getting the wailing and kicking baby in his walker. "Mom, his head is hot."

"What?" Not a fever, not now. Juliet took her screaming niece over to Robbie and squatted on the floor. "What's wrong, honey?"

She touched his head with the heel of her hand, then kissed his forehead. "Are you sick?"

Robbie just bucked and fought to get out. Juliet shifted Lily to her left arm and pulled Robbie out with her right. Zach disappeared, then she heard the water running in the hall bathroom. "Abe, find the thermometer in the kitchen drawer. I think Robbie's running a fever."

"Which drawer?"

"Just look for it, okay?" She was getting too short with her kids, but she'd had enough. Where was Holly?

"Why won't Lily stop crying?" Abe asked, digging loudly through a kitchen drawer.

"I don't know. She doesn't like bottles."

The dog started barking to go out, and the kids ignored him. Juliet was losing it. "Abe, take the dog out," she yelled. "Now!"

"But I was looking for the thermometer!"

Both babies' crying went up an octave. "Stop and take the dog out anyway."

Abe muttered under his breath and let the dog out, then followed him into the fenced-in yard.

When Zach came back, she told him to get the thermometer. When he found it, she handed him Lily. "Take her for a minute. Try to feed her."

Zach carefully took the infant, and Lily's screams seemed even more painful. "She hates me."

"No, she doesn't." Juliet held Robbie and put the thermometer in his ear. He fought it as if she were giving him a shot. When it beeped, she read the temperature. "A hundred. Yep, he's sick."

"What if Lily gets it? She's so little."

"She's still on breast milk, so she has Holly's immunities, but she could still get it, I suppose. Holly needs to take her home."

"Should you take her temperature too?" Zach asked.

Juliet found the alcohol and swabbed the thermometer. Thankfully, Lily didn't have a fever, but the thermometer only made her angrier. She was hysterical now, and she showed no sign of calming down.

Juliet threw up her hands. "Okay, time to call Holly."

She got the phone and clicked Holly on speed dial, but there was no answer. When it went to voice mail, Juliet said, "Holly, call me. Lily is very upset and needs her mom, and Robbie's running a fever."

She put Lily into her infant seat, which only irritated the baby more. She carried the seat into the bathroom and waited for Holly's call while she quickly bathed Robbie. Lily's screaming raised Juliet's blood pressure, creating a sense of panic, but she tried to stay calm so Robbie wouldn't start up again. When would the baby get tired and fall asleep? She checked her watch. Only ten thirty. If Holly kept her word, she'd be here at eleven.

But why wasn't she calling back?

Juliet got Robbie out of the bath and diapered and dressed him for bed. She always rocked him before bed and read a book, but how would she do that tonight? Just when he needed an extra dose of TLC, she couldn't provide it.

She could get Zach to do it, but first he needed to shower so he'd be ready for church tomorrow. Abe too. They should all be in bed by now. How had her life gotten so out of control?

When Holly wasn't home by eleven, Juliet had Abe Google Holly's taxi service to find the phone number. Maybe they could radio her and get her to call.

"Deluxe Taxi Service. What's your address?"

Juliet shook her head. "I don't need a cab. I need to get in touch with Holly Cramer. This is her sister. She's working tonight, and I need to see if you can radio her. She's not answering her phone."

The dispatcher hesitated a moment, then said, "Holly's not on the clock right now. She was, but she clocked out around eight thirty."

Juliet froze, letting that sink in. So Holly had lied to her.

Furious, she hung up and tried Holly's phone again. Still no answer.

So this was how it was going to be. Holly's flying right had only been temporary while she was pregnant, but now that she wasn't, she was going back to her old lifestyle? Lying and partying with her friends?

It was seeing those friends today that had done it. They'd lured her back. Juliet should have known the temptation would be too great.

She burst into tears as the baby screamed in her ear. She would do anything to make her niece feel better, and though Robbie wasn't crying now, she needed to get him to sleep.

Zach stood in the doorway. "Mom? Are you crying?"

"No!" she said. "I don't know where Holly is and I don't know what to do to comfort Lily. She won't eat."

"The bottle's cold now. Maybe if I warm it up again."

"You should be asleep," she said.

"But I'm not. I can help. Want me to call Aunt Cathy or Uncle Jay? They could come."

Juliet wiped her tears. "Yes, call Cathy. Tell her I'm having a mini meltdown, and I don't know where Holly is."

CHAPTER 18

In the dim illumination from a streetlight, Holly met Creed's eyes in her rearview mirror—sitting in her backseat and holding her gun on her.

"I need you to listen carefully," he said.

She tried to breathe. "Creed, this is crazy. What are you doing?"

"I should ask you the same question."

She didn't know what to say. She couldn't tell him that she was trying to find him so she could turn him over to the police. She thought of bringing up Lily, reminding him that she was a mother . . . but that didn't seem wise. "Creed, come on. Put the gun down."

"Brittany told me you were asking about me. As she was leaving, I saw your cab. Are you working for them?"

"Them who?"

He stared at her. "I want you to give me your phone and that camera."

She took them off her seat, handed them to him.

"Now you're going to get out of the car with me and come into the camper. We're going to drive it out of here. If you found me, the others will too."

She swallowed hard. "Yes, okay. Sure. Just . . . take it easy with that gun, will you? Point it somewhere else."

He looked down at the phone, probably checking to see if she'd called anyone about him. Then she heard him ejecting the gun's clip, no doubt making sure it was loaded. "All right, get out. I'll have the gun in my pocket, aimed at you as we walk. If you scream or do anything other than what I tell you, I'll shoot. Don't test me. I'll do it."

"Right. Okay. Whatever you say."

Her mind raced for an escape, but she couldn't run with a gun pointed at her back. He got out of the car, took the keys out of her hand and locked it. He prodded her. "Walk."

Stiffly, she crossed the street and passed several RVs, motor homes, and campers till they came to his motor home under the streetlight. He opened the door and motioned for her to go in. She stepped up and into it.

In the dim light she could see two small beds—one above the other—a table, and a small door that led into a bathroom. The driver's and passenger's seats were accessible from the living area.

"Nice place," she said in a metallic voice. "Is it yours?"

"Get in the driver's seat," he said.

"I don't know how to drive one of these. I'll wreck it."

"Do it!"

She slipped into the seat behind the steering wheel. Creed got into the passenger seat next to her. Now she could see that he looked pretty much the same as he had ten months ago. Dark hair a little too long, his face two or three days unshaven, those blue eyes that had done her in . . .

"Now pull out. I'll tell you where to go."

She started the engine, her hands shaking. "What about my cab?"

"I don't care about your cab."

"Well, I do. It's the way I make a living."

"I know about both your jobs, Holly. That's why I think you can help me."

Help him? Was he insane? "Who told you what I do?"

"Rio."

She sighed as she pulled the behemoth vehicle down the drive to the campground's exit. "He sure is chatty these days, isn't he? Just a treasure trove of information."

"You might say that."

They were quiet for a moment as she turned out of the RV park and onto the highway. What was Juliet going to think when Holly didn't show up to get Lily? Would she realize something had happened to her, or would she just assume that she had gone back to her old partying ways?

Holly looked over at Creed. His eyes were wide open—on high alert—as he scanned the cars on the road. He looked tired and scared.

Holly swallowed. "Listen, Creed. I know you're stressed out with the police looking for you and all. I don't know if you killed that guy or not, but I can tell you that taking me hostage right now is not going to help your situation."

"I'm not taking you hostage. You came here of your own free will."

"Well, I'm not in this motor home of my own free will! I have a baby who needs to be picked up from my sister's house! Juliet is going to think I ditched my child to go out partying. Can't I just call her?"

"No. You're not calling anybody."

"Creed, the baby needs to be fed soon."

He grew quiet, glancing from her to the highway, brooding in the darkness.

"Where are we going?"

"There's another RV park across town." He hesitated, frowning. "But that might not be a good idea. If they find me the same way you did, and they know I'm in a motor home now, then they'll be looking at all the campgrounds. No, there's got to be a better place."

The confusion and near panic in his voice gave her pause. He didn't seem quite so hardened now.

"Just drive. I'll show you where they're working on a new neighborhood. They're clearing land. We'll just park out there."

She didn't like the idea of being in some remote place alone with him.

"Creed," she tried again. "They're going to find you eventually. They're turning over every rock. Why don't you just turn yourself in and let the justice system sort this out?"

"Because I didn't do it. I didn't kill anybody, but if I turn myself in and tell them that, they won't believe me."

"Why do they consider you a suspect?"

"Because my stuff was at the scene. I was set up, and I don't know how strong the case against me is."

"If you got a lawyer, they could find out for you."

He gave her a glance. "If you found me, the bad guys can too. I'm a dead man."

Thick, heavy silence fell like a blanket over them. When her phone vibrated, she looked at him. "Creed, please. It's probably my sister, wondering when I'll be home."

He pulled it out of his pocket, read the text aloud: "When

are you coming to get Lily? You said eleven. She won't take the bottle and she's hungry."

Holly felt her let-down reflex react, and she twisted her face. "Please, Creed. Let me call her."

He stared at the phone for a long moment. "Is that what you named her?"

Holly hesitated. "Yes. Lily."

Silence for a moment. "You weren't even gonna tell me I had a child."

She swallowed. "I didn't think it would matter."

"You didn't think her father would want to know about her?"

That made Holly angry. "Excuse me for saying so, but you're holding a gun on me right now. Sorry if I didn't think you'd be that great an influence on her."

He took in a long breath, then dropped his shoulders as he exhaled. "I would have been a good dad if . . ." His voice trailed off.

If what? she thought. *If you hadn't gone into the criminal world? If you hadn't killed a guy? If you hadn't taken me hostage?*

He didn't speak again until he told her where to turn.

CHAPTER 19

Cathy sat at her desk in her small bedroom office, stuffing the envelopes for every news outlet she could find in the Florida, Georgia, and Alabama markets. The packet included her own plea for them to cover Michael's story as well as multiple articles highlighting his journey. On the top page she had typed in bold letters, "Should Governor Larimore Pardon Local Hero?"

She might be up all night getting the packages together.

But when the phone rang and Zach passed along Juliet's frustrated need for help, Cathy loaded the stacks of stapled papers and manila envelopes into her car and headed over. Maybe after she helped Juliet she would have time to work on this, and she could still get them in Monday's mail.

She found her sister's house in a rare state of chaos, so she took over with Lily while Juliet attended to Robbie. By this time, Lily was hungry enough to take her bottle, but every so often she would let the rubber nipple go and scream out again, as if in pain. "I hope she's not getting whatever Robbie has," Juliet said.

With two crying babies and two tweens—how had Juliet been handling all this alone? "Maybe Lily just misses her mother."

"She's not the only one," Juliet muttered.

When Robbie had finally fallen asleep and the boys were in bed, Cathy was still walking Lily from one end of the house to the other. The baby stayed quiet as long as she kept moving.

How could Holly put Juliet in this position? "Where is she?" Cathy said as Juliet came out of Robbie's room.

"Probably in some bar getting drunk with her friends."

That didn't sound like Juliet.

"She lied through her teeth," Juliet went on, "and said she wasn't going to meet them."

"Do you think she was really mugged the other day?"

"Yes, I think that part was true. I just need to figure out what to do about Lily. Do I keep babysitting her so Holly can go out and party? I was only doing it when she was trying to earn money, but I have my hands full, and I don't want to be used."

"If anybody needs a night out, it's you," Cathy said. "I'm just surprised at her. She's been so different lately."

"But those girls today, they really did a number on her. Pressuring her to go out with them."

"Still, she loves Lily so much. She hates being away from her."

Juliet checked her watch. "Well, it's past eleven now. When she gets here, I'm gonna let her have it. She hasn't even answered my texts yet. That's the least she could do so I don't imagine she's dead on the street."

"She's not dead on the street."

Juliet looked at her. "She could be. What if she got mugged again?"

"She's not working, remember? She wouldn't have picked up any strangers if she's not on the clock."

Tears escaped Juliet's eyes. "I'm just sad for Lily, if Holly's going back down this path. I understand her wanting some time with her friends, but I hate lying."

Cathy knew that lying was a knife in Juliet's injured heart. She might never overcome her husband's lies. Holly knew that. Why would she put Juliet through this? Even in Holly's worst years, she wasn't cruel. And maybe she *wouldn't* do this. Maybe they had it all wrong.

"Let's just calm down," Cathy said. "She's not that late yet. Maybe she's fine and just being inconsiderate."

But when midnight passed, Cathy's denial began to seem ridiculous. Juliet had no choice but to feed Lily formula. Lily's digestive system rejected it, and she promptly threw it up. Eventually she cried herself to sleep in the swing.

Afraid to move the baby to the portable Pack 'n Play bed, Juliet collapsed on the couch. "How did this become my life?"

"It's not so bad, honey. Just a stressful night."

Tears blurred Juliet's eyes, and she pulled her knees up and dabbed at her eyes. "I just sometimes think . . ."

When Juliet's voice trailed off, Cathy sat down next to her. "Think what?"

"That God is punishing me for something, and he's keeping the reason a secret."

So that was what Juliet had been thinking. Cathy studied her sister—she had been losing weight since Bob's death, and she was almost skin and bones. Lines had etched themselves deeper into her complexion, and shadows seemed darker around her mouth and under her eyes. "God's not punishing you. You're probably one of his favorites."

That made the tears fall. "No, I'm not. I can't be. All this stuff wouldn't keep happening."

Cathy sighed. "Someone really wise once told me that even Christians aren't immune to tragedy. That we can't use this fallen world to gauge our value to God."

Juliet must have remembered saying those words, because she smiled, but it only lasted a moment. "I just don't understand. Bob's whole life was a lie, and now mine is turned upside down. My kids have to go to counseling to deal with their feelings. I've had to work full-time to keep a roof over our heads, after having all the money I needed for most of my adult life. I barely make enough to pay my bills. Now my kid sister who I thought was finally flying right is going back off the cliff, but this time she has a baby. Why can't something go right?"

"When you're this tired and stressed, everything looks bad. Discouragement sets in. Then the devil gets a foothold."

"Are you going to keep quoting me all night?"

"Yes," Cathy said with a laugh. "You keep sounding like me and I'll keep sounding like you. Go to bed."

Juliet flipped on the television, turned to a movie channel. "Let's just watch something fun until she gets home."

Lily started to cry again, and Juliet drew in a deep breath. Cathy jumped up and got her out of the swing.

"Poor little thing," Juliet said. "She sounds miserable."

Cathy started walking again. It was going to be a long night if Holly didn't come soon.

CHAPTER 20

When they stopped, Creed took the battery out of Holly's phone and stuffed it into his pocket.

"What are you doing?"

"Making sure nobody tracks you."

She wished they *could* track her—but the truth was, her sisters didn't have the ability to track her phone unless they had her computer, where she had the Find My Phone app.

"Creed, you're killing me here. My sister is freaking out, thinking I'm getting wasted and doing all the things I did before I had a child to think about, but none of that is true."

"Tell me about it. My family's been told I'm a killer."

Holly leaned back in her seat, looking out the windshield into the night. "I'm not like I was when we met, you know. I don't go home with strangers."

"I know you don't."

"Oh really? How do you know?"

"Your friends seemed surprised that night. If you did it all the time, they wouldn't have been. Your family will get over it. Mine will too, if they ever learn the truth that I didn't walk up to some guy and put a gun to the back of his head and blow his skull off."

She stared at him, not sure she believed him. "Okay—what happened, then?"

"There was a big drug bust. Several dealers got arrested, and some idiot decided I was the snitch. They had to make an example of me."

"So I'm a sitting duck here with you, waiting for your maniac friends to come kill you if the police don't get here first?"

"It's not an ideal situation."

"Not ideal? Are you crazy? Do you know how many years you could get for kidnapping? That's what you're doing here, Creed. Kidnapping!"

"I'm not a criminal."

"You are now." She saw the war being waged on his face, so she changed her strategy. Lowering her voice, she said, "Let me go, and I won't tell the police. I can keep my mouth shut."

"Why would you? You don't believe me."

She honestly didn't know if she did. He seemed sincere, but criminals could be manipulators. "Creed, listen to me. When the cops came to my house looking for you, I researched you to see what was going on. There isn't a warrant out for your arrest yet. They just want you for questioning. You're just a person of interest. If you got a lawyer and turned yourself in, you could tell them what really happened. If you didn't do it, you probably have an alibi, right? Some proof of where you were?"

"That's the thing. I don't. They were holding me while it

happened. They planned it all out from the beginning. A way to take us both down. Me and Loco, the guy who was killed. I was there."

"At the murder scene?"

His mouth twitched as he seemed to struggle with his emotions. "It's all so insane, me dealing drugs. I was waiting tables and wasn't making enough. I could have gone to work for my dad, but I didn't want to depend on him. I needed to pay bills, and I didn't want to ask my parents for money, so I wound up selling weed. Then I figured I could make more selling coke. Just a little here and there, to friends who were going to buy anyway. But after a few weeks, I told my supplier I wanted out. Next thing I know, the DEA drug bust happens. I guess it looked suspicious that I got out right before that happened. My suppliers suspected Loco too, because he was arrested for dealing a few days before the bust, and then the police let him go with a tiny bond. They thought he had made a deal with the police, and if you ask me, he probably did."

"So you saw who killed him?"

"Yes. They shot him right in front of me." His face glistened with sweat, and his trembling hand came up to wipe his mouth. "It's not like in the movies. It was sick . . . worst thing I ever saw. One of the guys cut me . . . knife across the ribs."

He lifted his shirt, showed Holly the newly healing cut. She sucked in a breath.

"It wasn't a deep cut, but I was bleeding. Miller told me to take my shirt off to blot it, and when I did, he shoved the gun into my hand and put the knife into Loco's. I realized they were staging the scene, and I dropped my shirt and the gun and made a run for it. They shot at me and chased me, but I got away."

Holly tried to picture the scene. "Why didn't you go straight to the police?"

"You don't understand," he said. "Those guys have people there. They have people everywhere. They're looking for me. They want me dead."

"They're not omniscient, like God. Maybe you're overestimating them."

"I'm not, okay? I'm not."

Silence hung heavy over the motor home as Holly played out the scene in her head. Finally, Creed said, "I would have been a good father, I think. I had a great family. Good parents."

"Had? What are you, dead already?"

He didn't answer, and she realized that he didn't expect to survive this—which meant she might not either.

She looked down at her feet. "I followed your parents when I was looking for you."

"You what?"

"I didn't know where you were. I thought they might lead me to you. Anyway, they went to a T-ball game. Was that for your nephew?"

"Yeah, Brock. He's five, really a blast. Loves his Uncle Creed. I was supposed to go to that game too."

"Your parents seem nice."

"They're great. Best grandparents in the world. If they knew they had another grandbaby . . ."

The thought made Holly look away. She stared out into the night. "Creed, you talk like it's over for you, but it doesn't have to be. Turn yourself in."

"You don't get the drug trade, Holly. It's a tangled mess, and it reaches everywhere. Even some of the cops are tied up in this."

She sighed. "If you let me go, my sisters and I can try to help you."

She didn't know if she could keep that promise, but she would worry about that later.

He raked his hand through his hair. "I don't know," he said. "I have no idea what to do. I need to sleep."

"Go ahead," she said.

He breathed a mirthless laugh. "I'm not stupid. You'd get away. I have to tie you up."

"Tie me up? No! Come on, Creed. I've cooperated with you."

"Just so I can sleep. Just until daylight."

When he raised the gun back to her head, she understood she had no choice. Was it true that he couldn't pull the trigger and "blow her skull off," as he said? She couldn't count on it. He walked her to the bunk bed, made her lie down on the bottom bunk, and used plastic zip ties to secure her right hand to one end and her right foot to the other end. He made sure there was nothing around that she could reach, then he climbed onto the top bunk. In minutes, she heard his rhythmic breathing.

Holly tried to wriggle her hand and foot free, but he'd bound them too tightly. The ties were already cutting off her circulation. Her foot was going to sleep.

She thought of Lily crying for her mother. Was she distressed? Was Juliet able to calm her? She knew for sure her sister wouldn't let Lily be upset for long.

But the thought that her sisters would assume she was shirking her maternal responsibilities killed her. Why hadn't she just come clean with them and told them about Creed? She could have used their help, and they wouldn't have had to rely on their imaginations to figure out what had happened to her.

She lay on her back, looking at the bunk above her, and said a silent prayer for help. Only God could get her out of this now. She hoped he was paying attention.

CHAPTER 21

Lying in the dark, Holly looked around the motor home. She wondered whose it was. If it belonged to Creed's family, the police would have located it by now. There were a few personal touches—homemade curtains in the windows, a yellowed almanac in the pocket behind the driver's seat, a coffeepot on the small counter. But no pictures, nothing personal.

She dozed lightly off and on during the night, going rigid when she heard the sound of wind moving a branch against the motor home. Assuming Creed's story was true—what if the drug dealers found them? Would they kill her along with Creed? What story would her family believe about why she was here with him? What would they ultimately tell Lily?

When daylight finally came, she heard Creed stirring. He hung his legs over the side of the bunk above her and sat there for a moment, with only his feet in view. Then he slipped down to the floor.

"Can I please go home now?" she asked.

He didn't answer. His hair was sleep-tousled, and his face looked paler than last night. "Are you hungry?"

"Yes. I need to nurse, Creed. My daughter needs me."

"*Our* daughter needs you."

She opened her mouth to protest but decided it wasn't wise. "Then let me go to her."

He busied himself in the kitchen, pouring cereal. There was a small refrigerator under the counter, and he pulled out a carton of milk. Then he started the coffeepot.

She watched as he searched through a drawer, found some scissors, then picked up the gun again. Holding the Glock in his left hand, he cut her ties with his right. She sat up, rubbing her wrist. "Thank you."

"Come eat."

If it weren't for the gun he kept within reach, and the fact that she was painfully engorged and needing to nurse, it would have seemed like a normal breakfast. She ate the bowl of cereal.

"Want more?" he asked.

She shook her head. "Aren't you gonna eat?"

"Not hungry," he said, sipping his coffee.

After a moment, he said, "Well, I guess we should move the motor home in case contractors show up to work out here."

"Creed, please . . . the baby."

Creed bent over and peered out the window. "I was thinking. Maybe we should go get her."

Holly caught her breath. "Really?"

"We could let them think what they're already thinking. That you just spent the night with me last night, that I'm your latest boyfriend."

Her heart crashed. "No, I don't want to do that."

"It's believable. We go in there, and I keep the gun in my pocket in case you decide to go rogue. We get the baby—Lily—and thank them for keeping her. No explanations. Just get the baby. Then you can take care of her."

Holly didn't want to lie to Juliet again, but maybe she could give her a signal that would raise a red flag. Then again, if Juliet didn't get it and questioned her, Creed could realize what she was doing.

"I don't want them to think that of me," Holly said.

"They already think it of you. Let them. You can feed her then. I just want to see my baby before I can't anymore."

Holly dreaded the thought of bringing Lily into the motor home with a man who had kidnapped her mother at gunpoint. "Just let me go feed her and leave. I don't want to bring her into danger."

"Holly, I'm not going to hurt her."

Had he really said that with a straight face? "You've got a gun on me! Besides, if someone is after you, then she could get caught in the crossfire. Or if the police come, even then, she could get hurt. Why can't you just let me go? I thought about it all night, and I believe you. I'm not going to call the police. Just please, let me go back."

"I can't chance that. No, this is what we're going to do. We drive the motor home back to the campground where I was yesterday, then we park it somewhere and get your cab. We go get the baby—and if you try to signal your sister, I'll know it."

"And what? You'll kill me? You really want me to bring my baby to you when you've just threatened to kill me?"

"I don't have a choice!" he shouted, startling her. "What else am I gonna do? I know I'm in trouble, one way or another. I know my days are numbered. I just want to see my baby and have some time to think before my life is taken from me. We're going to do it this way, like it or not."

Holly could hear in his voice that she would never talk him out of it. "At least eat first so you're thinking clearly," she whispered. "I don't want you shooting me because of low blood sugar."

As if to appease her, he poured himself some cereal.

CHAPTER 22

Juliet woke to Lily's crying. For such a little thing, she had a big voice, a voice that created panic and urgency. When Juliet lifted the baby out of her vibrating seat, Lily screamed louder, wriggling and squirming as Juliet carried her into the kitchen and opened the container of powdered formula. "I know you're hungry, sweetie, but I don't know where your mommy is. Aunt Juliet's going to feed you, but you'll have to wait just a minute."

She heard Robbie crying from his bedroom. That was all she needed. She scooped formula into the only clean bottle she had and mixed it with bottled water.

Fatigue made her feel like she was moving through water, but her heart raced like she was sprinting. Today was Sunday. Should she even try to get Zach and Abe to church?

Cathy came up the hall with Robbie on her hip. "Look who's up."

Thankful Cathy had rescued him, Juliet smiled at her son, kissed his forehead. He was still feverish. Lily kept screaming.

"Anything I can do?" Cathy asked.

Juliet knew if Cathy set Robbie down and took Lily, he would get upset. She didn't want both babies to cry. She managed to get the nipple and top on the bottle, shake it up, and set it in the warmer. Lily continued to scream as the minutes crawled by. Relieved when the steamer finally beeped, Juliet tested the temperature before putting the nipple in Lily's mouth. The baby suckled greedily.

Silence. Beautiful silence.

"Okay," Juliet said to Cathy. "You come feed Lily, and I'll take Robbie."

Cathy took the baby and sat down on the couch. "So Holly never came home."

"And she never called me back or answered her phone. I left a dozen messages." Juliet met Cathy's eyes. "You don't think she's hurt or something, do you? Maybe she had a wreck or got mugged again."

"I can't imagine her just not calling. I'm getting worried."

Juliet took Robbie to his room and changed his diaper, then took him back to the kitchen and put him in his high chair. She gave him some Cheerios to satisfy him until she could get his bottle ready. Thankfully, he cooperated.

Suddenly the doorbell rang, followed by a loud knock. Juliet's stomach flipped. "Oh no. It's news about Holly."

Keeping the bottle in Lily's mouth, Cathy followed Juliet to the door. Juliet turned on the porch light and looked out through the peephole. "Thank God, it's her." She threw the door open.

There stood Holly with some guy Juliet had never seen

before. Just the sight of him made all the hours of stress explode in Juliet's chest. "Where have you been? I've been calling you all night. Your daughter needs you!"

Holly reached for her baby as she stepped inside, and Cathy surrendered her. "That's why I'm here," Holly said in a flat voice.

Juliet studied her, looking for clues of intoxication or a hangover. She looked disheveled, but not necessarily impaired.

"Who are you?" Cathy asked the man.

"This is my friend Deuce," Holly said before he could answer.

Deuce didn't bother to shake their hands. "Hi. How're you doing?"

"Been better," Juliet said.

Holly pushed past her toward the living room, Deuce following close behind. He wore a windbreaker, even though it was warm outside, and he was unshaven. He looked just like the kind of guy Holly would fall for. Dark and handsome, with that bad-boy look. Juliet wanted to throttle her sister.

Tears welled in Holly's eyes as she pulled her nursing cover out of her diaper bag. Juliet gaped at her. Holly was usually modest and didn't like nursing in front of people. "Hey, sweetheart," Holly whispered to Lily. "I'm so sorry I wasn't here." She looked up at Juliet. "Is she okay?"

"She's hungry," Juliet clipped. "I've been giving her formula."

"Formula upsets her stomach," Holly said. Juliet crossed her arms, livid, and shot Cathy a look.

"I came over to help because Robbie was sick and Lily was crying, and it was chaos," Cathy said.

"I'm really sorry," Holly whispered. As she fed Lily under the nursing cover, Deuce seemed transfixed by Lily's little feet.

"Can you do that in the car?" he asked.

Holly gave him a tense look. "She has to be in her seat while the car's moving. I can't nurse her there."

"You can give her the bottle."

"She needs to nurse," Holly said with irritation. "Can we just sit here for a few minutes?"

Juliet's mouth fell open. Was Holly honestly asking his permission?

Deuce kept one hand in his jacket pocket, but with his other he stroked Lily's foot. His knee bounced as if he were nervous.

Juliet stood over Holly, her arms crossed. "So . . . no explanation for last night? You said you'd be home at eleven, and you wind up coming back at five a.m.? No apology? No nothing?"

"I didn't plan that," Holly said weakly.

"No, I didn't think you did. It was spontaneous, right? You met a guy . . ."

Holly winced, tears beginning to rim her eyes. "I already knew him. I ran into him last night."

"So you decided, hey, why don't I go shack up with him for the night? Forget my baby and my sister who wasn't prepared for an overnight visit!"

More tears glistened in Holly's eyes as she looked at Deuce. When she brought her eyes back to Juliet, she said, "Can we talk about this later? She's calm now. Let her nurse in peace."

Juliet forced herself to calm down. Turning her back on her sister, she decided to get on with her day. "I have to feed Robbie."

As Juliet fed Robbie in his high chair, Holly nursed quietly, clearly brooding, and the guy—Deuce whatever—didn't say a word. Finally, after twenty minutes, Holly put herself back together and burped her baby.

Deuce watched with a look that Juliet couldn't place. It was more than simple interest. Almost a longing.

Suddenly it hit her. Was he the father?

Even if he was, that still didn't explain Holly's irresponsibility.

Finally, Holly got the diaper bag and swaddled Lily in a blanket. "Well, okay, we'll go now. Thank you for keeping her last night. I'll try to call you later."

Juliet couldn't think of a thing to say. As she fed Robbie bananas, she watched Holly head for the door, with Deuce right behind her.

Something wasn't right. She listened for the closing door, then went and locked it behind them. She looked through the curtains as Holly strapped Lily's seat in the backseat of her taxi. Then Deuce sat in the back with the baby, and Holly got behind the wheel.

Why would Holly trust that man with her child? It didn't make sense, even if he did turn out to be the father. With a sinking feeling and smothering discouragement, Juliet went back to the kitchen.

"So she's at it again," Cathy muttered.

"We can't control her," Juliet said. "We never could."

CHAPTER 23

Holly watched Creed in the rearview mirror as they drove back to the motor home. He couldn't keep his eyes off Lily. Though he kept the gun pointed at Holly's back with his right hand, he had given his left hand to Lily. She had his calloused finger clutched in her tiny fist.

Holly seethed. The last thing she needed was this man getting into her daughter's heart.

When they were almost back to the campground, she glanced back. "Creed, what do you want me to do now?"

"Leave your car here, and we'll walk the rest of the way to the camper. Then we'll move it. Maybe out of town."

"Out of town? No! I can't go out of town."

"Not that far. Just somewhere they won't look for me."

Holly was sick of this. "Why can't you go alone? What do you need us for?"

"I can't let you go and talk to the police."

"But I won't know where you are. I can't even lead them to you."

"You'll know I'm in a motor home."

"But so did Brittany. You didn't kidnap *her*."

"Brittany won't tell."

Holly pulled her car to a stop and shoved the gearshift into park. "How do you know?"

"Because she knows I couldn't kill anybody."

Holly turned and looked at him over the seat. "Is she your girlfriend?"

"No."

He got out of the car and unhooked the car seat. He'd clearly done it before, probably when his nephew was small.

He kept his gun in his pocket and carried Lily in her seat back to the motor home.

When they got inside, Holly bent to get the baby out of her seat, but he prodded her with the barrel of the gun again. "Drive first," he said. "Let's get out of here."

She had no choice, so she strapped Lily's seat onto one of the back bench seats, then climbed into the driver's seat. Lily slept as they rode north out of Southport.

"So we're almost to Pensacola," she said. "Isn't this far enough?"

"Probably." Creed stared down at his phone's GPS. "Take a left, go two miles, then a right into the Baymont RV park."

If she did as he said, would Creed let her walk away with Lily? How had she gotten into this?

She shouldn't have kept any of this from her sisters. If she hadn't, if she'd told them she was looking for Creed—the father of her child who was wanted for murder—then they would have known last night that something had happened to her.

In fact, why hadn't she told Creed last night that her sisters knew where she was and what she was doing? Even though it wasn't true, it might have frightened him into letting her go.

At the RV park, Creed made her go into the office and use her ID and cash to pay and sign in. She thought of telling the desk clerk that she and her baby were being held against their will, but what if that resulted in police surrounding them? Creed was out there with Lily. She couldn't risk putting her in even more danger.

Without alerting anyone, she went back to the motor home.

"Everything all right?" Creed asked her.

"Yeah," she said. "We're in space twenty-seven." She checked on Lily, slipped back into the driver's seat, and pulled into the space assigned to them.

Creed unlatched Lily's safety strap.

"Please don't get her out," Holly said. "She's sleeping."

He didn't listen—just put the gun in his pocket and lifted the sleeping child. Lily woke and stretched, arching her back, her little hands over her head. He smiled and brought her to his chest. "She's beautiful. She looks like you. My nose, maybe. She looks a lot like my nephew when he was a baby."

Holly couldn't breathe. Her maternal senses were on full alert. "I really wish you'd put her back down."

He shot her a sharp look. "She's my baby too, Holly."

"Why?" she demanded. "Because you picked up a girl in a bar? That doesn't make you a father, Creed."

"It made you a mother."

"I carried her for nine months. She came out of my body. I'm the one who loves her and takes care of her." She watched as he swayed back and forth, rocking her. His fatherly gentleness made her angry. "What do you want from me, Creed?"

He looked at her. "Nothing. I'm only holding you so you can't run to the police and tell them where I am."

"No, I mean what do you want . . . regarding Lily?"

He looked down at Lily again. Holly waited, but before he could get a word out, his face crumpled and his eyes filled with tears. This time he couldn't hold them back. "I don't know," he said just above a whisper. "But I don't take fatherhood lightly."

"Why not? Everybody else does! Doesn't everybody assume that one-night stands aren't supposed to turn into lifelong commitments? If you wind up in prison, do you want your daughter to grow up knowing her daddy's serving a life sentence for murder one?"

"I didn't do it," he bit out.

"Maybe not, but you can't possibly think that what you're doing now is making things better. Making you look innocent."

Lily's little head rolled to the side, and his hand came up to support it. He kissed the top of her head. "No, you're right. You probably did the right thing keeping me out of her life, especially since I'm in this mess." His voice broke. "But I would have been a fantastic dad."

She didn't know what to say. She looked away, sure he must be embarrassed by his tears. She tried to think. He didn't seem like a cold-blooded killer, someone who could shoot a guy execution-style in the back of the head. But even so, where did that leave her?

She had to get the gun away from him. She had to do what she could for herself and her child. Forcing herself to stay calm, she sat down next to him on the bench seat, within reach of the jacket pocket where he held her gun.

He held Lily in front of him, smiling as the baby looked up at him.

Now! In one quick move, Holly slipped her hand into his jacket and jerked the gun out.

"No!" he shouted, startling the baby.

Holly backed across the motor home, pointing the gun at the floor, unable and unwilling to aim it at him and her baby. Lily began to cry.

"Holly, give the gun back," he said as he brought Lily to his chest.

"I can't, Creed." Her hands were shaking. "I have to protect my child."

"Then don't aim a gun at her!"

"I'm not! Put Lily down now!" He made no move to do as she said.

The gun felt lighter than it should. She glanced down at it. It was her gun—the one he'd taken from her cab. She released the clip. It was empty.

Her mouth fell open. "It's not loaded?"

Creed just let out a long, weary sigh.

"Are you seriously telling me you've been holding me hostage all night long, and you didn't even have a loaded gun?"

"I took the bullets out. I didn't want it to accidentally go off."

She dropped the gun on the couch. "Give me my baby!" she shouted.

"No."

"Give her to me now!" She took Lily out of his arms, and the baby hushed. She backed away from him and sank into the front passenger seat, opened the glove compartment, and took out her phone and battery. She popped the battery back in, watched as it came to life and found a signal.

"Holly, don't call anyone. So help me . . ."

"What?" she asked, turning back to him. "You'll kill me? What will you do? Hit me over the head with the gun? Where are the bullets?"

He sighed. "They're in the console by the driver's seat."

She opened it, found six bullets, and put them into her pocket. "Unbelievable."

"I'm not a killer. I took them out when we were still in the cab. I just needed the threat."

She stalked across the trailer to the infant seat. "I'm leaving."

"Holly, I need your help. Please. I can help you too. You and your family."

She couldn't believe his gall. "What do you mean? With Lily?"

"No. I mean I know things. Things that can help you find your family's archenemy."

Her family's archenemy? Her mind began to race. There was only one. She stared at Creed for a long moment.

"I can help you find him. He was there when Loco was killed. I know people who can lead us to him."

Her heart stumbled. "Are we talking about . . . who I think we're talking about?"

"Yes," he said. "I can help you find Leonard Miller."

CHAPTER 24

Pushing through her exhaustion, Juliet dropped Zach and Abe off at church. As she drove home with Robbie, who still seemed slightly feverish, she drove past the office and saw that Cathy's car was there. She pulled in next to one of the old gas pumps, got Robbie out, and went in.

"What are you doing?" she asked Cathy, who sat behind Michael's desk.

"I wanted to use Michael's computer to look up that guy Deuce. Why didn't we get his last name?" Cathy asked.

"His last name? We didn't even get his *first* name. Deuce is probably a nickname." Juliet laid Robbie in the Pack 'n Play she and Holly kept there. He didn't protest, just curled up with his blankie.

"We're PIs," Cathy said. "We can find him. I'll do a search of the name Deuce in police records in Florida." She hit Send, then waited.

Juliet came around behind her to watch the screen. "Oh no," she said as names began to scroll up.

"Way more than I thought," Cathy said. "Seems to be a popular street name." There were at least a hundred people listed.

"Can you scroll through their mug shots?"

"I'll have to click on each one, but yeah, I'll do it. But if this guy doesn't have a rap sheet, we're barking up the wrong tree." She clicked through a few who weren't the guy, deleted them.

"Okay, I have an idea," Juliet said. "I'll call Holly's friends who were at the shower. She probably partied with them last night. They would know who he is." She paced in the other room as she called two of them. She had clearly awakened them. Neither admitted Holly had been with them last night, and both denied knowing anyone named Deuce, but they were gleefully intrigued by Holly's activities.

When Juliet got off the phone, she went back to Cathy and dropped into a chair. "Why are we doing this? It's a waste of time."

"Because we want to know who Holly is tangled up with."

"She's a grown woman. She can see anyone she wants. We can't stop her."

"But if we find out anything suspicious about him, at least we can tell her. Try to make her see reason. She's letting him be around Lily."

Juliet let out a hard sigh. "Cathy, do you think he could be the father?"

Cathy looked up at her, surprised. "No. I mean . . . what would make you think that?"

"He came with her to get Lily. That's kind of weird, don't you think? I mean, she's out all night with him, then introduces him to her child? Most women would want to pretend they're free and unencumbered. Most guys would run from a new mom with a baby."

"Yeah, it's weird, but—"

"Don't you think it's at least possible? The way he looked at Lily. He didn't just glance at her. He was very interested. He got this soft look on his face."

Cathy stopped clicking and stared at Juliet. "Well, *someone* is the father. I don't know why she refuses to tell us who. I always thought it was because . . ."

"Because she doesn't know?" Juliet saw from Cathy's eyes that she'd nailed it. "I don't think that's it. Holly was wild and reckless, but I don't think she would go through men like that. It would make her feel worthless."

"She did feel worthless," Cathy said. "Still does to some extent."

"But lately, she's had better judgment. Maybe we've got this all wrong."

"Okay, then what's going on? She stayed out all night with some guy we've never heard of." Cathy sighed as she read through the profiles coming up on the screen. "The first twenty or so aren't him. Still looking. I think I'll recognize him."

At least Lily was with her mom now. That was something. Juliet wished she hadn't invited Holly's old friends to the shower. Maybe they had been too much of a temptation. The whole single mom thing was overwhelming enough. "I should've helped her more," Juliet mumbled.

Cathy gaped at her. "Seriously? Juliet, in your tangled mind, how can this possibly be your fault?"

"I'm just thinking the pressure was so great. Maybe she—"

"Juliet!" Cathy turned away from the computer and faced

her sister. "Listen to yourself. You're grieving your husband, you've adopted his mistress's son, you've had to start earning a living, you're raising two boys alone, you've moved . . . Yes, Holly's had some struggles, but you get the trophy for tough times. And it hasn't sent *you* off the deep end."

"It's not a competition. I'm just worried about her. Something's not right."

When it was time for Juliet to pick up Zach and Abe from church, Cathy insisted on staying with Robbie.

"You sure you want to?" Juliet asked. "If he wakes up, he might be fussy. Besides, you must be as tired as I am."

"It's okay. I can handle fussy," Cathy told her. "And yeah, I'm tired, but I had planned to be up all night anyway to get my mailings ready for all the news outlets. I want to mail them tomorrow, but it might have to be Tuesday."

Juliet got her purse. "Well, let me help you. After I pick up Abe and Zach, we'll grab something to eat and then we'll all come back here and stuff envelopes."

"You don't have to do that. You need to nap."

"So do you, but we're in this together. Set up that long folding table. The four of us can get it knocked out. Maybe Robbie will sleep the whole time."

Cathy agreed gratefully. As she waited for Juliet and the boys, she used Michael's computer to search more rap sheets for Deuce. When Juliet and company arrived with fast food bags, Juliet joined her and Zach and Abe went to the back living area to eat and watch TV.

Juliet ate her salad at the desk while Cathy clicked through more mug shots. They heard a car door outside, and Juliet got up and went to the window. "It's Max and his dad."

Cathy looked up. "What are they doing here?"

"Did you tell them we were stuffing packets? Maybe they came to help."

Cathy shook her head. "No, I didn't tell them." She went to the door to greet the men as they came in, then directed them away from the table in the front room and into the office.

"Looking good in here," Jack said when they'd all taken a seat. "I haven't been here in months. We were driving by and saw your car. Thought we'd stop in. You're working on Sunday?"

"Not really," Cathy said. "We just stopped by to take care of a few things."

"A few things about the pardon efforts?" Max asked.

Cathy smiled at Juliet. "Yes, we're getting press packets ready."

"I've gotten the police department involved," Jack said. "I've gotten promises that they're going to write letters too."

Max grinned. "Dad got to talk to each shift, and all our people are ready to storm the governor's mailbox."

"And I know one of the governor's aides," Jack said. "He's the son of one of my former partners on the force. His dad owes me a favor."

"Dad saved his life," Max cut in.

Jack ignored that and went on. "He says he'll put a bug in the governor's ear too."

Tears filled Cathy's eyes. "Really? You guys, maybe we're getting somewhere. Maybe he'll consider it."

"Anyway," Jack said, sitting up in his chair. "I've been hearing about how you and your sisters are trying to keep the business running. That's a big help to Michael. Max said he's been giving you a hand. I thought if he could do it, I could offer my services too."

"Your services?" Cathy asked. "You mean here, in the business?"

"Yeah," Jack said. "God knows I need something to do with my time. I hate retirement. Max suggested I help hold down the fort while Michael's being held hostage by our flawed justice system . . ." He looked at the floor. "Leonard Miller's walking free—a known murderer—and Michael gets locked up. Don't get me started." He rubbed his jaw. "But I can help with these cases, take the load off you gals. I don't need pay. I have a decent pension. It's the least I can do to help my son."

Juliet and Cathy looked at each other and smiled. "We sure do need help," Cathy said. "We're in over our heads. Juliet's working full-time, and I'm trying to. Holly's about to start putting in more hours, but we still have more business than we can handle."

"Then what do you say?"

Juliet started to laugh. "I say . . . we're thrilled. You're a godsend."

"So what are you working on right now?" Max asked, glancing at the computer monitor, where the last mug shot Cathy had been looking at was still up.

"Well, honestly, we're not working on a paying case right now," Cathy said. "We've been researching Holly's new boyfriend."

Max frowned. "She has a new boyfriend?"

"Apparently," Juliet said. "She left me with the baby last night and lied about where she was going. Didn't call or anything all night. Then she shows up this morning . . ." Juliet let her voice trail off. "Never mind, I shouldn't be telling you that. I'm just a little miffed at her. We just want to see who this guy is."

Max came closer and leaned over the desk to see the monitor better. "What's his name?"

"Deuce. It's all we got."

"You say she didn't show up last night? Didn't call?"

"Right."

"Is that like her?"

"Used to be," Cathy said. "But not in the last year."

Cathy watched Max's face as he read through the rap sheet on the screen. "It's not him," she said. "We were just going through guys named Deuce. We haven't found him yet."

"So you saw the guy? Would you recognize him if you saw him again?"

"Yes," Cathy said.

"Mind if I try something?"

Cathy surrendered her chair. "Be my guest."

Cathy watched as Max typed in "Creed Kershaw." Frowning at Juliet, she waited. Suddenly, a driver's license picture came up.

Juliet caught her breath. "That's him! Max, how did you know?"

Max rubbed his temples, frowning.

"Max, who is this guy?" Cathy asked. "How did you know his name?"

"Holly told me."

"She told you she was seeing someone?"

"No," he said. "She's not seeing him. I think something's wrong. Holly could be in a lot of trouble."

Cathy stared at him. "What are you talking about?"

"I think you two need to sit down."

CHAPTER 25

"Why wouldn't she tell us that?" Juliet cried after Max told her what he knew. "How could she run off after a murderer and not have someone watching her back?"

"She was embarrassed. She didn't want you to know about him being the father," Max said.

"Why would she tell *you*?" Cathy demanded.

"Because she needed my help to find out things about him. I shouldn't have given her anything. I knew she was going to go off and do this."

"So let me get this straight," Cathy said. "Holly has been going to Southport to look for this guy, presumably so she can turn him in to the police and she won't have to deal with him coming back into her life . . ."

"Right. And it looks like she found him."

"So . . . what? Is he holding her hostage?"

"Juliet, I'm no expert on Holly, but if she didn't call last

127

night and didn't get her baby until this morning, and this guy was sticking to her side like glue, my guess is that she was under the gun. Literally."

Juliet felt light-headed. "He let her come get the baby, but he wouldn't let her get more than a few feet away. His hand was in his pocket the whole time."

"He had a gun," Cathy whispered. "Juliet, we've got to find her. He could kidnap Lily, or hurt them both. He could kill them! Max, can you put out an APB on her taxi? It can't be that hard to find. She could be here or in Southport, or anywhere in Northern Florida."

"Can you track her phone?" he asked.

Cathy hesitated. "I'll go to her house and try her computer. She probably has her laptop with her if she was searching for him, but she does have a desktop computer at home. It might be set up to track her phone if she loses it."

"Last night her phone was going straight to voice mail," Juliet said. "If he took the battery out, we can't track it."

"I'll go over there with you," Max said.

Cathy pulled up a database on the computer. "Max, do you have this guy's address?"

"Yes, but he's on the lam. I gave Holly his address, his parents', his sister's, and the place where he worked. That's all she had to start with."

"Do you think he really goes by Deuce?"

"No. That was probably just for you guys. So you wouldn't go looking him up under his real name."

Juliet picked up the desk phone and dialed her brother. "I'm calling Jay," she said. "I'll get him to keep the boys while we go look for Holly."

CHAPTER 26

The Southport police located Holly's taxi outside the gates of the RV park, but no one Juliet and Cathy questioned there had seen her. They followed her path to Creed's parents' house. To Cathy, it looked like a middle-class home with a well-manicured yard. The garage was closed and no cars sat in the driveway, and all the blinds were pulled.

"If they're home, do we tell them that Creed could be the father of Holly's baby?" Juliet asked.

"No, I don't think so. We tell them we're looking for our sister, and we think she's with him."

Juliet let out a ragged breath and covered her face. "I'm sick that I thought the worst of Holly when she was in danger. Of course she wouldn't have just run out on Lily without a good reason!"

"We can feel guilty later," Cathy said. "Right now let's just focus." She opened the car door. "Are you going to stay in the car with Robbie?"

"No," Juliet said. "I want to hear what they say. I'll take him with us. Maybe he'll make us seem less threatening."

Robbie was in a good mood after his nap, and his fever seemed to have broken. Juliet handed him a teething biscuit and got him out of his seat. When Cathy rang the bell, she heard footsteps, then felt as though someone was looking out the peephole. There was noise around the lock, then the door opened.

A woman who seemed about fifty looked suspiciously out at them. "Hello."

"Hi. I'm Cathy Cramer, and this is my sister Juliet, and her son Robbie."

The woman smiled at the baby. "What can I do for you?"

"We're looking for our sister, and we think she's with your son."

The smile vanished. "I don't know where he is. I'm sorry."

She started to close the door, but Cathy spoke again. "Please . . . could we come in and talk to you?"

"We're not police," Juliet said quickly. "Creed was at my house with our sister this morning, and something wasn't right. I was babysitting for her, and she picked up her daughter and they left together. Then we realized who he was. We think he's holding her hostage."

The door opened again, and now a man stood with the woman in the doorway. He looked outside for any other cars on the street, then ushered them in. "Come in."

The tidy house had been decorated with love—tchotchkes and family pictures covering the walls and every surface. Pictures of Creed when he was a kid, playing baseball, football, fishing with his dad, laughing with his family. He didn't look as rough as he had this morning. And he looked nothing like a killer. But killers didn't all look evil.

Sunshine poured in through the back windows of the

house, but it was quiet, and the TV was off. Mr. Kershaw led them to the kitchen table, where two Bibles lay open.

Christians, she thought. *This must be torturous for them.*

"Sit down," he said. "I'm Creed's dad, Frank."

They all shook hands, and Mrs. Kershaw—who told them to call her Sandra—offered them coffee, which they declined. When they'd all sat down, Frank asked them about the visit. "You say he was there this morning? At your house?"

Juliet told them about Holly's disappearance and her odd behavior this morning.

"Could she be a girlfriend?" his mother asked, deep lines of sorrow on her face.

"Our sister wasn't seeing anyone. She's a single mom, and she's got a lot on her plate. She knew him, but I don't think they'd seen each other in several months."

"So maybe she's helping him?"

"We don't think so. She would have given us some explanation. It was all very strange."

Sandra looked at Frank, her mouth compressed and twisted. "My son is a good boy. He didn't kill that man. He's gotten in with the wrong people . . . dangerous people. He's in over his head, but he wouldn't hurt a fly."

Frank rubbed his jaw. "He's had a hard time since graduating from high school. He didn't get into the college he wanted, so he went to community college, then dropped out and decided to just work. Waiting tables didn't support him. Then he started using drugs."

"What drugs?" Cathy asked.

"Marijuana at first, but then we think he graduated to cocaine. Couple of weeks ago he seemed to come to his senses. Told us he'd stopped using and wanted to quit waiting tables and come work for me. We felt like we had him back. Only now we hear that he might have been selling cocaine, and that this situation with this man he was supposed to have killed was a drug deal."

"We know he was doing something bad," Sandra said, wiping her face, "but if you knew him . . . he's got so much compassion for people. He once hurt a guy in a football game—broke his leg when he tackled him—and he cried about it for days. He would have taken the break himself if he could have. He would never take anybody's life."

Juliet turned Robbie on her lap so that he was facing out. He smiled at them, and the misery on Sandra's face faded slightly. She breathed a laugh and took his little hand.

"Mrs. Kershaw . . . Sandra," Cathy said, "can you tell us who his friends were? Who we might talk to to find our sister?"

"He had friends at the restaurant where he worked, but the police have questioned them. One of his closest friends there is a girl named Brittany."

Cathy wrote that down.

"I'm just so relieved to know that Creed is alive, that he was okay this morning." Sandra started to cry again, and Frank put his arm around her and stroked her back. "This isn't him," she said. "He's not like this. He's a good boy at heart. He just took a wrong turn."

Juliet met Cathy's eyes. How many times had they said the same about Holly?

Satisfied that his parents didn't know where Creed was, Cathy and Juliet went back to their car. "Where to?" Cathy asked. "His sister or Brittany?"

"Brittany," Juliet said. "I guarantee you Holly talked to her yesterday."

CHAPTER 27

Holly held Lily to her chest and stared at Creed. "What do you know about Leonard Miller?"

"I know people who work for him, people who could lead you to him. Back when your brother-in-law died, Miller moved up in the operation. He's back in town."

"How do you know? Have you seen him?"

"I told you—he was there when Loco was killed."

"You're sure it was Leonard Miller?"

"Yes. They called him Lenny, and I remembered him from all the news reports. His hair was different, but I knew his face. He was calling the shots."

"Did he kill Loco?"

"No, but he ordered it. When I got cut, it was Miller who stopped the dude who attacked me and told me to take off my shirt and put pressure on the wound. I thought he was protecting me. But he wanted my blood there and my prints on the gun. He wanted Loco and me both dead, and he was going to stage it to look like we killed each other."

"Why?"

"He thought we were snitches. He wanted his people to see what happens to traitors, and he didn't want the police looking for the real killer."

Holly could walk away right now, and there was nothing Creed could do to stop her. But Leonard Miller . . . they'd searched for him for so long. He'd killed people she cared about. People her sisters loved. He'd ruined so many lives.

"I don't even know how I'm still alive," Creed said. "There was this fence next to us, and a big drop-off down into a ravine. I got over it, rolled down. They shot at me, but somehow I didn't get hit. It was dark, so I was able to get away once I hit bottom. Miller must be furious that his plan failed. He won't stop until he finds me."

Holly moved her face to Lily's head, felt her child breathing on her neck. She tried to keep her voice calm. "He killed my sister's fiancé. Then he killed my brother-in-law. Michael's in jail because of him, and he's still out there murdering people."

Creed's eyebrows lifted, as if he'd finally wedged her door open. "That's right! Don't you want to find him? If you help me, I'll help you."

Holly touched the doorknob. "I can find him without you."

"Oh really? Have you seen him since he got away? Did you know he was back in town? Do you even have a starting place?"

She tried to think. "How do I know you even know anything? You could just be lying to keep me from turning you in."

He sighed. "I don't even own a gun. I had to steal yours, and then I took the bullets out so no one would get hurt. Do you really think I'd kill someone?"

"I don't know you!" she cried. "I don't know anything about you! You're just some guy that I was attracted to when I was too drunk to think! For all I know you *could* be a killer."

"Holly, I'm an idiot. I know that. I've done some really stupid things. I got myself into a mess, and I need help . . ." His voice broke off, and his face twisted. He turned away.

Holly's heart raced as she bent and put the baby into the car seat, snapped her in, then hooked her arm under the handle. She had to go before he stopped her.

"Rio said you're a PI," Creed said. "That they talked about you in the papers, all about how you and your sisters helped break up the drug ring. You know how to help me. I could help you find Miller, and you could help me prove I didn't kill that guy. I'm not under arrest yet. You said there's not even a warrant. I could get protection and a lawyer. Maybe your sister could represent me."

"Why would I trust you? You kidnapped me!"

"But I didn't hurt you. I didn't hurt Lily. I would never do anything to hurt my daughter."

"Don't call her that!"

"But it's true, Holly. She's my daughter."

Tears burned her eyes. "So . . . what? If you get off, if you don't go to jail and Miller doesn't kill you, what are you going to want from me? Custody? Visitation? What?"

"I don't know. I just want her to know she has a father who loves her."

"You don't love her. You just met her."

He tilted his head, and his face softened. "Did you love her the minute she was born?"

Holly didn't know why she was still here, arguing with him. She opened the door. "I'm leaving, Creed. I can't help you."

"Don't go, Holly. Please."

She looked out. No one seemed to be parked on the street watching them. She stepped down.

"Holly, they're going to kill me. I can only hide for so long."

She turned back, wishing she didn't care. "Creed, go turn yourself in. Tell them you can lead them to Miller. They might give you immunity if you help them. That's the right thing to do."

"How do I know they'll even listen?"

Holly hesitated. "I know people in the police department. Michael's brother Max . . . he wants his brother's murderer caught. He's a detective in Major Crimes. He'll listen."

"If I do . . . if I call them and turn myself in, will you wait here with me, Holly?"

Holly looked down at her sleeping baby. Where would she go if she left on foot? She could call a cab—one of her buddies would surely come—or she could notify the police herself. Cathy and Juliet would gladly come, but it would take awhile for them to get to Pensacola.

What would it hurt to just wait with him? Sometimes people needed help doing the right thing.

She stepped back in and closed the door. "Do you promise that you'll turn yourself in? That this isn't just a trick to make me stay?"

"I promise, Holly. I'll call right now."

She considered that, then blew out a ragged breath. "All right," she said. "Go ahead and call, and I'll wait here with you."

CHAPTER 28

The Gourmet Crab Bar and Grill in Southport was busy. Football lit up every screen in the dim restaurant, and both men and women sat with mugs of beer and seafood as they locked in on the games. Cathy led Juliet in—her sister holding Robbie on her hip. Cathy scoped the room, saw a blonde girl working at the bar. Moving closer, she read her name tag.

"That's her," she said. "Let's go sit at the bar."

Juliet gasped. "I can't do that!"

Cathy turned. "Why not?"

"Because I don't drink! What if someone from my church sees me?"

"Juliet, I think you'll be okay if you sit on a barstool."

"But with a baby? They'll think I'm a terrible mother."

"Who cares what they think?" Cathy whispered harshly. "We have to talk to her!"

Sighing, Juliet followed her. Cathy pulled out a barstool

for her, but Juliet couldn't make herself sit all the way on it. Uncommitted, she leaned against it, as if about to leave.

They watched the girl tending to the customers on the other side of the square bar. She seemed brooding, distracted, tired. After a few minutes, she made her way to them. "Help you?"

"Yes," Cathy said. "We were just at Creed Kershaw's parents' house, and we understand you're a friend of his."

Brittany stiffened. "Yeah. And?"

"And we think our sister might have come by to talk to you yesterday. Her name is Holly." Cathy showed her a picture. "She's blonde now, though. She doesn't have the pink anymore."

The girl glanced at the picture, then looked hard at each of them. "Yeah, I saw her, but it wasn't yesterday. Night before, maybe."

"She's not answering her phone. We're worried about her, and we know she's with Creed."

"No way," Brittany said. "She's not with him. Nobody knows where he is." She glanced away as she said that—a clear tell that she wasn't being honest. She twisted her face in angry puzzlement, then looked back at Cathy. "Why would you think she's with him?"

"Because she is," Juliet said. "They came to my house together this morning to get her baby. He was with her."

Brittany grunted. "Creed? Are you sure it was him?"

"Positive."

She frowned and considered that. "Were they in the motor home?"

So they were hiding in a motor home. That explained the proximity of Holly's cab to the RV park. "No, they were in her cab," Cathy said.

Brittany considered that. "That doesn't even make sense."

"What do you mean?" Juliet asked.

"He's . . . he doesn't want to be found. She asked me where he was but I didn't tell her . . ." She glanced away again. "Because I didn't know."

"When's the last time you saw him?" Cathy asked.

Brittany hesitated, then glanced at her boss near the kitchen. She got a rag and wiped the counter to appear busy. "The last time he worked, over a week ago."

"Are you sure?" Cathy asked.

Brittany hesitated. "Look, Creed didn't kill anybody. This police hunt . . . it's stupid. They're going to find out he's innocent."

"We're just looking for Holly," Juliet said. "Come on, help us out a little. She came here looking for him, and we saw them together, and now we think she's in danger."

"Danger from Creed? I told you, he's not dangerous, and he wouldn't be with her. He just wouldn't."

There was something there, Cathy thought. An attachment . . . jealousy. "Brittany, has he ever mentioned having a baby?"

"With me? We're not like that. We're not dating."

"No, with someone else. Has he told you that someone else just gave birth to his child?"

Now Brittany's face visibly reddened, and her hand stilled. "As a matter of fact, he has."

Juliet touched Cathy's hand, stopping her from going further.

"I know Holly's the one. She practically admitted it to me. Who knows? Maybe he contacted her. If he did after all the secrecy . . ." She threw her rag down and bit her bottom lip. "I have nothing else to say about Creed Kershaw." Shaking her head, she disappeared into the kitchen.

Realizing that they wouldn't get more, Cathy and Juliet headed out. "Why would you broadcast that about the baby?" Juliet whispered. "That's not our secret to share."

"I wanted to see her reaction. She and Creed may not have a relationship, but trust me, that's not because she doesn't want one. She definitely showed signs of jealousy. I thought she might get mad enough to stop protecting him."

They reached the car and Juliet put Robbie in his seat. "Still . . . do you think she told Holly anything about where he is?"

"Not a chance."

"So what would Holly have done?"

"Same thing we would have done—followed her after she got off work. Maybe for a couple of nights."

"And you think Brittany led her to Creed?"

"Maybe."

"But Holly's not stupid. She wouldn't have just knocked on his door, would she? And he sure wouldn't have answered. If what she told Max is true—that she wanted to find him to turn him in to the police—then that's what she would have done."

"They wound up together somehow. We know that."

"Motor home," Juliet said. "Her cab was found right outside that RV park. How many RV parks are there in this area?" Juliet used her phone to do a Google search.

"Nobody at that RV park had seen her," Cathy said.

"Maybe they've seen Creed," Juliet said. "Let's go back and show the park manager his picture and find out who checked out last night or this morning. Maybe that'll give us a tag number or a description of the motor home."

"They could be anywhere by now. They could have left town."

"While you drive," Juliet said, "I'll get a list of RV parks within a three-hundred-mile radius."

"Hang on, Holly," Cathy whispered, pulling back into traffic. "We're coming."

CHAPTER 29

Creed kept his word. Holly listened as he called Information to get the number for the Southport Police Department. Then he called the PD—on speakerphone so Holly could hear—and asked for the homicide unit. The town was too small to have one, so he was transferred to the criminal unit. As he waited on hold, he paced in front of the windows, peering out, nervous and watchful.

Uneasy, Holly sat with her arm through the car seat handle, ready to run out with Lily if necessary.

Finally someone picked up. "Yeah, hi," Creed said. "My name is Creed Kershaw. I understand you want me to come in for questioning about Emilio Juarez's murder."

Holly strained to hear the other voice, but suddenly Creed jerked back from the window. "Wait a minute," he said. "Hold on." He pointed. "It's them," he told Holly.

She stood and looked through the window. Two men stood at the door of the camper three spaces down, talking to someone inside. Across the driveway, another man was approaching the door of an RV.

"Cops?" she asked.

Creed shook his head. "No, I recognize one of them. They're Miller's men."

She swung around to face him. "Tell them!"

"Tell us what?" the detective asked on the phone. "What's going on?"

Creed looked panicked. "There's no way they'll get here in time," he told Holly. "We've got to get out of here." He put the phone back to his mouth. "I'll call back later. I'm really coming in . . . it's just . . . Leonard Miller's men are here. They're after me."

He clicked off the phone and headed to the driver's seat.

"I'm getting out," Holly said.

"No, they'll see you. They're dangerous."

"They don't know me!"

"Miller does, if he's with them."

He was right. She peered out again.

He started the engine. "You can't drive!" she said. "They'll see you." If they did, she and Lily might be caught in the crossfire.

"Then you drive," he said. "Hurry—pull out as fast as you can."

"What if they stop us?"

"Holly, this is life or death," he said. "These men have guns."

She slipped into the driver's seat and started the engine, keeping her eyes on the men. They had finished at the camper and were now approaching the RV in the next space. She shoved on the sunglasses on the dashboard, pulled straight out from their space, and turned toward the exit.

"Are they looking at you?" Creed asked, strapping Lily's

seat onto the bench seat. The urgency in his voice woke Lily, and she began to cry.

"Yes, they see me." She forced a smile and waved as she drove past. She glanced in the side mirror. They weren't looking at her.

"There's probably somebody waiting at the exit," he said. "I'm hiding. If they question you, don't tell them I'm in here— or we're all dead."

Lily kept screaming, and Holly felt sick. "Hang on, sweetie. I'll get you out as soon as I can."

As she approached the exit gate, she looked in the rearview mirror. Creed had vanished. He was probably hiding in the bathroom.

A man stepped in front of her at the gate, just as Creed had warned. She thought of bolting on through, but the last thing she wanted was to call attention to herself and make them chase her. She stopped and rolled her window down, trying to look unworried.

"Hi," she said to the man who looked like a linebacker.

He came to her window. "Ma'am, I'm from the Pensacola Police Department." He was wearing a T-shirt and jeans, and didn't offer credentials or show a badge.

"What can I do for you, Officer?"

Lily screamed louder.

"We're looking for a man who may be armed and dangerous. Have you seen this guy?" He held up a picture of Creed.

She shook her head. "No, why? Has he been here? How dangerous? What did he do?"

"I can't really say, but you're sure you haven't seen him?"

"No," she said. "But now you're freaking me out. We slept here last night. Was he here?"

Lily screamed harder, and Holly looked back. "Hang on, sweetie." She turned back. "I need to go buy diapers. It's kind of an emergency."

He leaned closer and looked through her window, his eyes roving over as much of the camper as he could see. Another man appeared at the opposite window. She powered that window down to appear accommodating. He looked toward the back, his eyes drawn to the screaming baby.

"If I see him I'll call the police," she said.

He nodded. "Right. Do that."

"You'll catch him, right? Maybe I should change RV parks."

"We're doing what we can."

The man stepped back, and Holly gave him another wave and pulled out of the park. As they disappeared from her rearview, Holly realized she was sweating.

She picked up speed, glancing back. "It's safe. You can come out."

Creed came out of the small bathroom. "Good job," he said. "You were totally convincing." He dug through Lily's diaper bag, found her pacifier, and put it in her mouth. "It's okay, Lily. Hold on. You're okay."

Lily stopped yelling and suckled.

Holly glanced back in the mirror. He was stroking Lily's hair, whispering to her.

She swallowed the knot in her throat. "So now I'm driving straight to the Southport Police Department so you can turn yourself in."

"Just get out of here and make sure they're not following."

She looked behind her in the traffic. She couldn't say for sure if any of the cars behind her belonged to Miller's men. "Did you know the man who talked to me?" she asked.

"I recognized his voice. He's one of Miller's guys, no question. I'm telling you, they want me dead."

"But if I could find you . . ."

"Exactly," he said. "I had only been in that park for a few hours when Brittany led you to me. I shouldn't have told her where I was, but she was a good friend, and she was bringing me food. Until then I was just driving around, sleeping in parking lots." He kept his voice low so he wouldn't disturb Lily. "I need to talk to a lawyer. I think that would be a better approach than just showing up at the police department and spilling my guts. You may be right. Maybe I could get immunity if I tell them everything I know. Your sister—"

Holly shook her head. "Cathy's not practicing anymore."

"But she could represent me, right?"

"I'm not sure. She writes a blog and does part-time PI work."

"But she would know how to advise me. Maybe she could meet us somewhere and we could talk, and then I could turn myself in, with her there."

Holly could only imagine how that conversation with Cathy would go. "She's not going to have a lot of sympathy for you once she realizes you kidnapped us."

"Come on," he said. "You could vouch for me."

No, she couldn't. How could she make either of her sisters trust him when she wasn't sure she could trust him herself? But if she at least contacted them and updated them, she'd feel safer. "All right," she said. "Give me my phone."

He got her phone out of her bag and handed it to her. The battery was only at five percent. If the call went through, it would drop before she could get anything out. "Battery's almost out," she said. "Let me use yours."

He handed her his phone. "You want me to talk to her?"

"No, let me do this. I'm sure she'll meet us, because she and Juliet are probably worried about my latest lapse in judgment." Before she punched in Cathy's number, she met his eyes in the rearview mirror again. "Am I acting as an accessory if I don't drive you directly to the police station?"

"Holly, I'm not charged with anything yet as far as we know, right? If you help me, you're not breaking the law."

"But I know they're looking for you."

"So you're driving me to see my lawyer."

"She's not your lawyer. She doesn't know you, and she's very stubborn."

"You can convince her."

Holly thought about that as she drove. She glanced back again, saw him still stroking Lily's head. He took the pacifier out of her mouth and she didn't cry. She had probably fallen back to sleep.

Holly could kick herself. What was wrong with her? She shouldn't trust Creed just because he was good with her baby. He could be lying about everything. Those could have even been police back there, and she'd lied to them. How did she know anything he told her was the truth?

But her gut told her it was. She could drive him straight to the police department, walk away, and never look back. But what would happen to him?

Besides, she wanted to find Miller. If she called them to meet her somewhere, Cathy would bring Max. She wouldn't take the chance of meeting Creed alone. Maybe that was best. Max wanted to find Miller as much as they all did.

She waited until she got to a red light, then quickly punched in Cathy's number.

CHAPTER 30

Cathy didn't recognize the number, but she answered eagerly.

Holly said, "It's me."

Cathy's heart lunged. "Holly? Where are you? Are you all right?"

"Yes, I'm fine. I'm still . . . with him."

Cathy put her phone on speakerphone and looked at Juliet, who had her hand over her chest. "We know you're with Creed Kershaw. Can you tell us where you are?"

"We'll come to you," Holly said. "We want to meet you somewhere."

"We? Do you still have Lily with you? Is she in danger?"

"Yes, she's with me, and no, she's not in danger," Holly said quickly. "Really, it's all right. He's not going to hurt us. I'll explain everything when we meet, but it's really important. It's about Leonard Miller."

"Miller?" Cathy spouted back. "What about him?"

"Just . . . wait until we're there. Let's meet in the Home Depot parking lot."

Cathy shook her head. "We're not going to get into the motor home. Someplace where we can be out in the open."

Holly hesitated, as if surprised that they knew she was in a motor home. "Okay, he said we can meet at the Dairy Queen on Alf Coleman Road. It's usually pretty empty this time of day. We can talk there."

"Holly, listen to me," Cathy said. "Are we on speakerphone?"

"No."

"If this is a trap, just use the word *discuss* instead of *talk*."

"It's not a trap," Holly said in a level voice. "I think it's legit. We just want to *talk* to you, because it involves Miller. Then Creed's going to turn himself in to the police. We'll meet you there in an hour."

Holly hung up, and Cathy stared at the phone. "What do you think?"

"I think he could have heard everything you said," Juliet said. "He could have been forcing her at gunpoint to say whatever he wanted. We can't trust any of it."

"So you don't want to go?"

"Of course we'll go," Juliet said. "But first we call Max and have him go with us. He can sit at another table. Creed won't know him, and Holly won't act like she knows Max if she's in danger."

"Okay, I'll call him. What about Robbie? Do we take him with us?"

"No," Juliet said. "I'll take him to Jay's. I can't take him into something that could be that dangerous." She stared out the windshield for a moment. "Wish I could take Lily to him too. There's no way they're not in danger."

CHAPTER 31

When Holly and Creed arrived in the motor home from Pensacola, Cathy and Juliet were already there, and just as Holly had expected, Max's car sat in the parking lot.

Cathy and Juliet met them outside, and Juliet hugged her fiercely, then took Lily from her and held her as if she had thought she'd never see her again. They filed inside, ordered drinks, and sat down in a corner booth—tension thick between them.

Holly took her baby back and Creed reached out for her. Holly hesitated to hand her over. "Please," he said softly. "Who knows when I'll get to hold her again after this?"

Reluctantly, Holly put Lily into his arms. Her sisters watched Creed with suspicion.

Holly glanced around at the other patrons—a couple of teenagers at a table near the front, and a man at another table, reading a newspaper. She glanced away from him, then looked back. Max.

She turned to Creed. "That guy over there is Max Hogan, a cop. I told you they'd bring him."

Cathy and Juliet looked surprised, and Holly realized they thought she was being held against her will.

Creed sighed and leaned on the table. "Look, I plan to turn myself in after this conversation, and I might as well just let him take me in, but first I wanted you to know what I know about Leonard Miller. I think I can lead you to him . . . or at least close. But I need your help."

Holly had never seen Cathy's eyes so intense, but Juliet's eyes remained locked on Lily, as if Creed might smother her at any moment.

"Let me start," Holly said in a low voice. "Creed is Lily's father. We'll talk about all that later." She paused and watched her sisters glance at each other. They had clearly already figured that out.

Juliet gave Creed a cold look. "When he came with you this morning, he had a gun, didn't he?"

Holly looked at Creed. "It wasn't loaded."

"Then why did you stay with him? Why didn't you just turn him in then?"

"I didn't know it wasn't loaded then," she said. "But he was desperate. He needs help."

"So let me get this straight," Juliet said. "You're hanging out with him because you choose to? You're not being forced? You're with a guy who's wanted for murder, and you and your baby are just sitting here with him like nothing's wrong?"

"Holly told me she'd checked with the police before she found me, that I'm not wanted for murder yet," Creed said, keeping his voice low. "They just want to question me. I've called them and told them I'm coming in. Do you want to hear about Miller or not?"

"I do," Cathy said.

"Then let him get his story out," Holly said, "and we'll be done."

Juliet regarded Creed, who was holding the baby up to his neck, stroking her back. Lily's little head was turned up to him, trusting, content.

"Go ahead," Cathy said.

"Okay," Creed said, carefully supporting Lily's head as he brought her down and put her in Holly's arms. He folded his arms on the table. "I got involved with him because I lost my job. I was depressed and I started using. Then I figured I could make a little money to pay my rent, since I didn't want to move back home." He rubbed his face then went on. "I started selling coke to my friends, only I made mistakes. I wasn't very street savvy."

"What kind of mistakes?"

He told them the story he had told Holly, and she listened carefully for any inconsistency. There wasn't any.

"Whose motor home is this?" Cathy asked.

"My friend Brittany's. It belongs to her family. She let me borrow it and brought me some clothes so I wouldn't have to go home. At first I was just hiding from Miller and his people, but then she told me the police were questioning my friends about me. I realized then what they'd done. They left my stuff at the scene to convince the police I did it."

Cathy was still skeptical. "But that doesn't make sense. They must know that if the police found you first, you could implicate them."

"Believe me—*they* expected to find me first. And they would make sure I couldn't tell anybody anything."

"Miller's gang was going door-to-door at the RV park," Holly said. "We just barely got out."

Creed went on. "I don't know exactly where Miller is, but I know where two of his guys live. I don't know the addresses— I'll have to lead you to their houses. If you follow them, watch them, you should be able to track down Miller. But in return, Cathy, I need your help to get immunity and protection."

Cathy looked hard at him, her eyes dull. "Why on earth would I represent you?"

"I've made a lot of mistakes, but I didn't kill anybody. I need someone to go with me when I turn myself in. I know I'm in trouble. I just don't want to go down for something I didn't do."

"You abducted my sister!"

"I'm not pressing charges," Holly said. "I believe his story."

Cathy turned astonished eyes to her. "Well, you're not always the best judge of character, are you?"

"Cathy," Holly said, keeping her voice quiet, "he's trying to help us. He knows how much it means to us to find Miller, but if he gets arrested and locked up, then he can't lead us to these people. He can't help us in any way. He's going to have to have an attorney. Why can't it be you?"

"Because I don't trust him," she bit out, looking at Creed. "I don't know him. He's some guy who abducted you and your baby at gunpoint and held you overnight. He could get thirty years for that alone, and I don't want to fight to keep him from paying for it!"

Holly leaned forward. "I know this is hard for you, but this is our chance to get Miller. Another chance to break up this drug ring once and for all. Haven't we suffered enough? Haven't we lost enough to that man?"

Juliet nodded. "Yes, we sure have."

"Well, he can pay without my having to represent this guy," Cathy said.

Creed tried again. "The fact is, I may not live through the rest of the week with Miller's goons after me. There's no guarantee that if the police let me go I'm going to survive." His voice broke. "I just need some help here. I got in over my head. I was stupid, and now I can't change any of it. I can't fix it."

Cathy considered him for a long moment, then looked from Holly to Juliet. Even Juliet seemed to be buying his story. Cathy cleared her throat, rubbed her face. Finally, she slammed her hand on the table and stood up. "I have to talk to Michael."

"It's not visiting day," Holly said.

"I'm his attorney. I'll get a private meeting with him. I need to get his advice and see what he thinks."

She waved toward Max, asked him to come over. He set his newspaper down and ambled over. Cathy slipped out of the booth. "Max, he wants to turn himself in. I need to talk to Michael before deciding if I want to represent him. If not, I'll find him someone else."

Max's frown cut deep. "What does he know about Miller?"

"We'll talk later," Cathy said. "Creed, until I decide, just stay quiet. Max, can he turn himself in to you? Can you keep him in custody until I talk to Michael?"

Max looked at Creed. "Yeah, I guess that would work. I could let Southport know I've got him."

Cathy lifted her eyebrows. "Will you agree to that, Creed?"

"I'm not arrested, right? There's still not a warrant, is there?"

Max shook his head. "No, not yet."

"Okay. Cathy, please tell Michael that I know he's been through a lot, and I can help you put this guy away if I live through this."

Cathy gave them all one last look and headed out.

CHAPTER 32

Cathy found a parking space a long way from the jail door, but it was worth the hike. Clutching her briefcase so she'd look more official, she walked as fast as she could to the jail doors.

She hated this place. The office where lawyers and bail bondsmen had to check in—where those charged with crimes were processed and booked—had the smell of Clorox, Lysol, and lice shampoo.

"Cathy Cramer," she told the inmate trustee sitting at the desk, wearing the same orange jumpsuit that the other inmates wore. "I'm here to see my client, Michael Hogan."

The man smirked, as if he doubted this was an official attorney/client meeting, but he put in the call for Michael.

She went through the usual metal detector and left her purse with the detective on duty, exposed the contents of her briefcase—papers that looked official—then went to the interview room. She waited, anxious to see Michael and be close to him for the first time in days.

The room was uncomfortably cold, as always, air conditioning used as a tool to control the inmates. As she waited, she paced, thinking about what she was going to do next. Would she go straight to the police department, fetch Creed, and take him to Southport to turn himself in? Should she support him at all?

Finally, after fifteen minutes, the door opened and a guard brought Michael in. His eyes were soft and smiling as he looked at her.

Knowing they were being watched via video, Cathy held herself in control. They waited until the guard had stepped outside, then they quickly hugged. She couldn't help letting her face linger against his for a moment too long.

"Didn't expect to see you tonight," he said. "Is something wrong? I've been worried since we talked. Did you find Holly?"

"Yes, she's okay." She pulled back, tried to rally her professionalism, but his face was tanned from working outside and there was a slight sunburn on his cheekbones. His charcoal gaze drew her deep. She didn't want to talk about Creed, but she forced herself to focus. "Michael, this guy, Creed, was holding her against her will. He even forced her to put Lily in danger, but now she's all on board with him. She wants me to represent him."

Michael shook his head. "Are you considering that?"

"Michael, he says he can lead us to Miller."

Michael was silent for a minute. "Tell me."

She launched into a quick recap of the meeting they had just had.

Michael was quiet as he thought it over. Finally, he said, "Okay, I think he could be telling the truth."

Cathy frowned. "But why?"

"Because I've talked to a couple of guys in here who said some things. From what I gather, Miller did take over when Bob was killed, and he's back in town. I saw him myself, and I met another guy who's seen him lately. If this guy Creed can lead us to him, then I think you need to represent him so you'll continue to have access. He needs someone safe to represent him. Somebody they can't pay off."

"He'll be safe in jail, right? If they arrest him?"

Michael shook his head. "No, I don't think so. You need to do your best to keep him out of jail. Put him in a safe house, somewhere Miller's people can't get to him." His breathing grew more rapid. "Cathy, if we could put Miller away for the rest of his life and make sure he never gets out, it would make all of this worth it."

She shook her head. "No, Michael. Nothing can make all this worth it."

His eyes misted as he looked at her. Taking her hands, he pulled her close and kissed her forehead.

"It's just a few months, babe. It won't be that bad."

But it *was* that bad; he was just trying to make her feel better. Sleeping in a cage at night, working in a Dr. Seuss suit on the side of the road, being among people who had actually committed crimes. She knew it was no picnic.

"I'm praying for you," he said.

She smiled. "You're praying for me? I'm not the one who needs prayer."

"Yes, you are," he whispered.

That was so like him.

Back in her car, she called to let Max know she would take Creed's case.

She had work to do while she waited for her life to begin again.

CHAPTER 33

Instead of a holding cell, Creed sat in an interview room while he waited for Cathy's decision. She had promised to send someone else if she wouldn't take him herself. Creed hoped she wouldn't renege on that.

He got up and paced in the small room, glancing occasionally at the camera in a corner near the ceiling. What would Michael tell Cathy to do? Would he tell her not to get tangled up in this mess? Would he fear the danger it could bring to her? Would he think Creed was nothing but a two-bit criminal with only bad news to offer her?

Creed sat down, lowered his face into his hands. His poor parents. They were probably sick with worry. He'd seen them a couple of days ago when he'd driven past the T-ball field. His mother looked as if she'd lost weight. She and his father had sat apart from the crowd in the bleachers, supporting their grandson but holding themselves aloof from friends. They were both normally gregarious and friendly. It killed him to see them cutting themselves off from others.

They shouldn't have to deal with all this negative publicity. They had raised him right. He knew better.

But when he'd turned to drugs, he hadn't thought clearly, and his stupidity had led him right into the most ludicrous decision of his life—selling drugs. Who ever would have thought he could do such a thing? Why had he thought he could dip his toe into the drug world and not fall in and drown?

He stood again and leaned back against the wall. He could very well end up going to prison. Just when he'd learned of his daughter and had the privilege of holding her . . . he might never see her again. The thing was, he really liked children. He would have been an awesome dad.

Would his daughter have to overcome the fact that her father was in prison?

The door opened, and he looked up. Max came in and Creed slid back into his chair. "Heard from Cathy?"

"Not yet," Max said. "But I did let Southport know I have you. I told them I needed to question you about a drug trafficking investigation, that I would transport you to them myself when I was done."

"Did they agree to that?"

"Nope. They sure didn't. They said they'd give us a couple of hours to interview you, and then they'll head over and question you here."

Creed set his elbows on the table and dropped his forehead against his fist. "I'm toast."

"Maybe. Maybe not."

"I can't talk to anybody without a lawyer. I do know enough to know that."

Max didn't press. "All right, but when you get lawyered up, your greatest protection will be telling us everything you can remember. A lawyer who makes you shut up and gets you out could get you killed."

Max started to leave again, but Creed said, "Detective Hogan?"

Max looked back.

"How bad do you think this is?"

"Pretty bad."

"So . . . am I going to wind up going to prison?"

"I can't say. It's not my homicide case."

As Max left, Creed hoped there would *be* an attorney. What if no one came? What if he was railroaded right onto Death Row?

He went to the door and peered out through the small vertical window of glass. Miller's goons were still looking for him. If they realized he was here, they would panic. They'd figure out a way to shut him up. What if an inmate or dirty cop saw him and told Miller? Was he safe even here?

He wiped sweat from his forehead and temples even though the air conditioner blew cold air through the vents overhead. He ran his fingers through his hair.

God, if you could work this out . . . if you could just help me here.

He didn't ask God to make Cathy his attorney. What if she wasn't the best one? It was just that she was Holly's sister, and that she had suffered the brutality of Miller and his cohorts. And she seemed to have integrity. She could be trusted, he was almost sure of that.

But what business did Creed have praying? God was surely sick of him. He had probably turned his back on him the moment Creed first got high. Then when he'd let greed take over and had decided to sell, God must have been even more revolted.

And here he was, praying, when he'd decided just weeks ago that he didn't even believe there was a God. He'd locked his childhood faith in a box at the back of his mind and declared God to be nonexistent so that he could justify doing what he wanted.

It had all been so nice and convenient—until he needed that God he'd so easily dismissed.

God will give you what you choose.

His father had said that to him years ago, when Creed's downward spiral had started in high school. After an all-nighter, Creed had come home drunk, and his father had waited until he woke up that afternoon, head gonging with pain, to say those words to him.

"You know, son, God will give you what you choose. And if you think about that real hard, it'll scare you to death. I don't think you're ready to suffer the consequences of those choices."

Why hadn't he listened?

Tears came to his eyes, and he hated himself for it. He stood and went to the other side of the table, put his back to the camera, then sat again. He dropped his head onto his squared arms and let it flow.

God, I know I chose, but is there any room for me to change my mind? I know you're there . . . if you could just forgive me.

He checked his watch. He'd already been here an hour. How much longer would Cathy make him wait?

CHAPTER 34

Cathy had taken only two clients in the last two years—her brother, Jay, when he was falsely accused of murder, and Michael when he was charged with violating probation. She'd been passionately involved in both those cases, but she didn't feel that way about this one. The last thing she wanted was to represent a guy who might be guilty of murder, someone whose case she might have ripped to shreds in her blog.

But as Michael had said, she had no choice if she wanted to find Leonard Miller.

Grudgingly, she showed up at the police station and declared herself Creed's attorney. She found him in the interview room.

"Okay, Creed," she said as she stepped into the room, "here's the deal. I'm going to represent you, and in exchange, you're going to tell us everything you know about Miller."

He let out a ragged breath. "Thank you!"

She bent over the table, fixing her eyes on him. "This may come as a surprise to you, but I don't like defending criminal cases. I've been disillusioned with the court system since my fiancé's killer walked free. I write for a living now, trying to influence justice from the outside. I'm only doing this because I want desperately to find Leonard Miller, and you're my best tool to do that right now. So I suggest that you not lie to me about *anything*. I don't have the patience for it. Got it?"

He nodded. "Scout's honor."

"Not good enough," she said. "Try again."

He reached out his hand to shake. "You have my word. And you'll see that I'll stand by it."

"You're a drug dealer. Sue me if I don't put a lot of stock in your word."

He wilted. "I *used* to deal drugs. I'd rather be starving on the street than be involved in that kind of life again."

"You realize that you deserve to go to jail for that, right?"

"For that, yes, but not for murder."

Cathy gazed into Creed's round, intense eyes, searching for dishonesty. He looked sincere. But sociopaths often did pull off the look of sincerity.

Still, she saw Lily in those eyes, and her heart softened a little.

She pulled out her chair and sat down. "So here's what we're going to do. We're going to offer information about Miller and his group in exchange for immunity. They won't give immunity for the murder—we'll have to prove that you're not the killer. But I think they'll give immunity for your involvement in Miller's drug trafficking. Once we get that, you need to let them pick your brain about minute details in the operation that you won't even think matter. I'm talking hours of questioning. No attitude, no impatience. You're their tool, and you let them jog your memory on everything you know."

He nodded. "Yes, ma'am. I'll do whatever I need to do. But Miller's men . . . they're going to keep trying to take me out. They'll be more desperate than ever."

"We'll find you a place to hide. I don't want to rely on the feds or the local police to do that. That's backfired on us before." She didn't mention that the safe house where the police had "hidden" her sister was the place from which her sister's children had been abducted a few months ago. Miller and his men had no trouble finding them. "But you're right. They'll be gunning for you more than ever. Even that could give us an opportunity to catch them. We'll need your absolute cooperation, and it's bound to get scary. But you've proven already that you're resourceful." She cleared her throat. "Can't say I like how resourceful you are, taking my sister and all, but still. You've managed to avoid the thugs so far, and that's pretty remarkable."

He looked less like a thug now than when she'd first seen him. Or was she just getting soft?

"Look, I know this isn't easy for you," he said. "But these guys are brutal. Miller is the worst of all. Making sure he gets caught along with all his guys is life or death for me. You have to believe that."

She stared at him a moment longer. "I think I do."

"So when do we start?"

She slid her chair back and stood up. "I have a lot of nego-tiating to do with the police and the prosecutors, both here and in Southport, so you may be here for a while. Maybe even overnight."

"Overnight? If you could get them to keep me in isolation . . .

just so Miller doesn't reach me from the inside . . . then I can deal with that."

"That will be part of our deal. Just sit tight. Don't talk to anybody about anything unless I'm with you. Got that?"

"Okay. But now that you're representing me, you'll have to watch your back. This guy is really dangerous."

"You don't have to tell me that," she said. "Miller has been on my mind every single day for over two years. He's going to get what's coming to him."

She shook his hand. "Now, what did I say about talking to anyone without me?"

"Don't do it."

"If they come to transport you, and you say, 'Look, guys, you don't have to treat me like a killer, because I didn't do it,' that could legally give them the authority to question you some more. If you open the conversation, they can use whatever you say. You don't discuss the case or anything about the case, not to them, not on the phone to your parents, not to the guards. Got that?"

"Yes. Cathy, thank you. You have no idea what this means to me."

"Oh, I have some idea."

Her hands were shaking as she left the room.

CHAPTER 35

Monday morning, Michael rode the elevator down with the rest of the work crew, some of the louder men talking trash about one of the female guards. The elevator door opened, and they lined up to sign out at the front desk before going to the van.

As he waited his turn with the clipboard, Michael looked back at the holding cells, wondering if Creed was in one of them. He walked over and glanced into their barred windows. There was someone there. Michael saw a man sitting back against the wall, his feet up on the bench. That could be him.

Michael's least favorite guard—the one he'd secretly dubbed Adolph—went to the cell door with a tray in his hands, holding a sandwich, an apple, and a cup of water. "You men hurry up. Van's waiting."

Michael signed the form, then glanced back as the guard unlocked the holding cell door. "Kershaw, here's your breakfast."

So that *was* him. Michael stepped back and watched as the

guy got up and hurried to grab the tray. Michael didn't recognize him. The cell door closed again.

Michael followed the crew to the sliding steel doors that led to the van and silently prayed that Kershaw would lead them to Leonard Miller.

In the holding cell, Creed devoured his sandwich—the first food he'd been given since coming in here. He finished off the cup of water in three gulps and picked up the apple, turned it over. It was bruised in places. He wasn't surprised. The inmates probably didn't get premium grade-A food. He bit into it. It was sour, so he chewed and swallowed quickly, then turned the apple over and took a bite from the other side. It left a horrible aftertaste in his mouth.

He wondered if the taste came from something they'd used to wash the apple. Whatever it was didn't taste right. He took one more bite, chewed it quickly, wincing, then decided it wasn't worth it. He spat the mouthful into his napkin.

He set the tray beside the door and went back to the bench. How much longer would this take? It was freezing in this place, and the benches were just metal bolted to the floor—no cushions. There was nothing to do. No television, no radio . . . just him and his self-loathing thoughts.

He didn't even know the time. He lay on his back, staring up at the ceiling tiles. What was Holly doing now? He pictured her sitting at home in a rocking chair, feeding Lily, feeling that sense of contentment he'd felt when he'd so briefly held his child. Would he ever see Lily again? Would Holly even give him the time of day now that he wasn't forcing her to?

How had he messed his life up so much?

He should get Cathy to call his parents. There would be comfort in letting them know that he was alive and safe. But shame stopped him. He had disgraced his family and now he was in jail.

The thought of their reaction nauseated him. His parents deserved better than this.

He sat up. The room seemed to be spinning slowly. He reached out to get his bearings, dropped his feet to the floor, and stood. The room tilted to the side . . .

He balanced himself against the wall. Sweat beaded on his forehead, over his lip. His breathing seemed blocked. He should call the teacher . . . no, it wasn't a teacher. He wasn't in school. He should call the . . . what did they call the man out there? The one in the costume . . . He shook his head. No, not a costume . . . uniform . . . The man who watched over him . . . the guard.

What was happening?

He turned to look at the food tray by the door. What had he eaten? He took a step toward it, called out for help. The room flipped. His face hit concrete. He forced himself to his knees, tried to sit up, tried to call out. The cell wouldn't stop spinning and the lights grew dimmer . . .

CHAPTER 36

The phone started ringing as Holly rinsed the shampoo from Lily's little head. She hadn't gotten adept yet at giving her baby a bath, and she tried to ignore the ringing. She would have to call them back.

She poured another cup of warm water over Lily's head. Lily started to kick and wiggle. "It's okay, sweetie. Mommy's not gonna let you drown." She heard her answering machine pick up, then Cathy's loud voice.

"Holly, pick up! It's an emergency."

An emergency? What now? She pulled Lily out of the bathtub, threw the hooded towel around her. Lily didn't like being wet and cold, and she wailed. Wrapping her in the towel, Holly made her way to the phone and snapped it up. "Hello?"

"Oh, good. You're there," Cathy said. "I knew you'd want to know. Creed was just taken to the hospital."

"The hospital? Why?"

"He collapsed at the jail. Nobody knows what's wrong with him, but he was really sick. I'm at the hospital now. I heard the paramedics saying that his heart rate was down to like 30, and his blood pressure is 70 over 30."

"*What?*" Holly said. "He could die! Where is he?"

"They brought him to Bay Medical. They're taking him for tests."

"I'm coming. I'll see you in a few minutes." Holly hung up. What could have caused this? He hadn't been sick earlier. Maybe that cut had gotten infected.

She dried the baby and quickly dressed her, though she screamed and wriggled. "We've got to go somewhere, honey," she said. "I hate to take you back out. I know you've had a rough couple of days, but something's wrong with your daddy."

She caught herself the moment she said those words, and her heart sank. Was she really going to think of him that way?

Why not? That's what he was.

She snapped Lily into her car seat, grabbed her diaper bag and her purse, and rushed out to her taxi. Lily cried all the way to the hospital.

Holly tried to think over her daughter's misery. Miller's goons were after Creed. They wanted to see him dead. Had they managed to get to him in the jail? No, Cathy would have told her if he'd been stabbed or beaten. And Max had promised to keep him isolated.

Holly's cell phone chimed. Cathy. She answered quickly.

"I just learned that he's vomiting. He had just eaten before he got sick. I think he was poisoned."

Holly just made it through a yellow light. "Miller has people in that jail."

"I just talked to Max. He's working on finding out who

fixed Creed's tray and who delivered the food," Cathy said. "Are you on your way?"

"Yes."

"I'm calling his family. They need to know about this."

"Cathy?" Holly's voice cracked. "Is he going to die?"

"I don't know how bad it is."

Holly felt sick herself as she navigated her way to the hospital. *God, I don't want him to die.*

When she got to the ER, they let her go back, but the doctors were in the room, so she waited with Cathy in the hallway. While they waited, Max and his partner, Al Forbes, showed up to wait for the results of the blood work.

It seemed an eternity before someone finally came with the initial lab report.

Cyanide poisoning.

Panic choked Holly. "How did they get to him?" she demanded of Max. "How did they poison him if he was isolated?"

Max set his jaw. "Miller has a long reach."

"But who had access to his food?"

"Could have been anybody who had kitchen duty."

"Inmates?"

"Yes. They handle all the food."

Holly wanted to scream. "Did it ever occur to you that Miller could have gotten messages to his compadres inside the jail? That they shouldn't be handling the food of the guy they want dead?"

"I couldn't let him sleep in the interview room!" Max said. "I had to put him somewhere." He jammed his fists into his pockets and paced a few steps up the hall, then back, then up the hall again. "We're going to put a guard out here to make sure no one else gets to him. We'll only let him eat what we bring to him."

Tears stung Holly's eyes. Cathy took a few steps across the hall, set her hands on her hips, and turned back. Holly could almost see the gears turning in her sister's brain. "Is anybody else sick at the jail?" Cathy asked.

"No. Nobody's reported anything."

"Did you get the food? Did you test it?"

"The tray had already been cleared and dumped into the same garbage where the other trays had been dumped."

Holly's reaction surprised even her. "Do people die of cyanide poisoning?"

"Maybe not," Max said. "They found him pretty early. He's in the right place. They might be able to save him."

Holly held her baby under her chin and kissed her sleeping head. *Please, God . . . help them get that out of his system . . .*

"Whoever helped with this is on Miller's team," Cathy said, "and whatever you can find out about him might lead us closer to Miller."

"Right," Max said. "We're on it, Cathy."

CHAPTER 37

Holly stood in the ER waiting room with her feather-haired baby, her nursing cover over her neck so the blanket would cover Lily's head, hopefully blocking germs as she slept. This was the last place a five-week-old baby should be. Holly said a silent prayer that her immunity would protect Lily, but what about those monstrous super-bugs that turn healthy organs to mush or fill up a grown man's lungs with fluid? Though the place smelled like Clorox, it was filled with disease, virus, and bacteria.

She tried not to touch anything, and from time to time she went to the hand sanitizer on the wall and pulled some anti-bacterial agent onto her hands. It dried them out and made them feel as rough as sandpaper, but if that's what it took to keep Lily healthy . . .

She didn't know if Creed was alive or dead, or if the antidote to the poison was readily available in this hospital, or if his organs were harmed or his brain was damaged . . . and not knowing gave her a sick, burning feeling in her gut.

She looked down through the round hole of her nursing cover. Lily slept in shadow, her little eyes moving under her eyelids as dreams made synapses fire in her brain. She grunted in her sleep, smiled, stuck her pointed little tongue between her lips, sighed . . . Holly wanted to kiss her, but she couldn't do it without collapsing the cloth protecting her and waking her from that fragile sleep.

The glass doors slid open with a hum, and she heard a commotion at the desk. She walked to the corner and looked around the wall. She recognized the man and woman who'd come in—Creed's parents. His mother looked a mess, eyes red and swollen, an expression of weary terror on her face. His father held it together and took charge at the desk, asking where his son was, if they could go back to see him.

The glass doors slid open again, and the woman Holly had seen at the T-ball park and assumed to be Creed's sister rushed in and joined them.

Holly stepped back behind the wall, trying to listen to what they were told. They would be allowed to go in because they were family. Only Cathy had been allowed to stay with him until now.

The woman behind the desk told them which room he was in. The double doors near Holly clicked and slowly opened when the receptionist disengaged the lock. Holly stayed against the wall, holding the grandchild they knew nothing about, as Creed's parents flew past her, along with his sister. None of them even noticed her.

When the doors closed, Holly wanted to cry. It didn't make sense, the emotion overwhelming her. It wasn't as if she was in love with Creed. She barely even liked him. She'd been angry with him for most of the last two days . . . yet there was an attachment there. They had things in common. Shame . . . regret . . . Lily.

She wiped the tears on her face and wondered if she should just take Lily home. There was nothing she could accomplish here if she couldn't even go in. Still, her heart stumbled with anxious possibilities, and she couldn't escape the feeling, however ludicrous, that her being here would somehow keep him alive.

"Holly, honey. What are you doing here?"

She turned and saw Juliet. "I wanted to . . . I'm worried he . . ." Holly's voice broke off at the cliff-edge of her emotions, and she didn't even try to go on. Juliet touched the back of Holly's head, pulled her close, and pressed a kiss on her forehead.

"Is he all right?" she asked.

"I don't know. I can't get any information. Cathy's back there but hasn't texted in a while. His family just went back."

"Honey, you shouldn't have Lily here. There are germs—"

"I know that," Holly said. "You think I don't realize that? I haven't touched anything except the hand sanitizer. I haven't even sat down, because the chair handles—"

"Why don't you let me take her home?"

Holly looked down at Lily. She didn't want to let her go. Life seemed so dangerous right now, and she wanted her close. "I don't know. Maybe he'll . . . need to see her or something. Maybe it'll make him fight harder." Holly burst into tears, and she hated herself for it. "We shouldn't have made him turn himself in there. Maybe if he'd gone to Southport, Miller's men wouldn't have had anyone there."

"This is not our fault, Holly."

"I know." Holly smeared the tears across her face. "I'm just scared because nothing will stop them, and now they know he's here."

"When Cathy called she said they're putting a guard outside his room. No one will get in."

Holly didn't trust the guards or the nurses or doctors . . . Anyone could pose as anything in here. An intern walked past, a name badge hanging from a lanyard around his neck. Anyone could fake a badge. Maybe they should instruct the guards not to let anyone in his room unless they recognized them.

Security policies had kept *her* from going back. If they did it right, maybe they would keep criminals out too.

She looked through the opening in her nursing cover again. Lily slept soundly now. Her little dream of puppies and kitties or gentle smiles of loving family members had eased now, and her mouth hung open. Holly should either leave here and take her home, or stay and let Juliet take her.

Holly let out a sorrowful sigh, took the nursing cover off her neck, and put it over Juliet's head. Quickly, gently, she transferred Lily to her. "Just feed her the formula you have if she wakes up. I won't stay here all night. Just until I know he's going to be all right."

Juliet made sure Lily was covered. She lowered her voice to keep from waking her. "What if he isn't?"

Holly's eyes filled again. "I don't know."

Juliet stared at her. "You went after him to make sure he stayed *out* of your lives. Now you don't know?"

Holly wiped her nose. "I know it doesn't make sense to you, but I spent time with him over the last couple of days, and he . . . he reminds me a lot of myself."

"How do you mean, honey?"

"I mean, he's made a lot of mistakes, and now the consequences are chasing him down, but he wants to change. There's still so much potential. People can change. I did, didn't I?"

Juliet's eyes filled now, and she reached with her free hand and pulled Holly into a maternal hug. "I'll take her home. She'll be fine. Just stay in touch, okay?"

"Don't touch anything on the way out. Do you have my key to get her seat out of the car?"

"No. I left it at home. She's too little for Robbie's car seat."

Holly would have to walk Juliet out and help her get the seat out of her car, but she didn't want to leave.

Just then, the double doors leading into the examining room hallway swooshed open, and she turned. Creed's sister stepped into the waiting room, and her eyes fell on Juliet. "Are you Holly?" she asked.

Juliet shook her head.

Holly spoke up. "I'm Holly."

Creed's sister came toward her. "I'm Kelsey. My brother wants to see you," she said. "His attorney—Cathy—said you were out here in the waiting room."

Gratitude pumped through Holly's heart. "He's awake, then? Conscious?"

"Yes, but he's really sick. They said some of his organs were shutting down when he was brought in. His kidneys, his liver . . ." Her voice trailed off, and she stared at Holly, myriad questions in her eyes. "Who *are* you?"

Holly met Juliet's gaze, unable to meet Kelsey's. "I'm just a friend."

"Just a friend," Kelsey repeated. "How are you involved in all this?"

Juliet adjusted Lily on her shoulder under the nursing cover and walked away, toward the chairs, swaying gently with each step.

"My sister's his attorney," Holly said. "I got her to represent him." But Holly knew that wasn't what Kelsey wanted. She wanted the rest of the truth, and Holly wasn't ready to give it.

"Were you at the ball field a couple of days ago? I saw you there."

Holly felt nailed. "Yeah. I was looking for Creed. I'd heard he was in trouble. I was just worried about him."

Kelsey's stare was skeptical. "So how long have you two known each other?"

Holly paused, looking at the floor. "About a year, give or take."

Thankfully, Kelsey didn't follow that trail. "Do you know who did this to him? Who poisoned him?"

Holly didn't dare reveal what Creed had confessed to her. He may never want his family to know what had led to this. "No. He was at the jail . . . not under arrest. He had turned himself in and they had him in protective custody." She wasn't even sure that was what it was called, but it didn't matter. "Can I go see him now?"

Kelsey seemed to shake herself out of the equation she was trying to solve. "Don't stay long. He doesn't have much energy, and he's not out of the woods."

Holly turned back to Juliet, and she signaled her to go on. Kelsey looked back at Juliet now, and her eyes lingered a moment too long, then she turned and went back through the open doors. Holly followed her up the hall to Creed's room. Kelsey opened his door and stepped aside to let Holly in. Cathy stood by his bed, Creed's parents on the other side. Creed looked as colorless as a corpse, his eyes sunken in, his lips pale.

"Here she is now," Cathy said, and motioned for Holly to come closer.

Creed reached out with the hand from which his IV line protruded. Holly took it in both of her own and looked down at him. "Creed, how do you feel?"

"Been better." She could barely hear him, so she leaned down to get closer. "They got me, didn't they?" he whispered.

She swallowed the knot in her throat. "I'm so sorry."

He turned his hand and stroked her thumb as if she were the victim. "I'm worried . . . about you and Lily."

She glanced up at his parents. Tears on their faces, they hung on every word. She turned back to Creed. "Do . . . do you think they'll come after us?"

"I don't know how much they've figured out," he said.

Holly straightened and looked at Cathy. She could see the worry in her eyes. "They can't poison all of us," Holly whispered.

"Just . . . be careful. I want you to go home and be with Lily."

Creed seemed to drift off to sleep, and Sandra, his mother, pulled his covers up, tucked them over his shoulders, felt his forehead. Then she looked up at Holly. "You're the one, aren't you?" his mother said. "The one his friend mentioned on the answering machine. The one who had his baby."

Holly felt like wild game frozen by a flashlight beam, waiting for the fatal bullet. She couldn't speak.

"Her name's Lily?" his mother asked, tears filling her eyes. "A little girl?"

The Pandora's box of Holly's life seemed pried open, secrets blowing out in the wind. As hard as she tried, she would never be able to catch them all to put them back in. She hadn't expected them to know already, but of course they did. They'd heard that answering machine message, when Rio spilled the beans. That was what had led the police to her house in the first place.

"I think . . . it would be better if we discussed this when he's awake. When he can be in on it."

"Can we . . . see the baby?" his father asked.

Dread filled her heart. Holly looked toward the door, wishing for an escape. Lily was right down the hall in the waiting room. Could she—should she—tell them no, that they couldn't see their grandchild?

Tears filled her eyes as she resigned herself to this. She nodded and went to the door. His parents told Kelsey to stay with her brother, then they followed her out into the cold, antiseptic hall to the double doors. Frank punched the green button, and the doors swooshed open.

Holly stepped through and saw Juliet, still standing and rocking, holding Lily with the ease of a woman who loved the baby she held. Holly went straight for the hand sanitizer, filled her palm with foam, then turned back to Creed's parents. "I'm worried about the germs in here. She's only five weeks old."

Both of his parents foamed their hands, then rubbed them until the alcohol dried. Holly went to Juliet, and her sister carefully surrendered Lily.

A sudden wave of fear blew like the air conditioner in the ventilation overhead. Lily was exposed now, to germs and bacteria and viruses and family. Holly turned around, letting them see her. Their eyes were appropriately awestruck as they looked her over, Sandra's hands out ready to scoop her up.

Swallowing hard, Holly lay Lily in Sandra's arms. As tears shimmered in her eyes, Sandra breathed in Lily's scent, her lips lingering on the feathery hair. She brought the baby to her shoulder, expertly supporting her head. Frank touched Lily's back. "All that hair," he said with a cracked voice.

"Like Creed," they said together.

Holly met Juliet's eyes. Juliet looked down at the floor, and Holly saw the tension on her face. She, like Holly, was clearly wondering if this was wise.

"She's beautiful," Sandra whispered. "So she really is our granddaughter?"

Again, silence. Holly wasn't ready to make that final admission, not to people who would want to entwine themselves in Lily's life. As she grappled for the right words for her evasion, she heard Cathy's voice behind her. She hadn't seen her following them out.

"Mr. and Mrs. Kershaw, there are things that Creed and Holly need to work out. Right now, we need to focus on his health and his legal issues."

Sandra's chin trembled. "It's just . . . if there's a bright side to all this . . . I'd like to know it."

Holly understood that, and she desperately wanted to accommodate the woman, but she just wasn't ready.

Cathy took charge. "We'll talk about that later. I just got a text from the DA's office. In light of what's happened, they have agreed to give Creed immunity on the drug charges, in exchange for information."

"And the murder charge?" Frank asked.

"Not the murder," Cathy said, "but he hasn't been charged with that yet. It's my hope that what he tells them will lead them to the real killer, so that may not wind up being an issue.

But I need to run out and get the documents, then bring them back and get his signature."

"Thank heaven," his father said, touching his wife's shoulder. He turned back to Cathy. "We can pay for your services. We'll do whatever we can to help him."

CHAPTER 38

When Holly arrived at the hospital the next morning, Creed had been moved to a room on the third floor. He was sitting up in bed, sipping broth, an IV still dripping fluid into his veins. Color had returned to his face, though he was still weak. He seemed glad to see her and asked about Lily.

"Juliet's keeping her for a couple of hours. She's going to interview some babysitters today. Hopefully she'll find one we both like so we can help with the Miller hunt full-time."

"My mother would probably love to babysit her," Creed said.

Holly wasn't ready for that. She looked down at the floor. "So . . . have your mom and dad talked to you about Lily?"

"Yeah, they asked me if she was mine. Of course I told them she is."

Holly sighed, but she didn't argue. It was true, after all.

"Their getting to meet her . . . it softened the blow of everything else. Mom said it was God's way of making all this bearable to them." Creed shook his head. "I can see the disappointment in their faces about the trouble I'm in. The confusion. I told them the truth, that I didn't kill that guy. They're scared to death. I can't believe I'm putting them through this, but they're still here supporting me, no matter what."

Holly nodded. "That's what families do."

He considered Holly for a long moment. "When Lily grows up, are you going to tell her about all this? That her daddy was a drug dealer? That he was accused of murder? That he ran with some people so horrible that they tried to kill him?"

He clearly didn't expect to be around to tell her himself. "I don't know what I'll tell Lily," she said, "but we have plenty of time to decide on that. Maybe what I'll tell her is that her dad's testimony led to the conviction of some major drug dealers in the area."

Creed closed his eyes. "That would be good."

"Or maybe you can tell her that yourself."

When he opened his eyes and let his gaze settle on her, she looked away. She wasn't even sure she meant that. Did she really want him to be around when Lily was old enough to understand? She honestly didn't know.

There was a quick knock on the door, and Cathy came in, dressed in her lawyer clothes, her face all business and her heels clicking across the cold floor. She looked surprised to see Holly here again, but she got straight to the point. "Okay, I finally got the paperwork for your immunity, but you can't sign until I get someone from the DA's office and a court reporter to come by. Do you think you're up to that now?"

Creed straightened. "Yeah, I don't want to wait. They might change their minds."

"Okay, I'll get them up here. You understand that if you're

charged with murder, it won't be impacted by this immunity? This is only for the drug charges."

"Right," he said. "But if we can find Miller, if we can untangle this mess, then I'll be able to prove that his people are the ones who killed Juarez, not me."

"So as soon as you check out of here, we'll go to the police station and they'll question you. They'll take you on a little tour of the city, where you'll point out everywhere anyone associated with this drug ring could be."

Holly crossed her arms. "Cathy, where is he going to stay? He can't go home."

"I've convinced them we need to set him up in a safe house."

Holly was skeptical. "We've had experience with safe houses. We can't trust that. Too many people know about those houses, and Miller clearly has contacts everywhere."

"I'm going to find one myself," Cathy said. "It'll be someplace no one knows about—not even the police." Her phone rang and she looked down. "It's Michael calling from the jail. I've got to take this."

When Cathy had stepped out into the hallway to take the call, Holly turned to Creed and studied his face. His eyes were still sunken, with deep circles under them. Though his skin had more color, his eyes were yellow. His hands shook as he sipped his broth. He set the cup down, wiped his mouth on a napkin. Holly took the empty cup from him.

"The doctor said he would probably let me go tomorrow. I want to get this over with."

"That poison was in your organs."

"They're all working fine now. Kidneys, liver . . . my numbers were good this morning."

"But you still don't look good, Creed."

"It's not like I'm going to go run a marathon. I'll take it easy until I'm a hundred percent."

"But their questioning could go on for hours . . . days. They could run you all over town."

"I think I can do it," he said.

Holly didn't like it, but she had no right to protest. "Have you told your mother?"

"No, she won't like it. Look, I appreciate your concern, but the doctor decides when I go. I don't have insurance, so I don't want to just sit in here if I don't need to. I'll be ten years paying off the bill as it is."

"Not if you're dead." Tears sprang to her eyes, surprising her.

He reached for her hand. "I'm not so sure I'm safe here. Even with the guard, there are constantly people I don't know coming in and out. I won't be completely safe until these guys are locked up. And even then . . ."

"Yeah . . . even then." Silence fell over them like a heavy, hot blanket.

"Helping the police catch Miller is my only hope."

She turned away and looked out the window, dabbed at the tears in the corners of her eyes.

"When I'm in the safe house, will you bring Lily so I can spend a little more time with her?"

Holly turned back. "I don't know."

Creed nodded quickly. "No, you're right. It's dangerous. I don't know what I was thinking. We need to keep her as far away from me as possible right now."

Holly could think of nothing to say.

CHAPTER 39

Out in the hall, Cathy's phone rang. She clicked it on and said, "Hello," then waited as the jail recording went through the long explanation that an inmate was calling her collect. The cost for these calls was astronomical, and she'd had to set up a prepaid account so she could accept calls on her cell phone. But if she had to go into debt to hear Michael's voice, she would happily do that.

When they connected, he spoke so fast she almost couldn't follow him. "Babe, listen, I heard about Creed being sick. Was it poison?"

"Yes," she said, walking away from the guard at Creed's door so he wouldn't hear. She reached the exit door, then stopped and turned back. "Cyanide, they're saying."

"Well, I was in the office near the holding cells yesterday, and I saw the guard taking the tray to him. It was a guard named Norris."

"First or last name?" Cathy asked.

"Last name," he said. "Sergeant Norris. I've also been checking to see who was working on the food crew then, and I've narrowed it down to five guys who might have made the sandwich or handled the apple. If you give these names to Max, he can pull all their phone call recordings and see what was said. You got a pen?"

"Yeah," she said, digging through her bag for a pen and paper. "Shoot."

Quickly, he whispered the names and she scribbled them down. She heard profanity and yelling in the background, the usual din of men with too much testosterone trapped in close quarters. "Michael, is anybody near you?"

"I don't think anybody's paying attention," he said in a low voice. "We're about to go to work."

"I don't want you getting into trouble with the other inmates. Be careful."

"Just get those names to Max, okay?"

"Right," Cathy said. "I'm on it. Michael, I wish you were here to help with this. I know you could track down Miller."

"I wish it too," he said, "but we work with what we have." He paused. "I'm praying for you."

She smiled, but her heart felt too big for her chest. Tears misted in her eyes—as always happened when he said that— and she blinked and looked up the hall. A nurse's aide was going into Creed's room with the rolling blood-pressure gauge. The guard stepped in behind her.

"I want you out of there," Cathy whispered.

"Don't dwell on it," he said. "You have work to do. Important work. I'm fine in here."

She knew that wasn't true. Cops didn't fare well in prison.

The fact that he hadn't been a cop in two years didn't really help. Some of the habituals had been arrested by Michael for prior offenses. Others distrusted him because he wasn't one of them. During his earliest days there, she had seen him with bruises and black eyes. She woke up in the wee hours every single night, obsessing over what could be happening to him. "You could get killed or maimed for asking the wrong questions."

"Stop," Michael said. "You're getting yourself all worked up, and it's nothing I can't handle. Just focus, okay? Focus on finding Miller."

His strength always calmed her temporarily, but today she couldn't shake that feeling of unease. "Be careful what you eat. I'll put some money on your account later today so you can get commissary food. The cafeteria food could be—"

"You're killing me," he cut in. "I don't want you worrying like this over me. Please, Cathy."

She was quiet. The recorded voice came on, warning that they had one minute left in the call. Her stomach sank.

"I'll call you as soon as I can get to the phone again. Is that all right? Am I running up the bill too high?"

"Michael, I don't care how much it costs. I want to talk to you whenever I can. Please don't ever even think about the money. We'll make it back."

"Okay," he said.

"I love you," she said quickly.

"I love you too. Hang in there, okay?"

She heard the click on the other end of the phone, then slowly clicked hers off. She missed him with an ache that throbbed through the marrow of her bones, burned like acid in her stomach, gonged in her head. If she could just get him out of that awful place. If they could just find Miller, get him out of their lives, bring him to justice once and for all . . .

She shook her head. She would have to stop dreaming and start acting. As Michael said, there was lots of work to do.

She started back into Creed's room, then paused and touched in Ned's number at the governor's mansion—a number she had memorized.

Her call was routed to his voice mail. "Me again," she said. "Cathy Cramer. Look, I just want to ask you one more time to please make sure the governor sees our clemency package and all those letters. This is an innocent man we're talking about. He's not safe in jail. He's a cop, and they don't take well to cops. Last night a guy was poisoned in there, and I'm scared that Michael could be next." Her voice broke off. She shouldn't have told him that. "Please, I'm begging you. I know you can't control the outcome, but if you could just make sure he sees it."

Her voice was growing more high-pitched, and she tried to temper it. "If anything happens to him in there . . . Please, just think about it. If it were you—" The voice mail beeped, ending the call, and she clicked the phone off and turned to the exit door, wiping her face before anyone could see her tears.

The exit door flew open and she jumped back as a doctor pushed through. "Excuse me." He held the door for her to go through, but she shook her head.

"No. I'm . . . thanks." She turned and headed back to Creed's room. She had work to do. She forced herself to change gears and think like a lawyer instead of a fiancée.

CHAPTER 40

The meeting with the assistant DA in Creed's room took three hours, since he and the court reporter stayed to get Creed's statement after he signed the immunity agreement. Cathy sat with him through his testimony, taking notes on everything he told them about Miller and his cohorts. When his energy seemed spent and he was being forced to repeat himself, Cathy called an end to the meeting.

As Cathy headed down the hallway toward the elevators, Holly stepped out of the waiting room. "Finally," she said.

Cathy gaped at her. "You've been here all afternoon?"

"No, I went home to feed Lily, and then she was sleeping so Juliet said I could leave her. Juliet's tracking down everything she can find on the names you texted us. I brought my computer up here to do the same."

Cathy followed Holly into the waiting room.

"Did it go okay?" Holly asked.

"Yeah, it went pretty well, I think." She looked at Holly for a moment, then opened her arms to her little sister. Holly hesitated, then came into them. Cathy held her tight. "I just want you to be all right."

"I am all right."

Cathy's phone rang, and she backed away, her eyes locked on Holly. Her sister had managed to smile.

Cathy dug through her bag, drew out her phone, and looked at the display. She sucked in a breath. "It's the governor's office. I have to take it." She clicked it on. "Ned, I can't believe you called me back. I guess you got my message today?"

"Yes." Was that a smile in his voice, instead of the usual irritation? "Girl, you're filling up my inbox."

"Yeah, sorry about that," Cathy said. "But this is getting very urgent."

"Well, Cathy, I'm calling to tell you I have good news."

Cathy touched her chest. "The governor's going to look at our package?"

Holly jumped and threw up both arms in a touchdown signal.

Ned chuckled. "He already did," he said.

Cathy grabbed Holly's shoulder. "He did? Ned, what did he say?"

"Cathy, I can't believe I'm telling you this, but something about your persistence really got through to him. It's the only pardon he's granted since being in office."

Cathy sank down, almost missing the chair, her heart pounding so hard she thought it must be visible through her blouse. "The only pardon? You mean he's going to . . ."

"He's granting Michael clemency!" Ned said. "Congratulations, Cathy. You did it."

Cathy sprang up, yelling unintelligible words as she threw her arms around Holly, the two of them hopping like little girls. She heard Ned laughing with her.

Cathy tried to think. "Wait," she said, breathless. "You're sure? He's going to grant a pardon for everything? Wipe his slate clean?"

"That's right," Ned said. "Michael will no longer have a conviction on his record. If he wants to go back to carrying a weapon, he can. If he wants to be a police officer again . . ."

She was sure she was going to hyperventilate. "How soon can we get this in writing?"

"I'm working on that right now," Ned said. "If you want, you can come by and pick up the paperwork. Take it to the jail. The governor's going to call them personally and tell them to release him today. Try to keep it out of the press until we set up a press conference for tomorrow. The governor wants to announce it and explain it himself."

Cathy didn't know when she'd gone from laughing to crying, but she was now in a full-fledged sob. "Ned, I'm going to make you a star in my blog. I'll call every news station in the state after the press conference. Thank you, thank you, thank you!"

"Glad it worked out. I'll see you when you get here."

When she hung up, Cathy hugged Holly and they spun around. "Call Juliet," she said. "Tell her everything. I'm going to get those papers and take them to the jail. Michael's getting out today!"

She wept all the way to her car.

CHAPTER 41

Michael had just gotten out of the shower after a scorching workday grooming the median along Highway 77, when he heard over the intercom, "Michael Hogan, you're needed downstairs."

From his cell, Michael looked through the reinforced Plexiglas to the control room where two guards sat. According to the clock on their wall, it was past time for visitation.

He hadn't done anything wrong, but that didn't mean someone hadn't lied about him. He could be in some kind of trouble without even knowing it. But if that were true, the others would be looking at him with amusement, and he would feel the tension in the air—predators circling and waiting for blood.

Maybe it was something else. Maybe they had a message to give him, some awful news from outside. Alarm pulsed through him. Had something bad happened? Were they notifying him of some tragedy? Had Miller made another hit?

Pulling his shirt over his wet head, he hurried out of his cell and across the pod to the doors. He waved, getting the attention of the detention officer, who came out of the control room and opened the door.

Michael stepped out. "Who's here?"

"Got me," the guard said. "I'll buzz you down. Report to Lancaster."

Michael braced himself as he stepped onto the elevator, a sick feeling in his stomach. What if his father had had a heart attack? His blood pressure had been too high ever since Michael's incarceration. Or his mother—what if something had happened to her?

Or was it Cathy? The thought of her being hurt made him almost physically sick, but he swallowed hard and drew in a deep breath. By the time the elevator hit the bottom floor, he was sweating as if he'd just jogged two miles.

He found Sergeant Lancaster standing in the guards' break room. Michael knocked. "You wanted to see me, Sarge?"

Lancaster glanced up at him, then looked down at the fax in his hand, reading as if he hadn't heard Michael. Then he pulled another sheet off the fax and read it as well. He shook his head and grinned. "Unbelievable."

"What?" Michael asked.

Lancaster looked at him. "Go back to your cell and pack up your stuff."

Michael felt himself stiffen. Surely they weren't going to transfer him to the state prison like they did all the other convicts. The judge had said he could serve out his sentence in the county jail, closer to home. He had promised him that small mercy so he could see his family and Cathy.

"Sergeant Lancaster," he began.

"Michael Hogan," Lancaster cut in, "you have officially been granted clemency by the governor of the state of Florida. You're being released today."

Michael just stood there, trying to absorb the words.

"Did you hear me?" Lancaster said, a smile stretching across his leathery face. "Son, you've been pardoned by the governor. You're done here."

It took a full minute for the news to sink in. "Are you kidding me? I'm getting out?"

"That's right. Your record's being expunged."

Michael gaped at him, certain he'd made a mistake.

"You might want to get down to the waiting area. There's somebody here to take you home."

Michael got hold of himself and left the office, jogged up the hall to the processing area—and saw Cathy, weeping and waving some papers. "Is it true?" he said.

"It's true!" she said, jumping like a game-show contestant. "Michael, you're free!"

She threw her arms around him, and he picked her up and spun her around. "How did this happen?"

"It happened because God answers prayers," Cathy said. "Hurry, go pack your things. I can't wait to get you out of here."

CHAPTER 42

Since word hadn't reached the press yet that Michael had been released, family and friends were able to quietly gather at his parents' house to celebrate his homecoming.

Holly and Lily rode to the celebration with Jay and his little boy, Jackson, who sat in the back and stroked the baby's hand. When they arrived, Michael quickly scooped Lily out of her seat and held her, awestruck, as if she were already a member of his family. He only put the baby down to eat the favorite foods his mother had prepared.

Holly helped clean up in the kitchen, knowing Lily was safe, surrounded by people who loved her. She found herself wishing Creed were there, then she mentally kicked herself. She barely knew him, and he was in so much trouble . . . yet she'd rather be at the hospital with him than here with her family.

Cathy shot through the kitchen, her phone at her ear, and

stepped into the pantry, the only quiet room in the house. Holly couldn't resist listening.

"Cameron, I hate to bother you tonight, but . . . are you still in Germany?"

Holly turned off the water. Who was Cameron, and what did he have to do with what was happening tonight?

"Great," Cathy said. "Listen, I have a big favor to ask from you. Huge." She told him about Michael's release. "The thing is, I don't think he's safe spending the night anywhere his enemies can find him tonight. If word gets out, he could be in danger. Add to that, I'm representing a client who's a witness against those same people, and I need to put him in a safe place too. I was thinking that your place would fill the bill, if you'd let us borrow it."

The safe house for Creed. Wiping her hands on a dish towel, Holly stepped toward the pantry. Cathy glanced at her, her expression hopeful. "Wonderful. Yes, we'll water your plants. No problem. Who has the key? Will you let her know I'm getting it? I'll put it back when we leave."

When she hung up, Cathy punched the air. "I can't believe it," she said. "My friend says they can use his house. He's in Germany for a month. His sister's been watching the house, watering his plants, but he said she'd be thrilled not to have to go over there for a few days. There's a key hidden there on the property, so Michael can stay there tonight. When Creed gets out, he can stay there too."

"Both of them together?"

"Yeah, I think it'll be all right."

It showed a tiny bit of trust in Creed, and Holly appreciated that. She hugged Cathy. "When I grow up, I want to be like you. You're amazing, you know. You got Michael out, you got Creed immunity, you've found a place for them to be safe."

Cathy waved that off. "You want to be like me? I wouldn't wish that on anybody."

Holly knew Cathy meant it. "Things are looking up," she said. "I think your life is about to change."

Cathy grinned like a little girl. She wasn't the squealing type, but the joy in her eyes was like that of a four-year-old on Christmas morning.

Holly watched as Cathy went back into the living room and told Michael what she'd arranged, then lifted the sleeping baby. With the child in her arms and Michael smiling next to her, Cathy looked as if motherhood might be the next thing on her priority list, as soon as she was married.

Cathy always did things in the right order, even when it was hard. Holly envied that. When the three sisters had begun talking about the upcoming wedding, Holly remembered the wedding dresses she'd had for her Barbie dolls as a kid—how she'd imagined herself wearing a veil, how she'd wanted to walk down the aisle with her father escorting her.

Now he was in a nursing home, a stranger who didn't recognize a soul, not even her. And that fairy-tale wedding seemed about as possible as Cinderella's pumpkin turning into a carriage.

She'd skipped steps and missed the good stuff, to get to some destination that seemed silly now. Yet she had the grace of Lily.

She stepped outside, where earlier Michael's dad and Max had started a fire in the fire pit. No one else was outside yet, so she picked up a stick, stirred the fire, then sat down in front of it.

She leaned back in the Adirondack chair and gazed up at the sky. What did God think about the goings-on of human beings down here? Was he sick of them, as he'd been before the flood? Did he get discouraged and wonder why he bothered?

"You okay?"

Holly looked behind her. Juliet was coming out. "Yeah. Robbie asleep?"

"Yeah, he drifted off on the couch. What are you thinking about out here alone?"

"I don't know," Holly whispered.

"Creed?" Juliet asked.

For a moment Holly didn't answer. She looked at Juliet's face. The orange glow of the fire flickered on it, making her look soft and vulnerable herself. She'd had a horrible year, yet she forged on, never giving up.

"I know you and Cathy are worried about me and Creed," Holly said. "I don't really know how I feel. A week ago, I had no feelings for him at all. I didn't want him to have any part in our lives."

"And now?"

"He's not who I thought he was. Just like I'm not who he thought I was. But I realize my gut doesn't always lead me right."

Juliet had the grace not to reply.

"I feel drawn to him . . . probably because he's good with Lily. I can't dislike anyone who has the good judgment to fall in love with her, but am I thinking so much about him because I long for a family for Lily? A mother and father who are her biggest fans? Or is this something God has worked out to bring us together? Is he giving me some gift I didn't expect or even ask for?"

Juliet seemed to consider that. "My gut tells me that you need to move very slowly and cautiously. But then, *my* gut hasn't always led me right either."

Holly drew in a long breath. "I look at Cathy and think how wonderful her wedding will be, and how great Michael will be as a husband, and when they have kids, Michael will be there to help her. Things won't be so hard. Why do I always make things so hard for myself?"

Juliet smiled as if surprised that those words had come out of Holly's mouth rather than her own.

Holly went on. "Sometimes I look back on my life and try to figure out which decision I made that started my crazy descent . . . if I could just go back to that minute and make a different choice. Maybe I would have gone to college, gotten a career, a decent job. Maybe I would have met a guy and gotten married and had Lily at the right time."

Juliet took her hand. "Honey, I think what matters is where you are right now, this minute, and what you do from now on."

"I know, but if I can't learn from my mistakes, how will I ever teach her?"

"The Bible says that if you ask for wisdom, God will give it without partiality. It's a promise."

"I know, but will I *use* that wisdom he gives me?" she asked with a grin. "Or will I convince myself that my own screechy voice is that wisdom? I have a very loud inner voice."

"Remember that scripture passage Dad made us memorize when we were little? Philippians 4:6–7?"

Holly hadn't thought of all that Scripture memorization in years. "Remind me."

"'Do not be anxious about anything . . . ,'" Juliet said.

Holly remembered now. "Right. 'But in every situation, by prayer and petition . . .'"

"'With thanksgiving . . .'"

"'Present your requests to God,'" Holly went on. "'And

the peace of God, which transcends all understanding, will guard your hearts and minds in Christ Jesus.'" She nodded. "I can't believe I still remember that."

"It's still in there," Juliet said. "Dad did leave some legacy, even though he didn't really live by it later on."

Holly sighed. "The peace of God. That's what I never wait for. I want that."

"That's not entirely true," Juliet said. "You felt peace about going through with the pregnancy. Not aborting."

Holly's eyebrows lifted. "That's true. So there have been times when I listened to God's wisdom instead of mine."

"You can do it again." Juliet hugged her. "You've grown up, sweetie. I doubted you a few nights ago, but I should have trusted you, because it's clear you've changed. I think you can trust that voice of God in your heart. He'll give you that peace if you let him lead you. This is hard for me to say, but I trust you to make the right decision this time."

Juliet went back inside, and Holly stayed there alone, watching the dancing fire. She leaned back again and moved her gaze back to the heavens. "I know I've said this before, Lord, but I'm so sorry for all the stupid choices I've made. I want to start over, with your guidance. I can't afford to make mistakes now. Will you turn up the volume on your voice, and turn mine down? Will you give me that wisdom you promised if we ask? And will you help me to make the right decision about how involved to get with Creed?"

She waited for some instant change in her heart, some quick neon sign in the flickering flames. There wasn't one, but she felt God's fondness for Creed. Maybe that was a sign that she could get to know him better.

Still, she would be cautious, just in case.

When she went back in the house, everyone was sitting around Cathy and Michael. Cathy still held Lily as she talked about the wedding.

"I don't want to wait," Michael was saying. "I want to find somebody to marry us tonight."

Cathy laughed. "We can't get married tonight. We need a marriage license."

Michael groaned. "We should have gone straight to the clerk of court and applied for one the minute I got out."

"Where would we get married?"

"There, at the courthouse," Michael said. "The sooner the better."

"No," Cathy said. "All this time you've been in jail, I've been dreaming about the wedding. And in those dreams, I was always walking down the aisle of your church. Maybe that's why I never booked a venue. I want to get married there."

Michael's eyes shimmered, and he touched her chin and turned her face toward him. "I didn't know you were thinking that way. I thought you wouldn't even consider my little church."

Holly knew that Cathy had been feeling the same revulsion against church as she had since their father's infidelity after years of preaching moral messages in the pulpit. The church's cruel reaction toward their family had soured them. In adulthood, both Cathy and Holly had strayed from organized religion, but Holly could see that Cathy was coming around.

"Do you mean that?" Michael asked. "You want to get married in my church?"

Cathy swallowed. "Our church. Our pastor can do it."

He took her face in both his hands and kissed her. Cheers went up around the table. His father and mother were as excited and happy as any of them. "All right," he said. "We'll do it whenever you want. Wedding dress, bridal party, reception, the whole works."

"She already has the dress," Becky, Michael's mother, said.

Michael looked over at her. "She does?"

Becky smiled at Cathy, tears in her eyes. "I went with you to try those dresses on, when you were going to marry Joe. I cried when you found the right one, remember? It was so gorgeous."

"But . . . I can't wear the dress I was going to wear for Joe."

"Why not?" Michael asked. "If it's the dress you dreamed of. I like the idea of Joe being a part of our wedding. He's still such a huge part of both our lives."

Holly smiled at Cathy and nodded, and Cathy looked around, taking a silent poll of the expressions on everyone's faces.

"If you do that, we don't have to wait months for a dress to come in," Juliet said.

Cathy's composure crumbled, and she covered her face. "That's the dress I'm always wearing in my dreams, but I didn't want to hurt anyone by wearing it."

"I think it would be a beautiful way to celebrate this day and honor Joe," Becky said, and Michael's father nodded.

"Then it's done," Michael said, grabbing a napkin from the table and dabbing his eyes. "So tell me when."

Cathy was quiet for a moment. "Let's try to get the Miller thing resolved first, so we can all truly celebrate. But it wouldn't hurt to go ahead and get the marriage license and talk to the pastor about when the church is available."

The family all cheered and hugged each other. Holly felt Cathy's joy seeping into her heart, reminding her that there was always hope.

CHAPTER 43

The next morning, Michael met Cathy at the police station, where the governor's press conference would be held. Michael didn't know what to expect from his former coworkers, now that they'd learned of his pardon, but he hoped he could get permission to listen in on the questioning of Creed—who'd been released from the hospital that morning.

The moment he stepped into the building, he was surrounded by old friends slapping his back, hugging him, and giving him high fives and fist bumps.

Chief Wilson, Michael's former boss, waited for everyone to congratulate him, then took him into his office.

"We're really happy for you, man," he said. "None of what happened to you was justice."

Cathy shot Michael a look that reminded him of Wilson's attitude the day he'd been fired, after his conviction came down. Wilson had taken his weapons and badge . . . effectively ending his career.

But what choice had the chief had?

Cathy hung back at the door, unwilling to enter, as if the office itself would defile her.

"It's not right," Wilson said. "We lost two good men, not just Joe. You left a huge void on the force."

Michael looked at his hands. "Thank you, sir."

"And when they charged you a few months ago, I personally called the prosecutor and the judge and tried to reason with them. But it went the way it went. I can tell you that morale has been low ever since, and that scumbag Miller still walks free."

"Well, maybe with Creed Kershaw's story we can change all that," Cathy said.

"Let's hope so," Wilson said. "I'd like for you to help us with that, Hogan. I want you back on the force."

Michael hadn't expected that. He met Cathy's eyes again. He couldn't tell what she was thinking, but he could imagine.

"Wow, Chief. That's very generous."

"Not at all," the chief said. "What do you say?"

Michael stared at him for a long moment. "I honestly don't know. I'll have to talk it over with Cathy and pray about it. We'll have to figure out what my future looks like, but I really appreciate the option. What I'd rather do for now is have consultant privileges, so I can work with the PCPD on the Miller case and other cases."

Chief Wilson leaned back. "Second-best option for me. You got it. I'll call up to Major Crimes and let everybody know. We're going to catch this monster once and for all."

Michael shook the chief's hand again as a rush of emotion pulled at his face. By the time they were back in the hallway, Cathy could see the glisten in his eyes.

"Michael, you sure you don't want your badge back?"

"No," he said. "I'm not sure. But we have all the time in the world to decide."

He kissed her again, and then read.

Finally, I want to thank Jehovah God, who has walked with me through all of this. He knows my heart. I promise I to vow that our lives will be smooth sailing, but he does promise not

The press conference on the steps of the police station was a celebration. Every news outlet in the state turned out for the announcement that Michael had been pardoned. Since Cathy couldn't be sure that they had received the packets she'd sent them, she passed out new copies so that the journalists could quickly review Michael's case and hopefully assure the public that the governor's decision had been the right one.

Governor Larimore made a somber statement about why he'd chosen to make an exception to his campaign promise. When it was Michael's turn at the microphone, he pulled Cathy with him.

They stared with his smile—that he

As cameras flashed and filmed, Michael swallowed the knot in his throat. "Thank you all for coming. I'm overwhelmed with the love and support I've received from the police force and from all of you." He cleared his throat. "Two years ago, my brother was murdered, and that was the beginning of a long, dark ordeal for Cathy and me. We haven't yet gotten justice for Joe's murder, but we hope that this generous and compassionate act by Governor Larimore will result in new beginnings. My hope now is that I can help resolve Joe's murder, as well as the related deaths that have occurred since then."

He thanked the governor and Ned for not letting politics stand in the way of his pardon. Then he kissed Cathy. "And I have to thank my bride-to-be, Cathy Cramer, for working tirelessly to bring this pardon about. As soon as I can get to a store, I plan to put a ring on her finger. Then we have a wedding to plan."

He kissed her again, and the crowd applauded.

"Finally, I want to thank Jehovah God, who has walked with me through all of these trials. He doesn't promise Christians that our lives will be smooth sailing, but he does promise not to leave or forsake us. He has kept his promise in my case."

After another round of applause, the journalists shot out questions for the governor and Michael. Through it all, Michael held Cathy's hand and thought he was the most blessed man in the world.

Though Michael had had deep concerns about Creed's authenticity, he had to admit after meeting him that the guy seemed real.

They started with his timeline—when he'd gotten into the drug business, who he'd worked with along the way, people he'd sold to, people who'd supplied him, where they'd met when, whom he'd spoken to, what he'd seen.

Creed gave up all that information and more, offering things they didn't even ask for. As new thoughts came to his mind, he'd interject them as clues that might help them find Miller.

Finally, after six hours of questioning, they brought an unmarked department SUV into the sally port of the adjacent jail and loaded Creed in, away from watching eyes. Cathy sat next to him on the bench seat behind the driver, and Michael climbed in behind her. Max drove, Forbes rode shotgun, and two more detectives joined them. Another unmarked carload of cops rode behind them, watching for any sign of ambush.

Creed took them to a place on a canal that led to the Gulf

of Mexico where he knew some deliveries of cocaine had been made. It was a new location behind a private residence, just as they'd seen before. The detectives scrambled to find out who owned the property, and several stayed behind to recon the place as Creed took the others on to more locations.

The guy who saw himself as low on the totem pole of the drug operation had more information than he'd realized. He took them to another location outside a local library and told them what day he'd met Miller's men there. A couple of detectives got busy getting the security video from the library's outdoor cameras.

Then he took them to the homes of two of his suppliers— guys he'd known by street names before he'd gotten into drug dealing himself. From the public records on those properties, they were able to track down the residents and get driver's license pictures and mug shots, which Creed used to identify them.

He was a gold mine of information, but none of it led directly to Miller.

Finally, when they were done, Cathy took Creed and Michael to the safe house her friend had loaned them. It was open to the beach but had a cinderblock wall ten feet high between it and the street in front of it. It wasn't Fort Knox, but it was unexpected. Miller would never find them there, and even the police weren't aware of the location.

Cathy left them alone to go get Holly, who wanted to come visit Creed. Michael chose a bedroom and laid out his firearms on the bed. Max had kept his personal weapons and returned them along with his holsters, his Kevlar vest, his rounds of ammunition . . . all reminders that he had been reinstated into his life.

Slowly, methodically, he cleaned his weapons, loaded them,

slipped them into their holsters, then strapped one to his ankle and the other to his belt. He sat on the bed, feeling the freedom of a soft mattress after months on a six-inch-thick piece of foam on a steel cot. How wonderful to sleep in a place that didn't smell of body odor and bad breath or urine covered over with Clorox. It was quiet . . . a sweet luxury he had too long been denied.

"Do you think they saw us going by their places?"

Michael turned at Creed's voice. Creed stood in the doorway, hands in his jeans pockets, concern on his face. "I don't think so. We didn't slow down at any of them."

"But if they did, they could have followed us here."

"We would have seen them. Trust me. I was watching for tails."

"But they're good. Miller . . . he's deadly."

Michael turned back to the bed, put his ammo into his duffel bag, along with his vest. "Tell me about it. I've been up close and personal with him."

Creed looked down at his feet. "It's not me I'm worried about, but my parents and sister . . ."

"My brother has guys watching their homes. If Miller or his goons try to approach them, they'll be stopped. I think right now they're just keeping their heads down."

"Do you think they know I talked?"

"By now, probably."

Creed was quiet for a moment, and Michael studied him. He still looked pale, and his body slumped, as if exhausted.

"Can I call my parents?" Creed asked. "My sister? Warn them that they could be in danger?"

"Not a chance," Michael said. "They know that. We're gonna get him. Just sit tight and let us work. There's a football game on. Florida State and Ole Miss. Go relax. Sleep a little. You're still sick."

Creed shrugged. "Yeah, I guess."

"And Cathy went to get Holly and the baby."

Creed looked alarmed. "That might not be a good idea. What if Miller has figured out my connection to Holly? What if he's staking out her house or Cathy's? He could follow them here."

"They have a plan to meet their brother, Jay, behind a shopping center, and they're going to switch cars with him to throw the thugs off if they get that far."

"He would do that?" Creed asked.

"Yeah, probably so Cathy and I can spend time together. That family's tight. They watch each other's backs."

"Then I would think I'm the last person their brother would want Holly to be with."

"He's heard the truth about what happened. Doesn't mean he's not concerned, but he trusts Juliet's and Cathy's opinions about Holly's judgment." Michael held Creed's gaze for a moment. "You know, I'm close to Holly. She's like a sister to me. Don't hurt her."

Creed regarded his shoes again. "I won't. I know my word doesn't carry a lot of weight with you. Drug dealer, accused of murder . . . big-time loser. But I don't want to hurt Holly, or Lily either." He nodded at Michael's holster. "Congratulations on your pardon. Sorry you have to spend your first day free here with me."

"It's better than jail." Michael walked out of the room, and Creed followed him into the living room. Michael turned the TV on, found the game.

"Your whole story makes me wonder if there's hope for me,"

Creed said, dropping to the couch. "To have the slate wiped clean, I mean."

Michael turned to him, looked at him fully. "You know, your slate can be wiped clean whether you go to prison or not."

"What do you mean?"

"It's called redemption."

"Oh, right," Creed said. "Yeah, I was raised in church. I know all about redemption. Jesus dying for our sins and all."

Michael could see he didn't really get it. The "and all" told Michael all he needed to know about Creed's faith. His nonchalance minimized Christ's sacrificial death, turning it into something mythical and false, and demonstrated a lack of awe.

He said a silent prayer that God would show Creed what true redemption was.

CHAPTER 44

Holly heard Cathy pulling into her driveway, so she grabbed up Lily and the diaper bag, set her house alarm system, then hurried out to the car. Cathy gave her a disgusted look as Holly strapped Lily's car seat in.

"You're wearing lipstick. You curled your hair."

Holly rolled her eyes. "So?"

"So . . . you never do that. You really like this guy, don't you?"

Holly didn't answer right away. She gave Lily her pacifier, then turned on a colorful video on her tablet and set it beside the seat. Lily looked content, so Holly got into the front to sit beside her sister.

"I just took a shower, okay? Sue me for grooming."

"I'm just saying . . ."

"I know what you're saying, Cathy. Enough. I haven't done anything wrong."

Cathy sighed. She made an unexpected turn, and Holly looked over at her. "Where are you going?"

"To meet Jay and do our bait and switch."

Holly twisted in the seat and looked out the back window. There was some traffic behind them, but no one turned when they did.

"Jay's getting us some Chinese takeout so we can take it with us."

"Why? I thought we were going to cook."

Cathy shook her head. "Didn't have time to go grocery shopping."

"I could have gone. I was looking forward to cooking. Creed said he likes to cook. He would have helped."

"Yeah, and you could act like a happy little family. No thanks."

Holly gaped at her. "I'm not a child, Cathy. I can cook for a man without falling for him."

"Come on, Holly. Don't play dumb with me. You wanted to come tonight. I didn't want you to, but you insisted. I'm going along with it, but I think it's a bad idea."

Holly hooked her seat belt and crossed her arms. "A, I'm not in love with him, and B, I don't see why it would be such a bad idea if I were. Hasn't he done everything he promised? Hasn't he given us information we didn't have before?"

Cathy considered that as she drove. "Yes, he's been very open and helpful."

"You were supportive yesterday when I was at the hospital. You seemed to understand the things I'm going through."

Cathy sighed. "I do. But that doesn't mean getting more involved with him is wise."

"So let me get this straight," Holly said. "You don't think

that if he's sorry for what he's done then he should be forgiven? Because if you don't think he can be redeemed, then maybe I can't be either."

"No, that's not what I'm saying."

"Then what?"

"Just that your life is fragile and hard enough. Why complicate things by getting involved with a guy who has huge legal problems?"

"You got him immunity. He's not guilty of murder, and as soon as all this is untangled, the police in Southport will know that. He hasn't even been charged yet."

"Holly, you can't be that dense. You know what I mean. There's a contract out on his life. People want him dead because of his involvement in a criminal drug ring."

"Which he's helping dismantle as we speak."

Cathy drove in silence for a long moment. Finally, she spoke again. "How many times have I heard you say that you wish you'd listened to me and Juliet and Jay? How many times, Holly?"

Cathy had her there. It had happened more times than Holly could count. Was this one of those times?

She looked out the window as "Twinkle, Twinkle, Little Star" played in the backseat. Was this different from all those other times? Was this just another case of Holly doing what she always did? Bolting headlong into a situation that would bring her heartache and pain?

She looked back at her daughter. In the mirror she'd hung on the headrest, she could see Lily drifting off to sleep. What a precious sight, her little daughter so satisfied . . .

Her heart ached for her. She wanted so much more for her. "He's her father," she said simply.

Cathy let out a long sigh. "I know, but . . . does that mean you have to . . . have a relationship with him?"

"Yes, I think it does."

"You know what I mean, Holly. Don't play stupid."

Holly got quiet again. Finally, she looked at her sister. "I don't know how I feel about Creed. A few days ago, he was the last person on earth I wanted to see, but like I told you, I see a lot of myself in him. The wild child who fell off the cliff . . . who has a whole body of brokenness that needs to be healed."

Cathy's face softened, and she met Holly's eyes. "But you don't have to be the one who heals him."

"I know I don't, but maybe I understand him."

"And maybe you don't."

"There's remorse, Cathy. He's trying to undo it. Doesn't that speak to his character, at least a little?"

"Not necessarily. When people are looking at prison, they're often remorseful."

"The whole time I was with him, he didn't use once. He's not an addict, he's just a stupid rebel like me, who makes wrong choices and then has to untangle himself from the consequences. And sometimes the consequences stick around." She looked back over the seat. "Sometimes they become blessings. Don't you think God can do something with a man like Creed? A girl like me?"

"You know I do," Cathy said. "I just don't want you to be hurt. I want you to be careful. Cautious."

"I want that too."

It wasn't a promise that she would be—just an acknowledgment that she wanted to be. She knew Cathy hadn't missed that.

Cathy came to a stoplight and looked over at Holly. Headlights lit up her face for a moment, and Cathy saw the little girl in Holly's eyes, the one abandoned by her father when he chose a mistress over all of them. She remembered Holly looking out the window at night, watching headlights and expecting him to come home, even though their mother had told her he wouldn't.

Her father's choices had cost them all, but Holly more than anyone. She had been a daddy's girl, the glimmer in his eye until the day he walked away. Cathy wondered if he'd thought about what his leaving would do to Holly. Had he considered how worthless it would make her feel? How she would think it was because of something she'd done, or something she'd lacked? That she'd fly through puberty a few years later like someone out to prove something? That it would take her years to land on solid ground?

She had been on solid ground since Lily, and her remorse was real, not some speech that she'd rehearsed. Holly *had* changed. Maybe she could be trusted with her own emotions this time. And if Cathy couldn't talk her out of a relationship with Creed, then she could at least work to keep him from becoming a convicted felon.

Without thinking, she leaned over and pressed a kiss on Holly's cheek.

"What?" Holly asked with a smile.

"Nothing," Cathy said. "Just . . . I love you."

"I love you too."

Someone behind her honked, and she saw that the light was green. She pressed the accelerator.

Holly looked back. "Is someone following us?"

Cathy turned again. "No, we're fine. Jay should be right up here."

When they reached the shopping center, they drove around back and stopped at the door of an empty store. Jay got out of his car and came to the back door to get Lily's seat.

"Sure you're doing the right thing?" he asked.

Holly hoped they weren't about to go over the whole thing again.

"I'm sure," Cathy said. "No one followed us, but if they did, they'll tail you instead of us when we come out of here. Go to the nearest grocery store parking lot and go into the store. When they see that you're not us, they'll think they've been tailing the wrong car."

"I wasn't talking about that," Jay said. "I was talking about Holly."

Holly got her purse and followed him to the backseat of his car, where he placed Lily's seat. "Please don't preach to me, Jay. Cathy just got finished."

He bent low and strapped the seat in, then straightened and looked down at her. "How would you see this if you were in my shoes?"

She sighed. "Like a big brother worried about his little sister who's been known to have big lapses in judgment. But why don't you pray for me instead of worrying or preaching?"

He smirked. "I'll do that."

"I think it's okay," Cathy said. "We've talked. Her head is on straight."

Jay hugged Holly, pressed a kiss on her cheek, then took the keys from Cathy. "Call me when you're ready to trade back."

"Be careful," Holly said as she got into the car.

Jay chuckled and got behind the wheel of Cathy's car.

CHAPTER 45

As the four of them ate, Holly and Creed were quiet while Cathy and Michael chattered, catching up on all they hadn't been able to tell each other in the last several months. Michael kept going back to wedding plans, but Cathy's conversation jumped from the cases they'd taken in his absence to Juliet's grief and strength after her husband's death to what had happened today.

When they finished, Holly cleaned up the leftovers, put them in the fridge, and began to hand wash the utensils they'd used. Creed had taken Lily out of her car seat, and he held her now, awe softening his features. "Is it okay if I just hold her while she sleeps?" he asked.

Holly smiled. "Sure, it's okay."

"She's satisfied and content," he said. "Isn't it all amazing?"

Holly dried her hands and looked back at him. "Isn't what amazing?"

"That you can provide exactly the amount of nutrition it takes to satisfy her."

Holly nodded. "The first few days of her life, Juliet never stopped pointing out to me all the ways God designed mothers so perfectly to nurture their children. Like the whole pregnancy thing. Everything the baby needs to grow and flourish for nine months. The way childbirth releases hormones that set things in motion—everything from a mother's attachment to her child, to the milk coming in. Did you know that a mother has contractions after birth, when she hears her baby crying? Her body physically responds. Just hearing Lily cry makes my hormones scream out. I can't stand it until I pick her up."

Creed hung on every word. She pulled out a barstool and offered it to him. He slipped onto it, swaying slightly with the baby. Holly pulled out another one and sat next to him. She smiled and touched the crown of Lily's head.

"Did you have a hard pregnancy?" he asked softly.

She shrugged. "It was okay. Had some morning sickness, but that was the least of my worries."

"Why?"

She breathed a laugh. "I was mostly just horrified at first."

"So did she kick a lot? Keep you awake nights? My sister didn't sleep the last two weeks of her pregnancy. She would bite your head off if you spoke to her."

Holly smiled. "I probably did that too. Yes, she kicked a lot. She likes her space. It was like she was trying to stretch out more room. She weighed seven pounds three ounces. She's about nine pounds now."

He looked down at the baby as if considering every ounce. "Was the delivery hard?"

"It was okay. My sisters were there. They would never have let me go through that alone."

He nodded. "My family's kind of like that." He looked at his daughter again, shook his head. Tears welled up in his eyes.

Holly looked away, but her gaze gravitated back.

"I'm sorry," he said, and he worked at his mouth, trying to get his voice. "I just . . . I can't believe I've let them down the way I have. Humiliated them. They wanted so much more for me. Believe it or not, they had higher dreams than for me to become a coke dealer."

"Don't apologize for feeling bad about that," she whispered. "I've been there. So what was Plan A?"

"For me, or for them?" He wiped his eyes with his thumb and laughed. "They wanted me to be an astrophysicist or the guy who cures cancer. I just wanted to be independent, so I ditched college and moved out. My dad always thought I was good with wood like him, so he tried to get me to go to trade school to be a carpenter. I could have worked for him. Instead I became a waiter, only the tips weren't enough, probably because I was always getting high instead of working. I didn't want to work for my dad because I knew what he'd expect of me."

"You must have made enough to pay rent, right?"

"Not really. That's when I decided to sell a little coke—just to my friends who were going to buy anyway. It was fast, easy cash. So I sold more and more. But the people I was dealing with started to scare me. I told my supplier I was quitting. I couldn't handle it anymore, even if I had to move back with my parents. Right after that the drug bust happened. I probably would've been there that day if I hadn't already quit, which is why Miller and his people got suspicious of me. Figured I had unloaded to the DEA."

"*Did* you tell the DEA?"

"No, I just wanted out. I wanted to start over. I thought I could until they tried to kill me."

"Well, my sisters tell me that acknowledging where you went wrong is half the battle. You aren't in denial about your part in it."

He met her eyes. "You always make me feel better, Holly."

Warmth rose to her cheeks. She glanced toward the kitchen door but didn't see Michael and Cathy. They must have gone outside to the deck.

"You know," Creed said, "there was a girl in high school I dated a couple times. A girl I really liked. She had this pink stripe in her platinum-blonde hair . . ."

"Like mine used to be."

"That's why I was drawn to you. She deigned to go out with me twice, only she threw me over for some dude who played guitar. She told somebody I was boring."

"Boring? If she could see you now."

"Yeah. She wound up serving ten years in jail for grand larceny."

"No way."

"Last time I saw her mug shot, she didn't look that attractive. Still had some of the pink stripe, you know, but it didn't look quite so edgy anymore." His smile faded. "The stupid things we do when we're kids. Have I told you about the tattoo on my chest that looks like a bad picture of a phoenix rising out of the ashes? It was the name of my band I had for about six months. Horrible band. The tattoo artist was a friend who swore he knew what he was doing. Came out bad. Now I hate to take off my shirt."

Holly slipped her shoe off and pulled down her sock. "Here's my embarrassment."

He winced. "What is that?"

"It used to be a Chinese phrase, only I didn't know what it said. Found out later when a Chinese friend read it to me. It's pretty much the worst obscenity they have in Mandarin. Yep, I had it inked on my body because it looked so interesting. When I found out, I had another tattoo artist black it out. So now I have a thick black line along the side of my foot. Looks like I stepped in tar."

His eyes met hers again, soft, serious, his laughter fading to a gentle smile. "The girl of my dreams."

She matched that smile. "You should dream bigger."

"It's not the tattoo," he said. "It's the confusion. The mistakes."

"The failures?"

"Not that you did them, but that you see backward so clearly. Like me."

"Yeah, I do a lot of things backward."

He laughed. "Well, you're doing better now. You own a house, right? You support yourself?"

"Yeah, driving a taxi."

"And working as a private eye. Don't sell yourself short. That's pretty impressive."

She thought about that for a moment. "I guess I'm just not that into impressing anybody anymore. I never thought I'd be able to do something I like so much and get paid for it. Private investigating work seems like something I do just for fun, you know? Maybe soon I can quit driving the cab and live off the PI work, especially now that Michael's out."

"And you're a great mom. A really, really great mom."

Her smile faded and she felt a knot in her throat, tears gathering in her eyes.

He took her hand, looked down at it. "I want to do better," he said. "I really do want to start over."

"It's not too late," she whispered.

"I don't know, Holly. I've done some bad things."

"So have I."

"Michael told me I could redeem myself. I'm going to try."

"Are you sure he said you could redeem *yourself*? Because I'm not sure you can do it yourself," Holly said. "Michael would tell you that it has nothing to do with you. That redemption comes from what Christ did on the cross. Taking our punishment for all the messes we've made. That the blood he shed for us was enough to wash us clean."

He narrowed his gaze. "Blood washing us clean. Interesting concept."

"Yeah, but I believe it." She stopped and thought about how to say it. "It's like . . . once I trusted that Jesus' death for me was enough . . . well, then I stopped hating myself and wallowing in guilt, and I started over, like someone who was fresh and clean. Someone who had a shot at life. And God . . . he's sent me a trail of bread crumbs to guide me, you know? And trust me, I needed a *lot* of crumbs. I still feel insecure and inferior sometimes, and that guilt pops back up, reminding me what I was."

Lily started to stir and whimpered a little. Creed handed her to Holly, and she settled back down.

"You think he'd send me some crumbs?" he whispered.

Holly stroked Lily's back. "I know he would."

"Do you think God has given up on me?"

She had asked that same question so many times. The familiarity of it filled her eyes with tears. "No, Creed. I used to think he was disgusted with me too, but sometimes he gives things back that we lost. He restores things. And I don't know . . . I just get the feeling that he's not mad at me. He wants better for me, and for you. He wants us to know peace. I bet he has big plans for you. He sure does for me."

"Wow. Big plans. That's something to get my head around. Sometimes it just feels like the end of the road. Like I've used up all those big plans."

"You haven't."

Creed wiped the tears from her cheek with his thumb. "You're a better person than I am."

She shook her head. "No, I'm not."

Another tear fell, and his own eyes misted. "Holly, I'm sorry for treating you . . . the way I did last year. You're a really cool person, and I missed out."

"I even had pink hair and everything."

More laughter.

Holly shrugged. "I treated *myself* with disrespect. You were just following my lead."

He slid off the stool and stroked Lily's hair. "I don't want to miss out anymore," he said. "I know things are complicated . . . with you and Lily . . . my part in her life . . . my legal mess. But I really want to get to know you better."

Their eyes locked for a long moment, then finally he leaned in and kissed her. Holly closed her eyes, melted at his touch, amazed that it felt so natural, so right . . .

What would her sisters say? Was she being stupid again, or was this a sweet provision that God was granting her? A way to give her daughter the father she hadn't expected? A way to fill in the blanks of her own broken life?

Was she following more bread crumbs, or straying off the path?

Holly wasn't sure, but she didn't pull away.

And when it was time to leave with Cathy, Holly kept it to herself. The kiss left her confused and strangely happy.

CHAPTER 46

H e's going to put a target on your back, you know," Cathy said as Michael drove to the police department. "I'm just feeling a little nervous."

"Then we need to catch him, get all this behind us. We'll get Holly and Juliet and my dad at the office today after we leave the department, and strategize our next moves."

Cathy couldn't help the anxiety coursing through her. She had even worried about Michael driving his own car, but he'd been aching to get back behind the wheel. He'd insisted on driving himself, picking up Cathy on the way in. At least he was armed. Early that morning, Max had gone by the safe house to return the rest of Michael's weapons to him. Now he wore his belt holster and a shin holster, prepared for any encounter with Miller now that the man knew Michael was out. Cathy rejoiced that he'd been reinstated as a function-ing, even necessary member of society, but the other part of her—the part who loved him and was weary from this long fight with Miller—dreaded the dangerous confrontations that would make weapons necessary.

"Are you sure Creed will be okay? I don't like having his escorts know where the house is."

"I know those two guys, and Max is close to them. We both trust them. Max wouldn't have sent anyone to escort Creed in who might give away our location. He doesn't want to lose another brother."

Cathy hoped he was right. Creed had a few more hours of questioning this morning, and Miller and his men would probably stop at nothing to shut him up.

She saw the police department coming up on their left, but Michael wasn't slowing. "You missed the turn."

"Nope," he said. "I'm not going there yet."

"Where are we going?"

He grinned. "I was thinking we could apply for our marriage license, since we have a little time before Creed gets here. It's just a block down the street. We're practically there already. Later today, we can go shop for that ring."

Her heaviness lifted, and she smiled. "Yes, let's get our license. But not the ring. We don't have time for that. Not today."

"But what kind of man doesn't buy his fiancée an engagement ring?"

"One who cares more about the marriage than the diamond. One who's just gotten out of jail and has a killer to hunt down."

"All very good points," he said. "But I'm still getting you a ring."

"Fine. But later, when we don't have a murder investigation hanging over our heads."

He slowed and turned into the courthouse parking lot. "You realize getting the license starts the clock, don't you? You'll have to marry me within a certain time frame, whatever it is, or the license will expire."

She leaned over and kissed him. "I'm ready to start the clock."

They drove down four buildings and found a space in the parking lot across from Bay County Courthouse. Holding hands, they crossed the street and ran up the steps.

They took selfies as they hurried up the hall to the clerk of court's office, laughed as they applied for their marriage license. The clerk didn't seem to appreciate their good moods.

"So we could get married immediately now?" Michael asked as he signed the application.

"Not unless you're from out of state."

Cathy frowned, wondering if the clerk hadn't noticed their local addresses. "We're residents."

"Then you have to wait three days after application before you can get married."

"So residents are penalized?"

"Not a penalty," the woman said. "Just a requirement. How do you plan to pay?"

Cathy glanced at Michael, amused. The woman's hair was pulled back in a tight ponytail that narrowed her eyes, and she had shaved her eyebrows and drawn them back in in a perpetually startled expression. The stubble of her real eyebrows had begun to grow back in. Her face glistened with perspiration.

"Cash," Michael said. "Will that be okay?"

"Yes," the woman said, peering past them toward the door, as if they didn't warrant a look in the eye.

Michael handed her the cash. "It's hot in here. I don't know how you stand it, constantly on your feet when it's eighty-something degrees in here."

The woman's hardness vanished. "The AC has been out all day. They're trying to get it fixed, but it's a hundred degrees outside. They should just close the offices if they can't get it fixed."

"Well, we appreciate your being open," he said. "We'll consider naming our first child after you."

The woman managed a grin. "You don't want to do that. My name is Matilda."

"I like it," Cathy teased.

Matilda seemed much more pleasant as she gave them a receipt, then printed out the license. As she shoved it into a white envelope, Cathy handed her her phone. "Would you mind taking a picture of us with the license, Matilda?"

"Sure," she said with a long sigh. She handed them the license and took the camera. Cathy and Michael posed.

They thanked her, and as they turned to leave, she actually said, "Congratulations."

"I think we won her over," Cathy said as they stepped into the hallway. "You're such a charmer."

"Not an easy task. She made me sweat."

"And here I thought you were getting cold feet."

"Fat chance. With the AC out, no wonder she's in a bad mood."

"Yeah, glad we're not getting married outside."

They stepped out onto the steps of the building, muggy hot air enveloping them. He slowed and kissed her. "We're one step closer to being Mr. and Mrs. Michael Hogan," he said. "I like the sound of that. Mrs. Hogan. My wife."

Cathy had liked the idea of being Mrs. Hogan back when she'd been engaged to Joe, but that seemed like so long

ago—decades rather than three years—and it felt as though
Michael had always been the love of her life. From the foundation of the world, Juliet would have said in her Bible-quoting
way. But it felt true.

He kissed her again, lifted her and spun her around. A
week ago she had thought their marriage was months away.
Now it could be just days. Gratitude brought tears to her eyes.

He took her hand and they crossed the street toward his
car. "Why don't you start the car remotely," she asked. "Get
that AC going."

He pulled his key fob out of his pocket. "I will if this thing
still works." He held it up and clicked it to start the car. They
heard a deafening *pop*, then a *whoosh*. Hot wind blasted them
back, the smell of tarry smoke . . .

"Get down!" Michael threw her behind a concrete light
pole, pulled her down. Flames and black smoke billowed up
from the area where they were parked. "Is that *your* car?" she
shouted.

"I don't know."

When the explosion was over, leaving only flames and
black, billowing smoke, they got up. Michael took her hand
and pulled her farther away, as if he feared another explosion.
Heat and smoke hazed around them. They heard the sounds
of sirens from the fire department two blocks down. They
reached the edge of the parking lot and turned to watch.

"It *was* your car!" Cathy cried. "Michael, it was a bomb!"

Michael just stood there staring, keenly aware that he could've
easily been behind the wheel cranking the engine on his own

when the explosion went off. That was the intent. He and Cathy were meant to be dead. He looked down at the key fob, still in his hand. Starting the car remotely had saved their lives.

He put his hand on his belt holster and looked around. There didn't seem to be anyone else in the parking lot. No one injured, and no suspects.

How would Miller and his people have known he'd be here? His mind raced. They didn't know where the safe house was, or they would have struck last night while he was with Creed. No, they must have been watching Cathy's house. They must have followed them from there, even though he thought he'd been watching for any sign of a tail.

If they had planted the bomb while he and Cathy were in the clerk of court's office, there would be security camera footage. He located the cameras on electric poles around the lot, including one just above the column they'd hunkered behind.

Afraid for Cathy, he ran her across the street. "I want you to wait inside," he said. "Don't come out until I come back to get you."

"What about you, Michael?" she said. "They want *you* dead, not me. You shouldn't be out there either."

"I'll be with the police," he said. "Just hold tight. I'll be right back."

CHAPTER 47

At the same moment that Michael and Cathy were stepping into the courthouse to get their marriage license, Creed was across town leaving the safe house. He got into the black SUV driven by the cop Detective Hogan had sent, escorted by another one. Creed sat in the backseat, anonymous behind the SUV's tinted glass windows. So far, so good.

If Miller and his men had known where Creed was staying last night, he was sure he would already be dead. But nothing had happened, which told him that no one who knew had leaked it.

He sat back in his seat. Was it true what Holly had said last night—that he could be redeemed? Was it possible that God had not given up on him? Creed had grappled with his Creator all night long, asking God to show him if there was still a chance. He had finally fallen into a fitful sleep and dreamed about Holly and the baby, years from now when Lily was four or five. They were a happy family in his dream, something too far outside the realm of possibility . . . just a wish processed by his active mind.

But he had kissed her last night, and she hadn't pulled away.

He was falling in love with his daughter, and maybe her mother too. Was that even something God would consider? Letting them become a family? Or was that ludicrous?

It was too soon, and there were too many hurdles to cross before that time came, but the thought gave him hope.

His mind drifted back to a conversation he'd had with his dad in his workshop when Creed was fourteen. Creed had been sanding a piece of furniture he'd helped build, and they'd been talking about girls.

"So like, how do you even know when it's the right girl, when so many of them *seem* right?"

His father sanded for a few minutes, not answering, until Creed wondered if he'd heard him. Finally, he blew the sawdust off and straightened, looked Creed hard in the eyes. "You know you're in love, son, when you meet the girl who makes you want to be a better you."

Creed hadn't understood it then. That hadn't even made sense. What was wrong with the way he was? That was before he'd gone downhill, thinking he knew more than God or his parents.

Now he understood. Holly made him want to *be* better, *do* better.

As they approached the police department, he watched out the window, dreading the day of interrogation. It was tedious and demanded constant repetition as the police dissected every sentence he spoke, testing for truth and jogging his memory for unnoticed details or things he'd forgotten.

As the officer pulled into the drive where he would be let out, Creed heard sirens somewhere a few blocks away. He looked toward the sound, saw smoke rising in the sky. Was there a building on fire somewhere?

Suddenly there was a burst of chatter on the police radio. He couldn't make out what they were saying. He leaned forward. "What happened?"

"Explosion up near the county courthouse, in the parking lot," his driver said.

"Anybody hurt?"

"Not sure yet. Come on, let's get you inside. I might need to head over there."

The officer got out of the driver's seat and came around to the back passenger side to open Creed's door. Creed slid out.

Something whizzed past his ear, and he instinctively ducked and pivoted. Had that been a gunshot?

"Get down!" the driver shouted.

But Creed froze at the sound of two more rounds, and a bullet whizzed past like knuckles across his cheekbone, knocking his head back. Blood sprayed his shirt, his hands. Before he could react, another one hit his forearm, then pinged into the body of the SUV.

Creed clutched his forearm as his knees buckled in pain. He hit the ground.

"Man down!" one of the cops was yelling into the radio. "Need an ambulance and backup, but the shooter is still active! Repeat, shooter is still active. Rounds are still being fired."

A cop covered Creed with his body then shoved him under the car.

Shot . . . he was shot! His head . . . his arm . . . blood all over him . . .

"I can't see the shooter," he heard someone bellowing into

the radio. "But it looks like it's coming from the roof of the jail. We need people up there to take the sniper down."

Creed's mind raced. The jail again? How would an inmate have gotten up there with a rifle without being noticed?

He was shivering . . . cold . . . and pain shot through the bones of his arm, through his shoulder and his neck and up through his skull. He rolled onto his back, trying not to cry out, praying for cover, for another chance . . . just one more.

It was Miller again. He desperately wanted Creed dead.

He heard more sirens, saw the wheels of more cars skidding to a stop near where he lay, doors slamming. Strong hands pulled him from under the car, pain shot through every nerve ending . . . blinding, heart-stopping pain . . .

Why was he even still alive?

"He's going into shock," someone said, dragging him to his feet.

Someone tightened a tourniquet around his arm, wrapped him in a blanket, rushed him through a doorway into the building. The hallway was too bright, and men and women ran past, firearms clutched in their hands. Would one of them blow him to pieces, right here in front of everyone? Did Miller's tentacles reach that far?

EMTs ran toward him with a gurney, and he felt his body being pushed down. He dropped his head back onto the pillow and closed his eyes as they rushed him back outside and into an ambulance. What if the sniper got him now?

They rolled him into the ambulance, slammed the doors shut. He felt a surge of nausea as the vehicle started moving. *Get me out of here*, he thought. *Far away, where no one is trying to kill me.*

He kept his eyes closed and lost himself inside the pain rooted in his arm as the ambulance sped away, siren blaring.

CHAPTER 48

From his third-floor desk, Max heard shots fired and ran down the stairs, along with several other detectives. Uniformed officers stampeded toward the side door, weapons drawn.

"It's coming from the roof of the jail!" someone shouted.

Max looked out the window, saw the commotion on the ground near the door. Someone had been hit.

"Forbes, let's cross over!" He ran down the stairs to the basement, which connected to the jail—several sets of footsteps running behind him—and crossed to the other building, then dashed up five flights of stairs. The guards were already on the stairwell, moving up to find the shooter. They stepped aside as Max and those with him passed.

As he reached the roof, the door flew open and Sergeant Norris came running in, out of breath and sweating. "Roof's clear," he said. "Whoever it is, is back inside."

Max pushed past him onto the roof. The men with him fanned out, searching behind the cooling tower and any other structures big enough to hide behind. As Norris had said, there was no one there.

Max went to the edge of the roof and looked down. He saw the ambulance driving up, Creed Kershaw being rolled into it on a gurney. So the shooter was probably connected to Miller, maybe the same inmate who had poisoned Creed.

He ran along the perimeter of the roof, looking over to see if anyone had dropped the weapon over the side of the building. As he suspected, there was a rifle caught in the bushes on the south side.

He radioed down that it was there, then turned back to Forbes, who was breathing like a tuberculosis patient. The man seriously needed to get in shape. Max tried to think. Norris had been dripping with sweat just now, much more than if he'd just gone out for a minute. And according to Michael, he was the one who'd delivered Creed his meal the other night.

"Norris," Max said. "We need to check his hands for gunpowder residue."

"We probably need to check every guard and any of the inmates who weren't in their cells."

"Yes, but Norris is the one. Trust me!" He radioed for someone to detain him. "Let's go get the security video."

When they reached the room from which they monitored every floor, the guard stood up. "Detective, I was taking care of a problem on the second floor when the shooting happened. The cameras were disabled while I was up there. We don't have any video."

Max went to the window and looked at the surrounding buildings. There were cameras on the police department building, but were there any on the roof? And would they have gotten video of this shooter?

There was a bank behind them, ten stories high. Maybe a camera there had gotten some video. He sent a detective to check.

Just then, he heard the transmission on the radio. "Exploded car bomb . . . Michael Hogan's car."

His breath caught in his chest. "Did you hear that?" he asked Forbes.

"Yeah, I heard it. They said it was Michael."

Max's gut lurched. He got on the radio. "Is Michael Hogan alive? Was he injured?"

Static was his reply, then finally, someone came back on. "Yes, he's alive, uninjured. Lucky man."

Max let out his breath and steadied himself. "I have to get over there," he said to Forbes. "Can you take it from here? Start interviewing the guards, starting with Norris. Make sure his skin and clothes are tested for residue."

"Sure thing. If it's him, we'll know soon enough."

CHAPTER 49

The call from Cathy came at ten as Holly was gathering things in the diaper bag to take Lily to Juliet's.

"Holly!" Cathy yelled. "Bomb . . . shooting . . . Creed . . ."

The phone was breaking up. Holly clutched it closer to her ear. "What? Cathy, I didn't hear you!" She could hear intermittent sirens in the background, staccato noises, cracked voices.

"Chaos here!" she heard Cathy say. "Bomb under Michael's car. Sniper . . . Creed was shot!"

Her lungs seized. "No," Holly said. "Did you say Creed was shot?"

"He's alive." The words allowed Holly to breathe again. "He's . . . hospital . . ."

Holly dropped the diaper bag.

"Michael and I . . . all right. Miller won't stop," Cathy said more clearly now, her voice vibrating as if she were walking.

Holly's heart was thudding so hard she couldn't hear Cathy's voice. "Which hospital?" she cried.

"The same hospital. Holly, be careful . . . crazy out here."

The signal disappeared, but Holly had heard enough. The hospital. She had to get to the hospital. She shoved the phone into her jeans pocket, grabbed Lily, and hurried out to her taxi in the garage. She loaded Lily into the car seat. Her hands trembled as she found the pacifier and gave it to her daughter. "It's okay, sweetie. Daddy's gonna be okay."

She struggled to find her key, digging through her purse in the front seat. She strained to see through her tears as she backed out of her driveway. "God, help him!" she whispered. "It seemed like a gift from you last night. That Lily's dad and I . . ."

She wiped her face. How could she have been so stupid, thinking he was a gift from God? A second chance? Maybe what she'd told him had been wrong. Maybe God hadn't redeemed her. Maybe he was all out of second chances.

"God, please! Just one more. Please . . ."

She called Juliet on the way, and Juliet agreed to meet her at the hospital and take Lily.

Holly wiped her face as she drove. *Please, God, don't let him die.*

What would she tell Lily if her dad was killed today? Would it be enough to tell her that he was a hero? That he was trying to do the right thing, trying to out a drug cartel that had ruined so many lives? She could tell her that he was courageous, that he was willing to sacrifice his life to do the right thing.

But she didn't want to tell her that.

God, please don't let that happen! I'm begging you.

She parked at the hospital, got Lily out of the car seat, grabbed the diaper bag and her purse, and headed inside. She went to the information desk, asked about Creed.

"Yes," the nurse said. "He came in half an hour ago, but no one can go back yet. Are you his wife?"

"No. Just . . . a friend."

"Well, we need someone in his family to fill out some paperwork. Do you know if he has insurance?"

"No . . . he doesn't. Can you just tell me . . . is he all right? Is he alive?"

"Yes, he's alive," she said. "I really can't give you any more information. I'll check and see if he's been taken to surgery."

Surgery? Then it was serious. She imagined ripped organs and internal bleeding, life draining out of him.

No sign yet of Juliet, so Holly went into the same waiting room where she'd waited that first night when Creed was poisoned. She held her baby against her chest and paced back and forth. She heard the sliding glass doors at the front open, a woman crying. She turned and saw Creed's parents coming in, his mother sobbing, his sister in tears too. His father went to the desk to get information.

Holly approached them. "Mrs. Kershaw?"

The woman turned. "Holly! Were you with Creed when it happened?"

"No," she said. "I just got a phone call."

"Is he alive? Is he going to make it? They said he was shot in the head!"

Holly's knees buckled, and she felt herself going down. His mother and sister caught her and lowered her into a chair. Sandra took the baby from Holly's arms.

"I didn't know that," Holly said, putting her head down between her knees. "I'm gonna be sick." No, she couldn't do this now. She had to be strong. She pulled herself back up.

"You're in love with him, aren't you?" His sister's question ripped through the air.

Holly didn't answer, just tried to control her breathing.

"Holly," his sister said again. "Are you two an item?"

Holly didn't have the energy or the inclination to lie. "I don't really know what we are." She looked around. "Are they going to let you go back? I have to know if he's all right."

The double doors flew open, and a nurse came out with a clipboard. "Kershaw family?"

His mother nodded and handed Lily back to Holly. "Frank, they're calling for us," she said.

His father left the paperwork and hurried toward the double doors. He didn't even see Holly and the baby as he raced by. Sandra stopped at the door. "Can she come with us?" she asked the nurse.

"Is she family?"

Holly stopped, expecting the nurse to block her.

"Yes," his mother said.

Holly bolted through the doors and followed them to Creed's room.

CHAPTER 50

Michael perspired under his Kevlar vest. The bomb that had been planted under his car was fairly sophisticated, rigged to his starter. If he hadn't used his remote key to start the engine, he would be dead, and so would Cathy.

Thank you, God.

"Creed's going into surgery this afternoon," Max said, clicking off his cell phone. "Bullet shattered two bones in his forearm. He was lucky. The other one only grazed the side of his head."

"Did it penetrate his skull?"

"No. Just the skin. A fraction of an inch and he'd be dead. Same as you. If you'd gotten into that car . . ."

"These people are ruthless," Michael said. "They don't care who they leave dead. So are there guards posted outside Creed's hospital room again?"

"Yeah. They've been there since he was admitted."

"Good. Miller isn't going to give up."

Michael wished he could focus on the evidence without the racing thoughts that he'd barely escaped the explosion. Cathy would have been in that car with him. She would be dead right along with him.

It helped a little that Creed's sniper was in custody. The guard who'd taken Creed his meal the other night—Sergeant Norris—was being questioned right now. He had apparently cut off the cameras in the jail before he did the shooting, but he hadn't realized that cameras from the bank behind the building would expose him.

"Has Norris confessed yet?" Michael asked.

"No," Max said. "He thinks they're questioning all the guards about which inmate could have done it. But Forbes says he smells like gunpowder, and we have the security video. I'm going to head over and watch the interrogation. I can't wait to lock that phlegm wad up in the same prison he guarded."

Miller's reach was so broad that it almost made Michael despair. Norris was just one of many men who did the drug broker's bidding. Norris had been the guard with the least compassion and the most sadistic bent. Michael figured Miller had bribed him with money or drugs. He wondered how long Norris had been dirty.

Feeling vulnerable, Michael looked around to see if anyone was on top of the surrounding buildings, taking aim again. His torso was protected, but his head was exposed. He needed to get out of here.

He stooped by his charred car, still hot and smoking. A CSI agent Michael had worked with before was taking pictures. "Brad, we weren't in the building that long," he told him. "Just long enough to get a marriage license. The bomb had to be planted fast."

"Looks like it was magnetic," Brad said. "It's still attached . . . here."

Michael slipped on a glove and touched the magnetic piece. He pulled it off, turned it over. The lab might be able to find a serial number or other evidence, but at the moment, there was nothing he could discern from the piece.

The bomb had been attached to the side of his SUV, facing away from the county clerk's office. "Still," Michael said. "They had to rig it to the starter somehow, right? How could they have done that so fast?"

"Not sure," Brad said. "We'll have to take the car into the lab and figure out what they did. They might have opened the hood somehow. Doors were blown off, so we can't tell yet if the glass was broken to give them access or if the door was jimmied."

"An adept car thief would have been able to get the door open without doing any of that."

"True," Max said. "So if they got in, they could have easily rigged it. Wouldn't take that long for a pro."

"How big is this operation?" the CSI asked.

"Big," Michael said. "Bigger and broader than you could imagine. Miller's my big fish, but he's not *the* big fish. It goes all the way to Colombia."

"Hey, Hogan!" Both Michael and Max turned as one of the other major crime detectives ducked under the yellow crime scene tape. "I got something!"

He was carrying an open laptop. Michael went toward him, Max following. "What is it?"

"Camera footage from this building over here," he said,

pointing to the building next to the parking lot. "Got a visual of the guy."

The sun made it hard to see the footage, but Michael shaded the screen with his hand. He saw a man coming across the parking lot with a backpack, ambling as if he had no particular place to go, then standing at the car door for a minute.

"He's using a pneumatic bladder to open the door," Max said.

The same thing cops used when people locked their keys inside their cars. Michael watched as the man opened the door, looking toward the courthouse building. Then he ducked inside and down to the floorboard. So far Michael hadn't been able to see his face—just his back and side.

The man backed out of the car, strung the wire out the driver's door and under the car, and bent to magnetically snap the rest of the device underneath the chassis. Michael wondered if he would have seen the cord when he approached the car. Maybe, maybe not.

The man stood, looked toward the building again, then turned and went back the way he'd come . . . toward the camera. His face was clear now.

"You guys know him?" Michael asked.

"Not me," Max said, glancing at his coworker. "You got an ID?"

"No, but Creed Kershaw might be able to tell us."

"Send me some stills of the guy," Max told him. "We'll head over there now and talk to him before he goes into surgery."

"What about the interrogation of Norris?" Michael asked.

"They're taping it."

"They won't let him go, will they?"

"No. We have too much on him. They're just going to let

him lie through his teeth and then hit him with the evidence. He's going to jail today. The judge will probably deny bond. I'd rather talk to Creed right now and track down this bomber. Come with me."

Michael stood and dusted off his hands.

"Let me know as soon as you get a name," the other detective said. "I'll get a warrant and we'll hunt him down."

Creed was just being prepped for surgery when Michael and Max got to the hospital. He'd been given the pre-anesthesia medications, and he looked like he was close to falling asleep. His speech was slurred, and he could barely hold his head up.

They cleared the room of his family and Holly and the baby so they could show him the photo. Creed tried to help, but he couldn't focus.

"Creed, it's real important, man. Can you tell us who this dude is?"

Creed lifted his head to look at the still picture on Max's phone. "That's who killed me?" he slurred.

Michael shook his head. "You're not dead, okay? No, he's not the guy. He's the one who tried to kill *me*."

"Really? What'd you do?"

"Nothing. We think he's working for Miller."

"Sure he is. Cousin or something. Did bombs in one of the Stans."

Michael gave Max a frustrated look. "One of the whats?"

"Afghanistan, I think . . . army."

Okay, that narrowed it down. "His name. Do you know his name?"

"Yeah. It's, uh . . . ." Creed closed his eyes, and his head fell back.

"Creed? Creed, stay with us for a minute. Tell us his name."

Creed's eyes opened again, and he looked at the picture on the laptop again. "That a Mac?"

"Yes. Creed, the guy. Tell us who this is."

Creed narrowed his heavy eyes on the screen again. "Yeah, that's Deep Dog. Name's Barks . . . Barker. Somethin' like that."

"You say he's Miller's cousin?"

"Yeah. He was there, driving for Miller . . . when they killed Loco."

The door opened and two nurses came in. "Okay, that's all, guys. We've got to go to the OR, get this arm fixed up. You doing okay, Mr. Kershaw?"

"Yeah . . . good." He closed his eyes, and this time Michael let him drift out.

"Barker or Barks," he told Max. "Nickname Deep Dog. Cousin. Army veteran. We can run with that, right?"

"That'll get us started," Max said. "Let's go."

CHAPTER 51

Leonard Miller sat on the deck of his four-thousand-square-foot beach home overlooking the Gulf. His jaw popped as he worked through his next move.

Jack, the attorney who had become his closest confidant these days, sat next to him, his body slouched, elbows on knees as he stared at Miller. "Lenny, this whole thing has turned the heat up on us. It's just a matter of time."

Miller's jaw popped again, his molars grinding together. He dropped his feet from the railing. "Tell me how this happened. How is it that Creed Kershaw survived . . . *three times*?"

"Norris was nowhere near as good a sniper as he said he was. Now he's being questioned. My guess is they know he poisoned Kershaw and that he was on the roof. If they don't already know Barker set the bomb, they will soon. He'll be next to go down."

"They won't talk. We'll funnel cash to their families."

"You really think they care that much about their families?"

"Then we offer your representation. Make sure—"

"You're kidding yourself, Lenny."

Miller got up, kicked his chair, then went through the French doors into his study. The furnishings had been here when he bought the place—things he never would have thought to buy. A decorator had done the place up to help it sell, and Miller had kept everything, down to the fake apples in a bowl on the counter. He'd had Jack offer cash under an Arab-sounding name. He'd walked right in with his clothes and his toothbrush.

No way had he believed as a kid he would ever live in a place like this. His mother would have loved it; she'd always dreamed of living on the beach. He wasn't willing to give it all up yet.

In the bedroom, his girlfriend Jasmine sat in the middle of the bed, a syringe on her lap and a tourniquet around her arm. "Wish you'd get into the heroin trade," she said in a raspy voice. "I wouldn't have to go get it myself."

"Stop whining. I've got the whole Panama City police force breathing down my neck, and you want me to diversify?"

He stood in the doorway as she found a vein and delivered the heroin to her bloodstream. The tension on her face melted, and she leaned back, eyes closed. That should keep her quiet for a while.

He turned to leave, but she called out. "Lenny?"

He looked back in. "What?"

"When I was at the dope house . . . there were these people . . ." Her voice drifted off, as if she'd lost her thought midsentence.

"What people? Jasmine?"

She rallied. "Huh?"

"You said there were people . . . what people? Was somebody following you?"

"No . . . not that. I woulda noticed. It was these tweekers, high outa their minds . . . bragging about mugging that taxi chick. Holly somebody . . ."

"Holly Cramer?" When she didn't answer, he crossed the room and bent over her, shook her. "Holly Cramer?"

She looked up at him with glazed eyes. "Yeah, her. They had her purse, credit cards, her IDs . . ."

He frowned and let her go. She wilted back against the pillows, her face flushing.

"Are they still there? At the house?"

"Were when I left."

"Floyd's house? On Evers Street?"

"Tha's the one," she slurred.

He wanted to slap her, but what good would it do? "What do you even go there for? You shouldn't be seen in places like that now that we're together."

"I'd be waiting all week," she whispered, tossing the syringe on the bed table. "Youdontrustanybodytacomehere . . . Wantedit . . . now."

Disgusted and wondering why he bothered with her, Miller went into the living room, sat down, and tried to think. Jack still sat on the deck, looking out at the ocean. "Jack, come here!" he called.

Jack turned and came back in. "What?"

"I'm getting an idea. Jasmine said she met these two tweekers when she was at the dope house."

"She's still going there? Somebody could follow her here. There are people who know she's with you now. You used to be smarter with all this stuff. You've been under the radar all this time, but they're looking for you, man. You gotta be more careful."

He slammed his foot against his coffee table. "Don't you think I know that? If the hits you set up had *worked*, we wouldn't be in this mess."

"Hits *I* set up? I was taking orders from you! I used your own cousin, who you said was a genius with bombs! Who could predict Hogan would use a remote to start his car? That the only person we could get who had access to the roof of the jail would miss and hit Kershaw's arm?"

Miller got up and went to the fireplace he had never used. He rubbed his lip, turned back. "What if we picked up those tweekers? Offered them a hunk of cash to break into Holly Cramer's house?"

"For what?"

Standing at the French doors, Miller scanned the beach from left to right, then back again. "To get her kid. Then we could get Creed where we want him."

"Where is that?"

"Dead."

"Lenny, what is it with you and kidnapping? You did that with her sister's kids, and everybody involved is either dead or in prison."

"Not everybody."

Jack shook his head with disgust. "Okay, so *you* got away. But your luck isn't going to hold forever." He sat down on the coffee table, knee to knee with Miller. "Listen to me, my friend. My advice is for you to get out of the country, or at least out of the state."

"I have business here. I'm supposed to pack up and leave all that?"

"Go somewhere else and use the same contacts. If you don't, once your contacts in Colombia realize the heat on you is building, they're going to quit doing business with you. They've probably gotten wind of it already. Get out of here while you can. Michael Hogan is not going to rest until he tracks you down, especially since he almost died today. He has a score to settle."

Miller didn't want to admit it, but Jack was right. If he didn't go, it was just a matter of time before he was locked up. As good an attorney as Jack was, he wasn't good enough to get him off all the charges he'd face. "The question is, how do I relocate and still keep my business booming?"

"Set up a meeting with your contact in Colombia, in some neutral location. Talk to him about your options. Move to another location and keep brokering. You could even broker for *this* area, but from a distant location. You don't have to be here. Or better—work for him in Colombia where you're safe, and keep up the flow to the states."

"What about Creed?"

Jack sat back, rubbed his temple. "Lenny, I'm trying to help you. Have someone else take care of Creed when things settle down. But you don't have to be anywhere near town."

It made sense. But it wasn't as easy as it sounded. "How do I get out of town with everybody looking for me?"

Jack thought that over for a moment. "You should've done it while the police were all over the bombing."

"So we need another distraction. But we have to take care of Creed before I leave town."

"What difference does it make? They have a boatload of evidence against you already. If they can't find you, you'll be okay."

"It matters because of what my people will think. That they can turn on us and get away with it. That they can talk to police and survive. What kind of operation will we have if people think we're soft?"

"He has the whole police force watching his back."

"So we get them to look away." He turned, an idea forming in his mind. As it took shape, a slow smile came to his face. "This could actually be fun."

Jack got up and shoved his hands through his hair. "I don't think fun should have anything to do with this. Fun is what sinks you every time. Fun lands people in prison."

Miller laughed. "Call one of the guys and have them pick up the tweekers who mugged Holly Cramer. I want to talk to them. I think we can use them."

"Bad idea," Jack said. "You gonna trust any of this to a couple of junkies who can't think straight?"

"They're just part of the plan. We'll send them to Holly Cramer's house."

"You don't think they'd get caught?"

"I don't *care* if they get caught. Set it up now, and let everybody know we'll need all hands on deck."

CHAPTER 52

Michael and the team learned pretty quickly that Barker, the one who'd planted the bomb, no longer lived at the address on his driver's license, but it didn't take long to track him to a new address. Michael and Max staked it out and took turns watching all night, but he didn't leave once. By morning, they, their father, and Al Forbes rode in three separate cars, ready to follow Barker the minute he came out. He finally pulled out of his driveway at ten a.m. and didn't seem to notice them staggered up and down the street. They followed him through town, three cars moving behind him, alternating the tail so the same car wasn't behind him all the time.

As Michael swapped with his father and came up behind Barker, he saw that he was on the phone. Then, without signaling, Barker made a sudden turn into a parking lot and drove into the alley behind the stores. Michael couldn't follow without being seen. None of them could go into the back driveway and remain unnoticed, so they blocked both ends of the driveway behind the building.

"What's he doing?" Max asked.

"Don't know, but I think he's on to us," Michael said. "Should we move in and make an arrest? He's not going to lead us to anybody if he saw us."

"Let me walk back there and see what I can see," Forbes said. "I'll act like an employee out smoking."

"All right," Michael said, "but stay back."

Forbes left his car and walked around the building, smoking like an employee who'd just stepped out the back of a store for a break. In the radio, Forbes told them what he saw. "Dude's parked like he's waiting for somebody," he said quietly. "He's on the phone, yelling, slamming his steering wheel. Something's not right. I'm guessing he made us and is calling for help."

"Time to make an arrest," Max said. "We've got him surrounded. There's a ten-foot cement block wall back there, so I don't think he can get away. If we block off the alley, we can get him. If we get this guy into custody, show him that we have evidence he's the one who planted the bomb under Michael's car, maybe we can make him talk."

Forbes came around the building, got back into Max's vehicle. They waited awhile, but Barker never came back out. Finally, Forbes—the only one they were sure Barker wouldn't recognize—went back around, cigarette in his mouth again.

After a few minutes, Forbes radioed back. "You're not going to believe this. Barker's gone. Car's empty."

Michael hit the steering wheel. "We have to check out every store. He had to go through a back door, or he has help here somewhere. It's doubtful he went over that wall at the back."

Forbes and Max drew their weapons and checked every back door. There were no unlocked doors, but if Barker had a friend working inside, someone could have let him in. They went around to the front and checked every store. No one admitted seeing anyone come in from the back in the last few minutes. While it was possible that someone was hiding Barker, the police couldn't search the back rooms of the stores without warrants.

Michael followed Max back out into the alley and looked up at the building. "There," Max said. "There's a camera. Let's find the building owner and get that video."

Time ticked by—time in which Barker could be getting away if he wasn't holed up in one of these stores. After an hour, the building owner showed up and gave them the day's video. They pulled it up on Max's computer and fast-forwarded to Barker's car pulling into the alley.

They watched, breath held, hoping they'd be able to see if someone let him in. They watched the footage of Forbes walking up, then leaving again. They couldn't see Barker inside the car, but suddenly, the driver's door opened and Barker got out. He climbed up on a Dumpster, got his balance, then leaped to the top of the cinderblock wall and disappeared on the other side.

Max cursed, and Michael kicked the building. "He could have gone a dozen different directions on the other side of that wall," Michael said. "Probably had somebody pick him up." He set his hands on his hips. "I can't believe we lost him."

"We'll just have to find him," Max said. "He's bound to go home eventually."

But Michael doubted it. Barker knew he was being followed. He wouldn't let his guard down now.

CHAPTER 53

For Holly, it had been an early morning after a sleep-interrupted night. Lily had demanded two feedings during the night, then had wakened for the day at five a.m. Between feedings, Holly's sleep had been shallow, and she'd dreamed of tragedies involving Creed.

She gave Lily a bath and dressed her for the day. Juliet would work at home today so that she could watch Lily and Robbie, since she hadn't yet been able to find a babysitter. Holly would go to the office and hunt down any facts she could find about Barker, the alleged bomber, and hope something she found might lead them to Leonard Miller.

She strapped Lily into her car seat and carried her out the side door from her kitchen into the garage, snapped the car seat into its base in the backseat of her taxi, and kissed her daughter's forehead. She'd probably be asleep before they'd driven a mile.

A crash turned her back to the house. Glass breaking . . . voices . . .

Her alarm system blared its warning. Holly went for the gun on her passenger seat as her phone began to ring. The alarm company.

She clicked it on and said, "Call the police. Someone's in my house!"

She left the call connected and dropped the phone into her pocket as she headed back in, leading with her firearm. Then she saw them . . . the two meth heads who'd mugged her days ago, awkwardly going back out the window the way they'd come in, as if they hadn't counted on the alarm going off.

"Hold it right there!" she shouted. "Don't move!"

But the girl kept scurrying through, cursing as she cut her hand on glass. The man pushed her out and dove out behind her.

Holly ran to the front door and bolted out. The two stumbled across the yard as the alarm kept blaring. Refusing to let them escape this time, Holly followed them, yelling for them to stop. She couldn't fire right here in a residential neighborhood, and they clearly weren't afraid of her.

Their drug abuse had taken its toll, and they weren't fast runners. Holly ran with all the strength she had, and when she caught up to them, she grabbed the girl's shirt and threw her against the man, knocking them both to the ground. "Stay down or I'll kill you!" she shouted. "Don't move your little finger!"

They cursed and lay facedown on the pavement as the sound of a siren swirled close.

"What did you take from my house?" she demanded, dripping with sweat.

"Nothing!" the girl shrieked. "We didn't have time! We

were told you weren't home and you didn't have a security system."

"Who told you that?" They didn't answer. "Who?"

When they still refused to speak, she bent and roughly searched their pockets, grabbed the girl's huge bag. She looked through it, trembling, and found her own wallet, her credit cards, her driver's license—things they'd taken from her purse the day they'd robbed her in her cab. It didn't look like they'd had time to get anything from her home.

How stupid could they be, breaking in through a window like that in broad daylight? What kind of idiots were these people?

When the police cars made it to her street, she waved them down to her. Keeping her gun on the thieves, she called out, "I'm Holly Cramer. I work for Michael Hogan. I have a concealed permit. These two just broke into my house."

The first cop out drew his weapon and shielded himself behind the door. "Drop the gun."

Holly tossed it toward them, out of the couple's reach. "Cuff them!" she shouted. "They mugged me a few days ago. There's a police report. You can check. I don't want them to get away."

The cop in the back car got out and got her gun. "I know her. I took her report. She's legit."

Holly breathed a sigh of relief as they gave her back her gun, cuffed the two thieves, then shoved them into the back of separate cars, the two foul-mouthed addicts cursing and spitting.

Holly wiped the sweat from her forehead. *Lily.* She had left Lily in the car. "Can we finish this at my house? My baby's in the car in my garage."

They agreed. Holly jogged back the few houses to her own house as the police cars moved into her driveway. She went back in the open front door, through the kitchen, and out to the closed garage, a police officer following her.

The back door of her taxi was still open.

Lily lay sound asleep in her car seat, undisturbed by the chaos. But then Holly saw it . . . wires weaving through the straps and clip over the baby's ribs. A device of some kind placed on the top of the seat near her head.

A bomb!

"No . . . dear . . . God . . ." She stood frozen, unable to move.

The cop stepped up behind her. "Ma'am?"

"A bomb . . . on the car seat. The break-in was just a distraction."

The cop began shouting into his radio as Holly's focus narrowed down to those wires.

CHAPTER 54

Creed was sick of the hospital gown and wanted desperately to change into his own clothes, but his sutures and the Velcro cast on his arm made it difficult. Maybe when his mother came back in he would get her to help him change into clothes that made him feel more human. Cathy sat next to the bed, questioning him and taking notes. Though the police had questioned him for hours already, she still grilled him, hoping to jog loose some additional memory—any memory—that would help them locate the man who had changed her life three years ago.

The hospital phone rang, and he jumped. Most people called him on his cell phone. He hadn't gotten a single call on the hospital room's phone since he'd been here. He tried to reach it with his right hand, but Cathy sprang up. "I'll get it."

She picked up the phone and handed it to him. "Hello?"

"Hello, Creed." It was a man's voice, one he couldn't quite place. "Do you know where your baby is?"

Creed sat up straighter. "Who is this?"

"A recent acquaintance," he said. "Sorry our little encounters didn't work out. But this one surely will."

Miller. He mouthed the name to Cathy and slid his legs off the bed, got to his feet. "What do you want?"

"I wanted to let you know there's a bomb on your baby's car seat. If anyone tries to move her out of it, she'll blow."

Creed bent over and drew in a breath. "What . . . do you want?"

"I want you to walk out of that hospital and drive to where I tell you."

Creed looked frantically around the room. Where were his clothes? "I . . . I don't have my car here. I was brought in an ambulance."

"Have someone drive you to your car. Come the rest of the way alone. Give me your cell phone number. I'll call you back in twenty minutes."

Creed almost couldn't breathe. He rattled off his number.

"Oh, and if you talk to Holly Cramer, tell her not to do anything stupid," Miller said. "Those wires have a hair trigger sometimes."

The phone clicked off.

"What did he say?" Cathy said. "What did he want?"

"Have to call Holly." He grabbed his cell phone off the bed table. "Get my clothes. They must be in the closet."

Creed's heart slammed against his sternum as he waited for Holly to pick up. Her phone rang once, then she clicked on. Her voice was quiet, trembling. "Creed . . ."

"Is she okay?" he asked.

"There's a bomb," she said just above a whisper. "The police are here but they can't move it or it might explode. She's sleeping, but if she wakes up and starts to move . . ."

"Holly, Miller wants me to leave the hospital. He'll call me back with instructions. Just hang on. I'll do whatever they say."

He heard the slurp of her sniffs, voices in the background. Finally, she whispered, "Be careful, Creed."

Creed hung up and Cathy handed him his clothes. "I have to get out of here," he said. "Help me get dressed."

Cathy did, then hammered him with questions as they headed out.

Max was waiting at Creed's car, which was parked in his parents' driveway. Thankfully, Creed's parents weren't home, or they would have tried to stop him. But it wasn't his own safety he cared about. It was Lily's.

"We wired your car so we can monitor what's going on," Max said.

"No, they'll find out and hurt Lily."

"He already knows we're all over this. There are police at Holly's house. They know you would have gotten us involved."

"I have to hurry. He's going to call any minute."

"Then leave the wire in place. We want to follow you to wherever he intends to send you."

"No, he said to come alone," Creed said. "I have to do what he says."

"All right, but we'll set up near where you are in case we have to move in."

"What if they find out and object to that?"

"Creed, we're not going to let you go off the grid with them. This is the way it has to be."

Creed didn't have time to argue. He got into his car and tried to think like his enemy. Why would Miller risk this, knowing the police were swarming around?

His phone rang as he pulled out of the driveway. He swiped it on and set it on speakerphone. "I'm alone. What do you want?"

"I want you, Creed. Come to 202 Sherman Avenue. It used to be a car wash, but it's out of business. Wait in the parking lot, and when I'm sure you're alone and no cops are in the vicinity, I'll give you further instructions."

Creed made a U-turn and headed in that direction. "Do you have a remote to detonate that bomb?"

Miller only laughed.

"Do you have a remote?" Creed yelled.

"As a matter of fact, I do. But it won't take the remote to blow that car up. Just a little movement."

Creed felt as if the wind had been knocked out of him. "If you hurt my baby, I will spend the rest of my life tracking you down . . . There won't be anywhere you can hide."

More laughter. "Just go to the address, Creed. Do as we say and things will go better for the baby." Miller ended the call.

Creed wiped the sweat from his forehead. His mouth was dry; he could hardly breathe. He pulled over for a moment, typed the address into his GPS, saw where to go. Then he clicked on Holly's number again, hoping she had it on vibrate so it wouldn't wake Lily.

Her voice was barely above a whisper. "Creed?"

"Have they gotten the bomb disconnected?"

"Not yet," she said, her voice trembling. "She's still sleeping. What do they want you to do?"

"He gave me the address of some car wash. I'm headed there now."

"He's going to make you do something devastating. Commit a crime, kill somebody . . ."

"I'll do what I have to do."

"I don't want you to die. I just . . . found you."

He noticed a helicopter circling overhead. "You weren't looking for me."

"No, I wasn't, but now . . ."

"Holly, there's no choice," he cut in. "It was stuff I did that got me into this. Whatever happens, I caused it. I can't let Lily or you suffer for my sins. If I have to die for my daughter, so be it."

Holly was silent for a long moment. Creed saw the car wash up ahead, and a building in back. "I'm there now. I'll call you back."

"Creed?"

He hung up and pulled into the parking lot. No cars, no sign of life. He drove into a bay.

The phone rang again and Creed clicked the speakerphone. "I'm here."

"Go into the building. Door's unlocked. I'll be watching you through the security camera. I'll see every move you make." Creed got out of his car and started toward the building, the pain in his arm shooting through his bones.

"Now, listen carefully," Miller said. "You're going to walk in there and go to the desk in the office. In the top drawer, you'll find a loaded revolver."

Creed felt sick. They *were* going to make him kill somebody.

He opened the door and went in, found the office and the .38. He took it out of the drawer and checked; it was fully loaded. "What do you want me to do with this?"

"Walk to the middle of the lobby where the tarp is. Sit down on the tarp, then finish the job we started."

Creed's mind raced. What was Miller telling him to do? The gun . . . the tarp . . . the job . . .

Suddenly it hit him. They wanted him to be his own victim.

CHAPTER 55

Two men from the bomb squad, clad in padded gear and helmets like those Holly had seen in war movies, tried to get her to back away from the car. She refused.

"I'm the only one who can keep my baby calm," she said in a voice as quiet as she could manage. "If the bomb goes off and kills her, let it kill me too."

"We don't have that option, ma'am," Saginaw, the lead bomb expert, told her. "We have to clear the area. This bomb looks powerful enough to maim, dismember, or kill everyone within its radius."

Sweat dripped into Holly's eyes. "You're wasting time," she said. "I'm staying with my baby, so leave me alone. Get. The bomb. Off of her."

They conferred for a moment, and she fully expected someone to tackle her and cuff her and haul her away from her daughter. But no one did. Clearly the others were taking the bomb seriously enough not to want to walk into its radius to remove her, or risk making noise enough to wake Lily.

"Ma'am, we're trying to protect you."

"Stop calling me ma'am and focus on my daughter instead of me."

"We're not sure the bomb is hooked up," Saginaw told her. "First of all, he didn't have a lot of time to plant it. We can't see where the wires are connected."

She let out a ragged breath. "He's fast. He set the bomb under Michael's car, and he didn't have much time then either. Don't take any chances, please."

"The bomb does appear to be live. It's the same type of device that was put under Michael Hogan's car. That had considerable power, and add to that the gasoline in the car's gas tank . . . They might have this thing set up to detonate remotely, but we can't locate the detonator without moving the baby. Disconnecting the car seat from the base might be the trigger to detonate, but we're seventy percent sure that these wires wrapped around the seat are just for show."

Seventy percent wasn't good enough. "He had time to plant it. It didn't take him long with Michael's car."

"We're considering everything, ma'am." The other guy opened the opposite car door after examining it for wires, then slipped onto the seat, videoing the wires on that side of the car seat.

Holly couldn't breathe.

———

The moment Michael heard of the standoff at Holly's house, he notified Cathy, Juliet, and Jay, all of whom rushed to be there for their sister, even though the police had closed off the street, evacuated the surrounding homes, and roped off a perimeter far beyond the bomb's reach.

Cathy got Holly on the phone. "Honey, are you all right?"

"Yes," Holly whispered. "Lily isn't."

"You need to get out of there," Cathy said. "Let the bomb squad work on it, but you don't have to be there."

"I'm not leaving," Holly repeated. "If Lily goes, I go. If she wakes up, I need to be here."

Cathy burst into tears. "What can we do, honey?"

"Just pray," Holly whispered. "That's what we need."

CHAPTER 56

Max and his men set up a mobile command center in the parking lot of a skating rink just blocks away from the car wash where Creed had been sent. Michael paced outside the van, his phone to his ear. He'd found the owner of the car wash, learned it was rented to an LLC called Denton Enterprises. "I need to know about that building. Is the power still on?"

"Yes," the owner said. "We're trying to sell the car wash, so we've kept the power on."

"What about a security camera? Do you have one inside?"

"Yes, and it's still functional too."

"Does it save video to a hard drive on the premises, or is there a wireless link that sends the image somewhere else?"

"Wireless link," the owner said. "I can give you the login info if you want to get on that wireless network, but I don't know who's monitoring it right now."

Michael took down the info, then stepped into the van. "Which one of you is the computer tech?"

A young, bald guy with Buddy Holly glasses lifted his hand. Michael told him about the camera. "If we get on their network, what can we find out?"

The computer guy—who went by the name of Dex— scratched his ear. "I could pretty quickly locate the computer monitoring the image. I could also set up a feed so we could monitor it as well. But I need to get close enough to the building that I can access their wireless signal."

"The owner said it's video only, no audio. He told me the location of the camera, right over the front door. I think we could go in through a window in another room at the back and not be seen. Then, while you work on getting on the network, I can assess the situation."

Max didn't like it. "It's too dangerous. They could have snipers all around that place, or it could be rigged with bombs too. It could be a trap."

"Send a team ahead of us to scour the area for snipers," Michael said. "But if he has people on the premises, he wouldn't have to monitor things on camera. He would have had them kill Creed and be done with it. No, he set this whole thing up so that he could manage it from a distance."

"Or so you would come."

"I'm willing to risk it, Max. We have to find this guy. He killed our brother and he's not going to kill that baby!"

Max turned on him. "You think I don't know that? But I'm still on the police force. I have to follow protocol. We have policies and procedures for good reasons. If you go in there like an action hero and get blown to smithereens, I have to deal with another dead brother! You want me to face Mom with that bit of information?"

Michael sat down on a crate, his head in his hands. "Then

let's think this through. Barker is Miller's bomb guy. We were watching him all night and all day, until he got away in the alley. We know the bomb was placed on the baby's car seat in the past hour. He's only had time to go to Holly's and plant the bomb. No time for a car wash."

"He could have rigged the place yesterday."

Michael thought it over. "No, I don't think so. Miller expected Creed and me to both be dead. He needed time to regroup after his failures yesterday. I doubt he would have instantly had a Plan B. He probably came up with this plan last night, at the earliest, and we know that Barker didn't leave his house last night."

"The question is, are you willing to stake your life on that?"

Michael checked his watch. Time was running out. "Yes, Max. I am. I trust my gut on this."

Max turned to Dex. "Do *you* trust his gut?"

"No," Dex said. "But I do trust his facts. I'm willing to go. It'll make a great story to attract chicks." He grinned.

Michael glanced at Dex, wondering if the kid was taking this seriously enough. He turned to the satellite image of the car wash and pointed out his route. "We'll go on foot, come up through the woods."

Max stared at the map for a moment.

"It could work. I can do this, Max. You know I can."

"But what about Dex? He sits in an office all day."

Dex shoved his glasses up his nose. "Throw me this bone so I can prove I've got some chops. I'm all in."

Michael smiled.

Max raked his hand through his hair, then nodded. "All right. But whatever you do, don't let Miller see you on camera. And give Creed a warning not to give away the fact that he sees you or is talking to you. If Miller has a detonator, we don't want to give him a reason to set it off."

While the team went ahead of them to search for snipers, Michael armed himself, then made sure Dex was armed. Though the computer whiz might be rusty with a gun, he would have had some training before joining the force. Dex loaded his computer into a backpack, and they set out to run through the woods to the building, with Michael praying that Dex would be a help and not a bumbling detriment.

They hid in the trees just behind the car wash. The team hadn't found any sign of snipers, but a helicopter circled suspiciously overhead, lower than Michael would have expected this far from an airport. Did Miller have someone monitoring the building from the air, or was that a police helicopter? No, Max never would have ordered air surveillance. He would know it could set Miller off. It had to be Miller's.

When the chopper turned north and vanished from view, Michael signaled to Dex and they both ran to the building. Pressed against the wall, they worked their way to the door. It was still unlocked, but they couldn't use it, because the camera would pick them up.

Michael went to a window on the side where the camera was mounted. He looked in, saw Creed sitting on the tarp, talking into his phone. Slowly, he opened the window. Creed jerked, but Michael held out a hand to silence him.

He could hear Miller's voice taunting Creed on Creed's speakerphone, telling him to pull the trigger and save his child. So that was what he wanted. Michael climbed in. He pressed flat against the wall in the camera's blind spot. Dex came in the window behind him, set his stuff on the floor as quietly as possible, and pulled out his laptop.

Michael pointed to the camera overhead, showed Creed that he was out of the camera's sight. Creed seemed to understand. He kept talking into the phone. "You want me dead, free my child. Until then, we don't have anything to talk about."

"You're not running this show, Creed. I am."

Michael signaled for Creed to cut the call off.

"Call me back when my daughter is out of danger." Creed ended the call and looked down at the tarp.

"They can't hear us unless you're on the phone," Michael said in a normal voice, "and we're out of the camera's view. They don't know we're here, so keep looking down, and don't let them see you talking to us."

Creed covered his mouth and kept his eyes on the floor. "Have you freed Lily?"

"Not yet, but I'm told that the bomb may not even be connected. It may be just for show. Just keep putting him off. You're doing great."

A vein on Creed's forehead had swollen with the strain. "I'll do what I have to do to protect my child," he said behind his hand. "If I have to . . ."

"Creed, listen to me. Nothing will be gained if you kill yourself. If he has the power, he could still blow up Lily after you've done what he says. Just hold on."

Creed looked up at the camera, his skin shining with sweat. He still held the gun to his head.

"Lower the gun," Michael said. "You don't know that weapon. It could have a hair trigger. Keep it down."

Creed slowly lowered the gun, pointed it toward the floor.

Michael glanced at Dex. He was typing feverishly. "Every cop in Southport is working on this, Creed. We're trying to track the link where this camera is being monitored. This is

Dex. He's working on it right now, and it'll tell us the location of the computer linked to it."

Creed glanced at them but didn't let his gaze linger.

"If we can find the computer monitoring this camera, maybe it'll lead us to Miller, but I need you to hold out. I need you to promise me that you're not gonna pull that trigger. Can you do that?"

Creed gritted his teeth. "No, I don't think so," he muttered without moving his mouth.

Michael tried again. "Creed, your life is more valuable than this."

"No, it's not," he said behind his hand. "It's not more valuable than hers."

"Both of your lives are valuable. You're her father. She needs you."

"I'm dispensable," he said.

"You're not. Don't give Miller that power."

Creed just kept his eyes on the floor.

The phone rang again. Creed looked down. "It's a different number every time," he muttered behind his hand. Michael signaled for him to answer.

Dex continued to work frantically.

"Don't hang up on me again," Miller said. "And put that gun back to your head."

"Is my baby free yet?" Creed asked.

"Of course not. Looks like we have a standoff here."

Creed swallowed, and the vein on his forehead throbbed.

Miller's voice sounded impatient. "The ball's in your court."

Creed looked up at the camera. "This is not a negotiation."

"Come on, Creed, what have you got to lose?" Miller asked, his voice as slick as pond sludge. "You're going to be charged with murder, you've shamed your family, you have all of us gunning for you, you've brought nothing but danger to your baby and her mother. Let's face it, kid. You have nothing to live for."

"I have a daughter," Creed choked out.

"Not for much longer. She'll be waking up soon."

Creed swallowed and closed his hand over the gun. "If I do it . . . how will you free her? The bomb could still go off."

"I'll call Holly and tell her how to disconnect it."

Michael shook his head, signaling Creed.

"I'm hanging up now, Creed. The minute you do the deed, your baby will be safe. I'm watching you."

"Why should I trust you? You're a sadistic, psychopathic liar."

"Yes, but I'm all you've got." The phone clicked off, and Creed wilted.

"If that bomb is connected," Michael said, "he's going to kill her no matter what you do. If it's not, then what a waste that would be."

"I just want this to be over," Creed muttered under his hand as he rubbed his face to hide his words. "Why can't they disconnect that bomb? What is taking them so long?"

Dex was sweating, working frantically on his computer.

"Creed, just drag it out a little longer."

Creed's face twisted in confusion, and the gun shook in his hand. He dropped his head as sobs overtook him. "I don't know what to do."

Finally, Dex shouted, "Got it!"

Michael knelt beside him, studied the monitor, saw the server and the address where the camera was linked. "We have an address, Creed!"

Creed looked up at the camera.

"Do you hear me?" Michael asked. "Put the gun down. Your daughter and her mother need you."

Creed didn't answer.

"I'm patching this feed into the command center so we can keep monitoring him," Dex said.

As soon as Dex had closed his laptop and loaded it into his backpack, Michael said, "Creed, we have to go, but you're not alone. The command center is watching you now too. All you have to do is trust me, and believe that your life has value. God isn't finished with you, Creed. I don't think Holly is either."

Creed lowered the gun, stared down at it. Michael didn't know if he'd gotten through to him, but he had to go. He motioned for Dex to climb back out the window, then he followed.

They paused outside and listened for the telltale whine of the helicopter's engine. They couldn't hear it, so they cut back through the woods, running back to the command center. On the way, Michael called Max. "Did you get the address Dex sent?" he asked, out of breath.

"Yeah. Good work. And the patch works—we can see and hear everything. Creed's really sweating. Is he gonna hold out?"

"Does he have the gun to his head?" Michael asked.

"Not right now," Max said.

"Let's get the SWAT team assembled and get over there." Michael prayed Creed would give them time.

CHAPTER 57

It seemed to Holly that the three men on the bomb team worked as slowly as an underwater dance team, videotaping the car seat from every angle, examining it via a camera out of the bomb's range. Holly stood against the wall of her garage in the hot, padded jumpsuit they'd forced her to put on. When her baby's head turned and her sleepy eyes came open, Holly lunged toward her.

"Stay back!" Saginaw told her.

"But she's going to kick and cry. The wires . . . she'll hit them."

She could see the sheen of his sweat under the mask and helmet. The suit must weigh fifty pounds, and the padding was suffocating.

"It's okay, sweetie," she said in a soft voice.

Lily looked around, disoriented. She grunted and swung a tiny fist.

Holly couldn't breathe. "I have some breast milk in bottles in that bag on the floorboard," she said. "I could try to feed her. It would keep her still and calm."

"Too dangerous."

When Lily began to cry, Holly moved anyway. Wiping the sweat off her forehead, she reached for the baby bag on the floorboard. There were no wires attached to the bag—she had heard the bomb techs say that earlier. She slid the bag as slowly as she could until she had it out of the car.

Lily saw her mother and cried more loudly, her arms flailing.

Holly unzipped the diaper bag. She had six bottles there, each with three or four ounces. Five had been refrigerated, but one was still warm from her latest pump before leaving. She pulled out the small bottle and, making sure not to jiggle a wire, put it gently into Lily's mouth.

Lily instantly stilled and began to suck. Holly drew in a deep, long breath.

The bomb tech in the backseat bent down and moved some screwdriver-shaped object along the wires. When would this be over? What would she do with Lily when the bottle was empty?

She concentrated on keeping her hands steady as she fed her daughter. Lily wasn't in distress. She didn't know any of the danger surrounding her. If only Holly could unsnap her seat from its base and take her out of harm's way. If she could just hold her tight in her arms, smell her little head . . .

The phone vibrated, and Holly saw that it was Creed. She grabbed the phone. "Hey."

"How is Lily?"

"She's awake."

"No, God . . ."

"She's feeding from a bottle. She's still for now."

"For now," he repeated.

"Creed, they told me what he's ordered you to do. Just wait, please. They're working on it."

Creed cut the call off, and Holly's face twisted in anguish. She wiped her eyes with her sleeve.

After a few minutes, the bottle was empty, and Lily opened her eyes and looked up at her mother, kicking again. Holly started to sing in a wobbly voice. "Hush little baby, don't say a word, Mama's gonna buy you a mockingbird . . ."

As she sang, she stroked the center of Lily's forehead softly with her index finger, and Lily relaxed and stopped moving. Slowly, her eyes drifted shut again. As long as Holly kept singing, maybe her baby would be all right.

The address linked to the car wash camera was in Ashland Park, an upscale neighborhood on St. Andrews Bay. Michael drove by to do a threat assessment. The two-story house, built several feet above sea level, had a circular driveway, and the front doors were ornate with custom leaded glass. It didn't look like a place where someone like Miller would live. Michael had pictured a cave with decaying rodents stinking up the place.

He headed to the parking lot on 23rd Street where the SWAT team would meet him. Waiting in his car, he did a Google search of the address. A real estate listing from six months ago came up, with twenty-five photos of the interior of the house. He studied the pictures, drawing a crude blueprint of the house in his small notebook. There were images of various views of the yard. The backyard was on the bay, though there was a pool close to the house. He counted three back doors, plus the door into the garage and the front door. They would have to cover them all.

There were ten windows on the front—four on the first floor, six on the second, and the back of the house was mostly glass—French doors and floor-to-ceiling windows. He did a quick search to see who had bought the property. It was a Pakistani-sounding name—Palash Khan—and there was no mortgage. Someone had paid cash.

That was the way a drug kingpin would do it. He'd hire a lawyer to make the deal, pay cash under an assumed name. If this was indeed Miller's house, he had plunked down $1,340,000 for the property two months ago.

Michael couldn't believe Miller had been living right here in Panama City in plain sight.

He did one more drive-by, this time analyzing the terrain, certain Miller's guards would be watching for any sign of intruders or police. The SWAT team wouldn't have much time once they got there. They would have to do a high-risk entry, ramming the doors at two or three breach points, then moving through the house with speed and precision, restraining anyone they found inside.

Miller wouldn't go down without a fight. He would be willing to kill anybody in his path to get away.

He hoped Lily and Creed had time to wait for the SWAT team to get here. Anxiety pulsed through him as he waited. He picked up the phone, called Cathy.

"What's the status?" he asked when she answered.

"They're telling us Lily woke up. Holly's kept her quiet, but she's right there, in the bomb radius."

"We found Miller's digs. I'm waiting for the SWAT team."

"Are you sure it's his?"

"It's where Creed's camera is being monitored from. It's a 1.3-million-dollar house, so it's not just some hideout. I think we've got him."

Cathy drew in a deep breath. "I wish I were there."

"Don't worry, I won't let him get away this time. I can't go in with the SWAT team since I'm not on the force, but I'll be outside, waiting for them to drag him out."

"Be careful, Michael. He'll shoot his way out. I don't want to lose another fiancé."

"I don't want you to either."

"I want to live with you for the rest of my life. I want to have babies with you. I want to see your face the first time you hold our son or daughter . . ." Her voice broke off.

"You will, baby."

"Please be careful. Let the SWAT team do the heavy lifting."

When Max arrived with the SWAT team, Michael's adrenaline surged as he put on his Kevlar vest. These guys, many of whom worked as patrol officers or detectives and gathered for SWAT operations only when they were needed, had trained for years to do this kind of thing. Their choreography for high-risk entries was precise and well rehearsed. There was no need to go over what they were to do when they got inside.

Michael showed them the pictures of the house and the blueprint he'd drawn, and he quickly went over the terrain and layout with them.

Max added, "You can count on these people being armed. We have no idea how many are in the house."

"The three-car garage is closed," Michael said, "and there aren't any cars in the driveway out front. I'm hoping that means there aren't a lot of people inside. Miller likes to keep himself separated from others in his operation so they can't identify him. Occasionally, he screws up, like with Creed, but for the most part, he's got a small inner circle. So the place is probably not full of people, but the ones who are there will be dangerous."

The SWAT team, outfitted in all their gear, loaded into the van, and the van pulled onto the street and headed to Gulfmoor Avenue.

It pulled to a quick stop just out of sight of the house, in case Miller or his men looked out the window, and the SWAT members unloaded like Navy Seals at war. Michael waited in the van. A few of the lead men had cameras on their weapons, and he watched their progress on the video screen with Dex.

They entered with no trouble, and from what Michael could see on the monitor, the foyer was empty as they criss-crossed inside. He heard what sounded like a door closing, footsteps running.

They cleared the living room just past the foyer, the kitchen and pantry, the dining room. There was a smoking bong pipe lying on its side.

Someone motioned for them to go down the hall toward the right. They found an office with a computer, and when the SWAT team's camera was pointed at the display, there was Creed live on the screen, drenched with sweat and still holding that gun. Miller was nowhere in sight.

Michael heard screaming, and Dex pointed to the square that showed the video feed of another room. Michael saw a woman on the bed being handcuffed. They pulled her up, and she staggered. "I didn't do anything. It's him you want. Not me!"

"Where is Leonard Miller?" someone asked.

"He left me here. I don't know where he is."

"How long ago did he leave?"

"I don't know," she cried. "Half an hour, maybe."

Michael glanced at the other squares, feeds from the other cameras moving through the house. There didn't seem to be anyone else anywhere in the house.

"I'm on probation," she said. "I can't go back to jail. I didn't do anything. I was just sleeping here."

"Tell us where he is."

"I told you, I don't know. He's with Jack."

"Jack who?"

"Jack, the attorney. I don't know his last name."

Michael got on the radio. "That would be Jack Humphrey, guys. I'm getting his address now."

He waited as Dex typed in Humphrey's name, and the address came up. It was a house about six blocks away. "Got it," he said into the radio. "Let's leave someone to take care of her, but we need to get over there."

Satisfied that the house was empty, the SWAT team filed back into the van and raced toward the new address. As they drove, Max called the DA. "I need a search warrant at Jack Humphrey's house," he said, and gave the address. "Leonard Miller is with him. We think they went there."

The DA, who wanted Miller almost as badly as the Hogans did, texted him a file with the warrant. Dex quickly printed it out. Humphrey's house turned out to be a swanky modern home also on the beach. Clearly, representing criminals of this caliber paid well.

As the SWAT team filed out again, Michael waited in the van. He watched on the monitor as the doors were rammed in, and the team called out, "Police! Search warrant!"

He heard a staccato roar overhead and looked out the van's window. There was a helicopter overhead, circling the house. Then he saw Leonard Miller, waiting on the roof. Michael grabbed the radio mike. "He's on the roof. Repeat, he's on the roof, and a helicopter is about to land."

He grabbed his rifle and jumped out of the van, aiming at the roof. Gunfire shattered the air, and one of the SWAT men guarding the front windows dropped.

Michael saw Miller, rifle in his arms, darting across the peak of the roof to the side of the house. "Man down!" Michael shouted into the radio. "Subject still on the roof!"

The downed man—a buff ex-marine who'd been shot in the knee—dragged himself closer to the house, out of range of the shooter.

"Hang on, help is coming," Michael said.

Michael got behind the SUV in the driveway and scanned the roof again. He couldn't see Miller now, but he must still be up there. The helicopter had circled south. Michael might be able to find a way onto the roof through the house, but by then Miller might be able to get away. Rifle butt against his shoulder, his eye focusing through the gun scope, Michael slowly scanned the roof. No sign of Miller now.

When another SWAT member came out of the house to cover the front, Michael slowly made his way around the house, watching the roof.

There was nothing to climb on the side of the house, but in the back was a deck several feet off the sand, and an open arbor over it. Michael quietly climbed the steps to the deck, then stood on the rail to reach the top of the arbor and pull himself up. He found a foothold that allowed him to see over the edge of the roof.

There he was. Miller crouched next to the chimney, his back to Michael. Michael heard the hum of the helicopter returning, hovering over the flatter part of the roof on the back of the house. Miller went toward it, hair whipping in the helicopter's wind.

Michael fired but missed. Miller dropped, then came back up firing. Michael crouched as bullets whizzed over his head, from both Miller and the helicopter. The bird lifted and fled south again, leaving the roof quiet.

Michael heard footsteps across the roof. He peered over the edge again; Miller had vanished.

Michael pulled himself onto the roof, got his footing, and headed for the chimney in the center of the roof. Across from it was the door through which Miller had come to the roof. He saw Max stick his head out, nod that he saw Michael, and then step onto the roof, followed by another team member. Quietly, deftly, they crouched, rifles poised. Michael pointed to the area behind them, and they turned and separated. Michael made sure his side of the roof was clear, then followed his brother.

Then he saw him—Miller moving behind a ridgeline, his automatic rifle aimed at Max. Michael fired. The impact of the bullets bounced Miller, and he dropped his weapon.

"Got him!" Michael headed for Miller to get the rifle and restrain him, but Miller grabbed the rifle again, pointed it toward Michael . . .

Michael pulled the trigger again, spraying bullets at the man who had brought so much terror and grief to his family . . . the man who had terrorized Cathy and Juliet and Holly . . . the man who had put the baby and Juliet's kids in so much danger. Miller convulsed again as the bullets relieved him of any further chance to kill. He dropped the rifle, and his body jerked and twisted until he stopped moving, facedown on the hot roof.

The helicopter came back, rocking from side to side as it lowered. Someone inside began firing. Max ducked behind the chimney and returned fire. The pilot banked and flew away, trailing black smoke.

Max moved closer to Miller, his weapon ready. Careful not to slip on the incline, he stooped next to him and checked for a pulse.

"Maggot meat," he said, breathless. "He can rot in hell."

"What about the others?" Michael asked.

"We got the maid and Jack Humphrey downstairs," Max said. "I think one or both of them might talk if we make their lives miserable enough."

"Can I question him about the bomb?"

"Go ahead."

Michael went down the staircase into the house and found Humphrey lying facedown on the hardwood floor, hands and feet bound. Michael pulled him up and shoved him into a chair. "Your buddy's dead, and things aren't looking good for you. There's a bomb on a baby's car seat. If it goes off, you'll be a co-conspirator in the murder of an infant. I don't have to tell you how a jury will feel about that."

Humphrey closed his eyes. "There's no detonator. The guy who set it didn't have enough time to get everything connected. If you don't believe me, check my cell phone. Barker texted me that he didn't have time to get it right."

Michael looked around. "Who has his phone?"

The cop who had taken Humphrey's phone pulled it out of the evidence bag. Michael slipped on rubber gloves and checked the messages. Around the time that the bomb on Lily's seat was discovered, someone had texted: *Task completed. No time to connect things. Made it look convincing.*

He made a few quick calls to check the source of the message, and when they concluded that it was, indeed, Barker, he called the bomb squad and told them. He hoped Holly would soon be free.

The next call he made was to Creed.

———

Michael's call didn't completely convince the bomb squad, who were trained to expect tricks from those who meant to do harm. As Lily began to fuss and cry again, they gently pulled on the wires entangled with the latch across her rib cage, and the wires moved freely. They continued pulling until they saw the end of the wire, which had been simply wrapped around the wire at the underside of the car seat.

Saginaw unlatched the belt holding Lily, slipped the straps from her shoulders, and pulled the crying baby out. Holly took her quickly, holding her tight and weeping with gratitude.

"We need you to get out of the radius. It's still a live bomb, even though there's no detonator."

Holly did what she was told this time and ran through the house and out the front door with her baby, across the yard to her sisters and brother who waited in Juliet's van on the other side of the barricade. She got into the backseat and held her baby close, rocking back and forth. "Thank you, God. Thank you for my baby . . ."

When Lily had calmed and Holly could think, she called Creed. "She's all right. We got Lily out, and we're safe."

She could hear the emotion in his voice. "Michael told me. Thank God. I thought . . ."

"Me too. But Miller's dead. It's really over."

She heard Creed's rush of breath, sob-like sounds . . .

"Lily will grow up knowing her daddy is a hero."

CHAPTER 58

Creed put the gun on the floor and slid it away from him across the tarp as the sound of sirens came from the distance. He knelt on the blue plastic. He would have been wrapped up in the tarp and dragged out like a discarded rug.

But God had come through. Trembling, he covered his face and wept.

The door flew open, and police moved inside, weapons drawn, making sure it wasn't a trap. "Creed Kershaw?"

"Yeah, that's me."

"Are you able to stand?"

Creed didn't know why they would think that he wasn't capable of standing. He got to his feet, cradling his casted arm. "I'm fine. I just want to see my baby."

"We need a statement from you at the police department. Your daughter and her mother will meet you there."

In the backseat of the police car, Creed leaned his head

against the seat. He could handle anything, he thought. If he had to go to jail for his crimes, he would. If he still had to face a murder charge, he would survive. Whatever happened now, he knew that God wasn't finished with him. God had heard his prayers, acted on his behalf. The poignancy in that fact brought him to tears again.

As he entered the police station, he saw Holly across the room, holding Lily to her shoulder under a blanket. His heart almost burst. He crossed the room and hugged her fiercely. She kissed his neck.

He bent and kissed Lily's sweet face. She was calm now, sleeping, content and unharmed. It was a miracle.

Smiling softly, Holly handed Lily to him, and he took his daughter in his arms and held her against his heart, nuzzling her feathery little head. When Holly slid her arms around his neck and kissed his stubbled cheek, Creed began to weep again.

Michael found Cathy later that night, sitting on the beach across the street from her house. He sat down beside her in the sand and kissed her cheek. Her face was wet, and strands of hair blew into her face and stuck to her skin. He stroked them away.

She took his hand, pressed her lips to his palm. "I can't believe he's gone."

"Joe?"

She smiled sadly. "No, not Joe. I came to terms with that months ago. I can't believe Miller is out of our lives. That it's really over. He took so many things from us . . . so many people. He destroyed so much . . ."

Michael looked out over the water. "But God has a way of giving things back."

She slipped her arms around his waist and leaned into him, and he held her as she wept. Finally, when her tears were spent, she drew in a long breath. "So when are you going to marry me?"

He smiled. "Now?"

She laughed. "How about a week from Saturday? We'll see if the church is free Saturday night, and we'll call everyone we want to come. We can ask our families to help us call everybody."

"And you already have your dress."

She shook her head. "There's a sample sale at the bridal store this week. I know I can find a dress I like. I can go tomorrow and buy a sample off the rack."

"What about . . . your other dress?"

She sighed. "I don't want to marry you in the dress I was going to wear to marry Joe. I want to start fresh with you. You're not an extension of Joe. I can donate that dress to someone who can't afford one. That way it'll get used."

Michael framed her face in his calloused hands and pulled back to look at her clearly. "Are you sure?"

He saw no doubt in her eyes. "I'm positive. I don't want to wait a day longer than we have to. We've already waited so long."

Michael kissed her then, and Cathy got to her feet, smiling, grabbed his hand, and pulled him down the beach to where the waves broke against the sand. As the breeze whispered across the water, she kick-splashed him and yelled, "We're getting married!"

Laughing with her, he picked her up. A wave crashed into

them, knocking him off balance, and he fell with her in his arms. Laughter scored the night as they sat wet on the sand with waves splashing around them, settling into the idea of a new life without the pall of Leonard Miller hanging over them.

CHAPTER 59

The moment Leonard Miller was buried, Holly felt a surprising sense of freedom and hope. The DEA had taken the case and had gotten reams of information from Jack Humphrey about Miller's contacts and cohorts, who were now being rounded up and charged with multiple counts of drug trafficking. The names of the rest of his contacts were found in a twenty-dollar file cabinet in Miller's office. Though he'd been careful to keep his identity from most of his contacts, he hadn't been as careful with their names and contact information.

The cocaine trade in the Florida panhandle had been seriously curtailed—at least for a while, until someone else filled the vacuum. As long as there were buyers, there would be someone to sell. But for now, things were harder for those who made their living from other people's destruction.

Because the wedding was simple, with only Max and Juliet

standing up for Michael and Cathy, Holly sat in the front row of the church with Creed and Lily.

On the days leading up to the ceremony, Holly and Creed had been inseparable except when he was working. His father had hired him to work in his construction business, and despite his wounded arm, Creed had attacked the job with zeal. Every day after work he had dinner with Holly and Lily. Holly's immediate comfort with him was a portrait of grace in her life, a reminder that God cared more for her than she had ever cared for herself.

The small wedding chapel at Michael and Cathy's church had been decked out with white roses, their scent lingering on the air.

"With this ring, I thee wed," Michael was saying, his voice wobbling. Cathy was lovely as she smiled at her groom through a shimmer of tears.

Their father—his expression vacant, since Alzheimer's had ravaged his brain—sat next to Holly, unaware of where he was. Juliet had gotten him from the nursing home and dressed him in a suit and tie, and he reminded Holly of the man who'd stood in the pulpit years ago, before his choices had injured her faith. But today was a healing day. Jesus' presence overshadowed the pain and doubt and revived the truth they'd always known.

Lily lay quietly in the crook of Holly's arm, dressed in a long white gown. Creed touched Holly's left ring finger. His eyes were moist as he leaned toward her ear and whispered, "I'm in love with you, Holly."

Holly sucked in a breath. As Michael said, "Till death do us part," she whispered, "I love you too."

Cathy began to repeat the vows to Michael. As she did,

Holly looked down at Lily. Her eyes were open wide, looking from her mother to her father, as if somehow in the center of her awareness she knew what was happening.

As Cathy repeated the vows, Holly leaned into Creed, kissed him on the cheek. They hadn't known each other long, but they had grown so close in such a short period. They needed time to get to know each other even better, but Holly had no doubt where this was going. Creed had quietly stated his intentions toward both her and her daughter, and she had accepted with no trumpets or fanfare. Just a soft, gentle peace and an open heart, full of the perfect love that could only exist in a heart wiped clean.

A NOTE FROM THE AUTHOR

As I write this, I'm so aware that many of you are suffering. It's always been that way, and Jesus warned that it would be. "In this world you will have trouble," He said. "But take heart! I have overcome the world" (John 16:33). But lately, as I deal with issues in my own life and the lives of my friends and family members, I see more suffering than usual. It's as if the enemy only has a few days left, so he's kicking as much dirt as he can into the eyes of his opponents. In my own case, it's not comforting when people tell me that his attacks are so blatant against me because I'm a threat to his work. Knowing that does not lessen the severity of those attacks, though it does give them some meaning.

I find that his assaults against me are to keep me busy and distracted, sick and hurting, so that I'm not doing my part in prayer, and it's nearly impossible to do the work I'm called to. If he's scheming to take each of us off the battlefield as he ramps up his attacks on the world, are we falling for it? If I were to be honest, I'd have to admit that I sometimes do. It's never been more important to pray, yet I sometimes feel paralyzed in my prayer life. And I see that same phenomenon with one Christian friend after another.

I wish I could say that I handle my trials well, that I fit in to the category of The Faithful who take their blows with class and grace. But sometimes I fear that I'm falling into that category of the seeds choked out by the worries of the world (Mark 4:18–19). If I allow the enemy to knock me out so that I'm not praying or staying in communion with God, then the enemy has won a victory over me. As Paul so often says in Scripture, "May it never be!"

If you're experiencing this, too, you are not alone. This is a spiritual battle, and we are not equipped to fight it without the armor of God. And as I've written before, the armor of God doesn't just spring up overnight. It comes with much prayer and study and with a deep knowledge of, and faith in, God's Word. Those things build up our armor. Those who haven't put in the time getting to know their savior lack that armor, and that's why we see so many fall away from faith.

This is an all-out war against true believers. Instead of schemes, the enemy sometimes uses a sledge-hammer on us. Just remember—*he hates our guts* and wants to paralyze us.

When I talk to friends about what could be happening— why so many Christians seem to be suffering—they sometimes say that the American church needs to be pruned, that we have it so easy here that we're shallow and flabby. There are people all over the world who are persecuted for their faith. In Iraq, many Christians are being slaughtered for refusing to convert to Islam, yet they demonstrate such deep faith that they don't fall away, even when it means their death. Let's face it, American Christians do have it easy by comparison. However, I don't think that the shallowness in the American church has made God overlook us or turn His back on us. Instead of pruning us corporately, the way He does in countries where persecution is rampant and deadly, He works in our lives individually to prune us in different ways. Yes, we are blessed with peace and the freedom to worship as we want, so we often take that for granted. But He loves us enough to work in our lives anyway. That means that He sometimes allows the enemy to persecute us individually—through grief, sickness, physical and emotional pain, disappointment, financial hardship, legal issues, etc., *in order to deepen our faith.* I have to remind myself that He chooses how much we're pruned. Satan can do nothing without God's permission. Our Creator is in control.

I can either rail at God and wave my fists at Him—and fall away from faith—or I can trust that whatever He's allowing into my life is for a reason, and it will make me the kind of Christian He wants me to be. In other words, He isn't letting us off the hook just because we enjoy so many freedoms. He works in the lives of each individual Christian—shallow or deep, insightful or dense—and matures us through specific, custom-designed trials. Peter said, "Beloved, do not be surprised at the fiery ordeal among you, which comes upon you for your testing, as though some strange thing were happening to you; but to the degree that you share the sufferings of Christ, keep on rejoicing, so that also at the revelation of His glory you may rejoice with exultation" (1 Peter 4:12–13 NASB).

I guess it comes down to trust in God. Can we trust Him with our development as Christians, even if it hurts? I was just listening to an interview by a burn victim, who talked about the process of debriding his skin each day—having it scrubbed in an excruciating attempt to keep it from getting infected so it would heal. If that hadn't happened, he wouldn't be here today, but what a horrible thing to endure each day. Still, he came out on the other side, and while I'm sure he still has massive scars, he's a different person because of it. Maybe it's the same way with us. What God allows to get us where He wants us can be agonizing, and it can leave scars. But Jesus has scars, too, and He will use that pain for good if we let Him.

This life is not about our comfort. We have an eternity for that. I really think this is about training and testing. We will have work to do in Heaven, work that is fulfilling and perfect for us. God needs to develop certain skill sets in us before that time. That may be what this life is about.

As I close this, I'm praying for you, for all of us, that we will be found faithful and that these assaults bring us closer to our Lord rather than knocking us away from Him. May we never let the enemy have the victory.

"Consider it all joy, my brethren, when you encounter various trials, knowing that the testing of your faith produces endurance. And let endurance have its perfect result, so that you may be perfect and complete, lacking in nothing" (James 1:2–4 NASB).

DISCUSSION QUESTIONS

1. How do you feel about Holly's and Creed's relationship? Is Holly making a mistake?
2. Was Holly right to keep Creed in the dark about Lily?
3. How has Creed redeemed himself? Or has he?
4. Have there been times in your life when you felt God was disgusted with you?
5. Do you think Holly is a good mother? Is Creed a good father? What makes a good parent?
6. Were you bothered by the author's handling of Holly's "single mom" status?
7. Does God have a plan for broken people who've made mistakes? Does He send an ambulance or a firing squad?
8. Discuss Michael's reaction to his hard times. How did he remain positive?
9. How did faith play a role in each character's life?
10. How have you grown through reading about Holly?

ACKNOWLEDGMENTS

Over the years, I've been blessed to work with some of the finest publishing professionals in the business, so I wanted to take a moment to acknowledge one of them now. One of the first people I met when I switched to writing Christian fiction was David Lambert. I had worked with many New York editors in my career, but I quickly saw that Dave was by far the best. Though he is brutal with every manuscript I turn in, he never fails to spark ideas and motivate me into taking my book to the next level. It's hard work pleasing him, but I have to give him credit for much of my success. Some people think I'm a glutton for punishment when I ask for him time after time, but I know that he's the one who can make me work the hardest to deliver an entertaining read. So thank you, Dave, for all you've done to make me the author I am today.

And to all the other editors I work with to polish and perfect my work (though it will never be perfect)—among them

Ellen Tarver, Amanda Bostic, Susan Brower, Karen Ball, Bob Hudson, and Ami McConnell—I want to thank you too. You have each invested something important in me, something that has helped me mature as a writer, and you've made my books more readable, more entertaining, and more spiritually challenging.

I would not be here if it weren't for all of you.

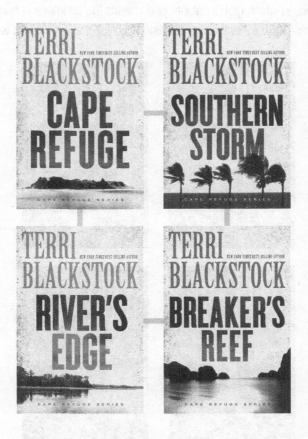

In the face of a crisis that sweeps an entire high-tech planet back to the age before electricity, the Brannings face a choice. Will they hoard their possessions to survive—or trust God to provide as they offer their resources to others? Terri Blackstock weaves a masterful what-if series in which global catastrophe reveals the darkness in human hearts—and lights the way to restoration for a self-centered world.

Terri Blackstock loves to hear from readers, receiving your letters and visiting via social media and her newsletter. Connect with her at www.TerriBlackstock.com or on Facebook at https://www.facebook.com/tblackstock.

Other great books from Terri Blackstock

INTERVENTION SERIES

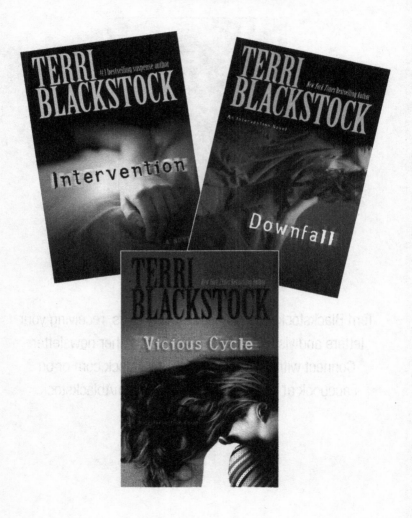

Available in stores and online!

ABOUT THE AUTHOR

Photo by Deryll Stegall

Terri Blackstock has sold over seven million books world-wide and is a *New York Times* bestselling author. She is the award-winning author of *Intervention*, *Vicious Cycle*, and *Downfall*, as well as such series as Cape Refuge, Newpointe 911, the SunCoast Chronicles, and Restoration.

www.terriblackstock.com

Facebook: tblackstock

Twitter: @terriblackstock